MORE THAN JUST A HAIRDRESSER

MORE THAN JUST A WEDDING

Also by Nia Pritchard

MORE THAN JUST A HAIRDRESSER

MORE THAN JUST A WEDDING

by

Nia Pritchard

Published by Honno
'Ailsa Craig', Heol y Cawl, Dinas Powys,
South Glamorgan, Wales, CF64 4AH

1 2 3 4 5 6 7 8 9 10

The author would like to stress that
this is a work of fiction and no resemblance
to any actual individual or institution
is intended or implied.

A catalogue record for this book is available from
The British Library.

Published with the financial support of the
Welsh Books Council.

ISBN 978-1-906784-12-6

Cover illustration: Kim Smith
Cover design: Graham Preston
Text design: Jenks Design
Printed in Wales by Gomer Press

For my mum, x

Acknowledgements

Caroline Oakley, for her continued support
and guidance, and all my lovely friends,
who kept me going by asking, 'When's the next
one out?'!

ONE

'Jason there's another box ready for you love,' Shirley called out to her teenage son from the front door.

He looked over towards her, sighed and put his thumb up. He jumped down from the back of the Transit van and made his way up the path to meet Shirley, followed closely behind by his mate Digo who looked exhausted. Shirley put the final mug wrapped in newspaper in the box, the kettle on top, and sealed it all up with masking tape. She wrote 'kitchen stuff' on the box in black felt tip and tapped it with her left hand.

'There you go love last one.' She looked up at Jason and smiled.

'Thank God for that. I'm knackered. Come on Digo you can lock up the van,' Jason said directing his mate with his head.

'Come on kid nearly done now,' Oli said almost running down the path jingling his keys.

'Are you gonna come back here, babe, after you've dropped the stuff off,' Shirley called.

'Aye, ok, babe. I'll come back and we'll have a little toast to say tara, eh?' Oli called back to Shirley who waved them off from the front door.

It was quite unbelievable, only last year Oli wouldn't even attempt to ride a bike, now he'd managed to take up driving lessons and not just pass but have the confidence to drive the removal van, albeit only a Transit. Oli learning to drive had become inevitable if they were to continue combining their two thriving businesses successfully. She'd been shocked when he suggested it, but was delighted that he had. The driving lessons hadn't been short on dramas but with the help of a few Valium here and there, and lots of support and encouragement, Oli had managed to pass his test at the second time of asking and was now Liverpool's queen of the road.

Shirley walked back into the empty house and wandered into the living room. She looked around, slowly, touching the wall at her side. This house held so many memories, happy as well as sad. She had moved into the house with Mike when they first got married, had brought her two beautiful babies back to the house after they were born, shared happy times when they lived all together as a family, and then shed tears when Mike had left her and gone off with another woman. She walked over to the window to the place where her phone had previously stood. She remembered the day her father had died and she'd received the news from her distraught mum. The pain and sorrow remained, although time was a great healer and the pain wasn't so sharp now.

Oli had been such a great source of support for Shirley and the kids. She loved him so much, and smiled as she remembered all the fun times they'd had. Taking him on to her mobile hairdressing service…The start of their detective work, the planning, organising and researching… The parties and the girlie nights in – all brought a smile to her face. As she walked through to the small dining area she remembered her early dates with David and smiled. She still had to pinch herself when she thought that in six weeks' time she would be his wife. That was the reason for the move; Ms Shirley Cartwright was shortly to become Mrs Shirley Wilmore. The wedding was planned, a new home had been mortgaged and a whole new life lay ahead for Shirley. The new four bedroom house, in a nice neighbourhood, wasn't going to be ready to move in to until two days before the wedding so David was keeping his place on till then and Shirley and the kids were moving in with Oli till after the wedding. Accompanied by Jason, Oli was on his way to take Shirley's possessions into storage for the six weeks till the new house was ready. Angie had offered to look after Shirley's stuff, but Oli had talked Shirley out of it… 'I don't think it's a good idea, babe, I know she's our mate but to be honest with ya I wouldn't trust her as far as I could throw her.'

Angie, lovable rogue that she was, had good form for pulling fast ones and scams and Shirley wasn't convinced that a few of her items might not accidently get 'lost' while in storage at Angie's. Shirley decided that a secure storage unit would be far better and probably cheaper in the long run!

'Hiya, Mum,' came a voice from nowhere startling her out of her reverie.

'The workforce is here,' Shirley's own mum announced, barging into the kitchen holding a carrier bag full of cleaning products.

'What do you mean?' Shirley asked looking surprised.

Shaz, Fiona's best mate, stood in the door way holding a brush in one hand and a mop in the other. Fiona was holding the mop bucket.

'Nan wants us all to help out and clean the place up,' Fiona said grimly.

'I'll help out an' all, Shirley,' Shaz said. She was wearing her usual mini skirt, crop top and orange fake tan. Today's added extra was a pair of bright pink Marigold gloves trimmed with fake leopard skin. 'Aren't they boss, Shirl? Me mum had them for

Crimbo from some fella she was seeing at the time,' Shaz added flashing the gloves.

'But I've all ready done it. I've spent ages cleaning,' Shirley protested ignoring Shaz's enthusiasm for the gloves.

'Oh I don't think so, Shirley, love. We have to make sure. You do realise it's Doreen Smith's daughter who's moving in here after you, don't you? I can't be having her say she moved into a dirty house,' replied her mum.

'Now girls, you do the bathroom. Shirley, you and I can crack on with the kitchen.'

Thursday, April 12th
12 midday

I can't believe today has finally arrived. I've had mixed feelings about it for ages. I'm so excited about the move and the start of this new chapter in my life, but I feel so emotional about leaving this place behind... All me memories, the good ones and the bad. I've been sat here holding me diary in me hand for ages now thinking about everything, me mum and dad, Mike, the kids, Oli and me mates. Goin over everything that's happened here...

Everything that's happened to me while I've lived here all added to make me who I am. It feels dead weird to see the place empty. Everyone says it's only bricks and mortar, our houses aren't who we are, but this place has been more than a house. It's been a home.

Anyway I can't get that maudlin now me bloody mum's turned up with Fi and Shaz and is about to get all ' How clean is your house?' on me!! Friggin' 'ell.

Shaz led the way up to the bathroom giving Digo and Jason an eyefull as she ungracefully wiggled up the stairs.

'Oh God, that's put me off me tea,' Digo complained to Jason as they both stood by the front door.

'Well, if you were doing what you were meant to be doing instead of standing around…' Shirley's mother scolded.' Now come on, get on with it, you two can give the lawn a mow and then give it a brush with the yard brush,' she added.

'Brush the lawn?' Jason asked, horrified.

'Oh, yes. I always make sure that my gardener Bill brushes me lawn after mowing it,' she informed them.

'But why?' Jason asked.

'Makes sure the grass all sits the same way, of course. Now get on with it,' she said pushing them out of the front door.

Tripping over themselves the boys reluctantly went to get the lawn mower back out of the already packed van.

'I don't think there's much cleaning going on up there,' her mother complained, joining Shirley in the already adequately clean kitchen. 'That Shaz is using it as an excuse to show herself to the lads. 'Anyway what's Oli up to? Haven't seen him getting his hands dirty, yet.'

'Hey, now come on, Mum, Oli's been a star,' Shirley insisted.

'Mmm, well it's all hands on deck, Shirley, love, many hands and all that. Now then, how's your oven doing?' her mother asked opening the oven door.

'That should be like a new pin given the use it gets.' Oli laughed, walking into the kitchen holding a flask. 'Fancy a coffee? I was very forward thinking, made a flask of coffee for us for when we were all done and dusted,' he said taking the lid off the flask.

'Done and dusted? Done and dusted?' Shirley's mother squealed. 'What's this?' she asked, scooping something that resembled a lump of coal from inside the oven.

11

'Oh, looks like an old roast spud to me,' Oli said seriously, examining the hard piece of charcoal.

'Oh well…it'll never be perfect,' Shirley said, matter of factly.

'Hey, babe, when did you last do roasties?' Oli asked still studying the incinerated vegetable. 'Wasn't it when you did that Sunday dinner for all of us in between Crimbo and New Year?'

Shirley's mother took a sharp intake of breath.

'Well it must have fallen down the back…' Shirley answered, slightly embarrassed.

Oli raised his eyebrows and her mother frantically sprayed the inside of the oven with a generous amount of oven cleaner.

'I did wonder why the oven kept smoking. Oh well, that's a relief, I thought it might explode on the new people. I have been a bit worried,' Shirley whispered to Oli as her mother vigorously scrubbed the oven.

Three hours later and they were finally done. House sparkling, oven gleaming and lawn brushed it was finally time to close the door on the old life.

6pm

Well we've finally made it to Oli's bag and baggage. It's been murder sorting out what clothes to bring. I have put a few things in storage – reluctantly – but even supermodel Oli put his foot down about finding space for six suitcases full so I've made do with four.

He's taken our stuff to the storage, so tonight we've decided on a takeaway, bottle or two of wine and probably another bit of a cry from me. I feel so emotional about leaving me house.

I don't know how Oli will cope with us for the next few weeks. His house is like a new pin and I've got the teenagers from hell coming with me. They are both as bad as each other. Well, in fact I think Fi is worse than Jason. Clothes everywhere. She didn't sort out her stuff before packing like she promised. Everything was piled into black bin bags and off she went. We had to rescue them from the skip at one stage cos Digo threw them in thinking they were the rubbish from her room!

Oli's invited Digo and Shaz over tonight an' all, which, to be honest, I can do without but he did say they'd both worked hard today helping us out so I should to say ta like. To be honest Shaz did sweet FA but I'd have felt dead tight not including her. They are due over at seven. I'm off to have a quick shower now, to freshen meself up before they arrive. I'll have to bunk up with our Fi for the next few weeks. Oli's got three bedrooms, so obviously he's in one, Jason's got the box room and Fi and I are in the other double. I did ask me mum an' all, just so's she didn't feel left out – plus she cleaned for Britain today – but she said she was too tired and just wanted a cuppa and to put her feet up. I didn't argue cos it would have been me that would be traipsing across town to pick up and drop her off, and I want to relax with a bottle of wine and have a bit of a cry in peace without her telling me to pull meself together. David is away overnight on a course with school, so it'll help take me mind off him an' all.

Oli set his large glass dining table with six little Chinese bowls, six pairs of chop sticks proudly sat on six blue fish chopstick holders. They all rested neatly on the bamboo placemats that Oli loved so much. The wine glasses were poised expectantly, and a vase of fresh flowers and three lit tea lights in oriental holders completed the perfect scene.

'Bloody 'ell who the 'ell's coming? Shaz'll pee her pants when she sees this set up,' Fi said as she walked into the beautifully set dining room.

'Isn't it lovely, eh, Fi? Oli's got such taste,' Shirley announced.

'Ah, ta kid. I like to have nice things and to make the effort, even if tonight it's for the Clampits.' Oli giggled.

'Hey I hope that doesn't include us, babe?' Shirley asked looking playfully wounded.

'Never, queen,' Oli said, grabbing Shirley and giving her a big hug and a kiss.

'Thanks for this Oli; we really appreciate it, you putting us up an' all. I love you.'

'I love you, all of you an' all, kid. You're all more than welcome here.'

'Yeah, but will he still be saying that three weeks from now, eh, Mum?' Fiona asked cheerfully.

11.45pm

In me bed, thank God. Had a lovely evening but I'm knackered – physically and emotionally. Had a few tears and Oli wiped them away bless him. I have to share a room with Fi, so I'm gonna have to be careful where I keep me little pink diary, but I have to keep a note of everything just so as I remember every last detail.

We had our Chinese delivered, so we've had a few wines. Fi and Shaz were on the Bacardi Breezers and Jason and Digo on the beers, so Oli and I had the wine just to ourselves. Fi's warned me not to snore after but looking over at her now, she's flat out – the cheek!

I wonder what kind of room David's got in that hotel tonight… He did text me earlier to say he was missing me, bless him. He's gone on a two day course on health and safety, or something. It was booked ages ago and he was gutted when he found out he wouldn't be around to help with my move. We didn't know the date, then. Anyway we've managed without out him; he's staying put till our house is ready. I'd love to be moving in with him till the wedding, but there just isn't the room. All good things come to those that wait, I suppose.

Shirley closed the little pink diary and put it in the side pocket of her handbag. As she had become more intimate in her diary entries, Shirley had invested in a little pink padlock with a secret code to ensure that wherever her diary was left there was no way anyone would be able to take a look.

Shirley leaned back in bed and took in her bedroom for the next few weeks. Oli had great taste and was regularly either decorating or buying more new and unique things for his house. Oli was comfortable financially and the extra money from the detective work was free money to do with as he wanted; extra pocket money to fritter away, so fritter he did on the house and on clothes. The bedroom was white and orange, the double bed Shirley had to share with Fi stood proudly in the middle of the room. It had been laden with orange and white fluffy cushions, Fi's favourite items. Shirley's favourite was the retro orange lamp perched on the vintage white plastic bedside table. There was attention to detail everywhere from the white 70s radio on the window sill to the nostalgic 70s phone on the little table by the door and the large orange glass lamp shade. It was like a show home, not a thing out of place.

Shirley leaned over to blow Fiona a kiss before carefully switching the little orange lamp off and within minutes she was snoring away like a trooper.

Friday, April 13th
11am

I'd forgotten it's Friday the thirteenth today and already I've had some bad luck. I've spilt coffee on Oli's white fluffy rug in the living room. As usual Oli was dead nice about it and he'd got one of them stain removers, thank God. I got it all out, mind – it's all probably going to go tits up from now on isn't it?

Shirley was devastated that she'd already got the day off to a bad start what with the coffee spillage and decided the best place for her was work.

'Come on you lot, school, you're gonna be late. We've gorra get off an' all, you know, we've gorra busy day, today,' Shirley announced while clearing up the breakfast things.

'You gonna give us a lift to school, Mum? We have to get two buses otherwise,' Jason complained.

'Well if you'd managed to pass your bloody test, Lewis Hamilton, we wouldn't have to would we?' Fi pointed out.

Jason looked annoyed as he pushed his cereal bowl into the sink. 'I can flamin' drive. I just can't pass me friggin' test. It's luck on the day.'

Shirley looked at Oli, who in return looked at Shirley, and they both raised their eyebrows.

'Have you booked your next test, Jay, babe?' Oli enquired, sheepishly.

'Nah, not yet, Oli. I'm waiting for a morning slot at the beginning of the month. I've been told that's the best time to pass. They're only allowed to pass so many a month, y'know, so if you have one like mine have been – at the end of the month – basically, you're knackered,' Jason went on, convincing no one but himself.

'Oh right, so the last test – number four, was it? – when did you take that, then?' Fiona asked smugly.

16

'Fi, shut up will you, love, and get yourself ready for school,' Shirley said, knowing a full scale row was about to break out.

'When was it again?' Oli whispered to Shirley, who was busy rinsing out her mug.

'Jan 3rd at nine o clock,' Shirley muttered under her breath, pulling a face.

'That was because the fella had a huge hangover, he'd been on the ale since before Christmas,' Jason protested, looking daggers at all three of them.

'Oh right, not because you mounted the pavement with two wheels and nearly ran over a man coming out of the newsagents, then...' Fi smirked, standing up from the kitchen table.

'Ok, we'll give you both a lift kids. Off we go.' Oli intervened and headed for the door.

After dropping the kids off at school, Shirley and Oli headed off for West Haven nursing home. Half an hour, later, Shirley pulled up in the car park and took her seat belt off.

'It's not the same here now, is it, since the old misses have gone?' she said, sadly.

'I know, babe. I don't half miss them,' Oli replied.

'Gone to a better place, though, some might say,'

'It'd do me babe,' Oli said in a day dream. 'Imagine finding a son, after all them years, and him taking you and your sister in to live in luxury on a massive farm in Wales...'

'Aye. All that fresh air, and they've got people that work for them, an' holiday cottages on the land. We'll have to go and visit them you know. They invited us.'

'Yeah, kid. Not sure I could stomach the smell of a farm... Anyway, come on, stop your jangling we've got work to do,' said Oli, marching on to do his worst for the blue rinse brigade.

Friday, April 13th
6pm

After a busy morning at the home we had the afternoon with the factory girls. Ali was sat legs akimbo wearing a brown gypsy skirt, orange blouse and sand coloured suede boots.

'Bloody hell Ali babe if I wasn't gay you'd be my number three fantasy girl,' Oli announced.

'Would I love? Who's numbers one and two?' she asked him.

'Anne Widdecombe and Cherie Blair.'

Poor old Ali just looked at him, bless her. I've been thinking about writing to one of them TV makeover shows...see if they can do anything with her, but, like Oli said, it would only be a waste cos her old fella's worse than she is. Why waste it on him!

They were full of their usual chat. Kelly had her nose buried in a magazine.

'Hey, Susan, tell Shirl and Oli about that thing in that mag, babe,' Angie shouted over the dryer to her mate. Anyway, it turns out that according to this article if you write down on a piece of paper everything that's happened to you in your life and look at it as if it's someone else's then you'll see if your life has turned out any good, like. They've all done it down the factory. 'How's yours Angie, babe?' Oli asked. 'Friggin' crap,' came the answer!

I've just done mine. I didn't want to do it in the factory in front of all of them lot. Mine's not too bad...it's certainly got better in the last year or so! Thank you, Mr Wilmore.

Anyway, we're back home now. I hope Oli doesn't get pissed off working with me all day and spending all evening with me an' all! We're gonna have an Indian takeaway tonight. David is coming over. Oli will be out on the pull I suppose – it is a Friday after all. I hope he doesn't think he has to make himself scarce all the time just for me. I don't want him to be a stranger in his own home, do I? I do hope he buggers off tonight, though. The kids will be out and I could do with a bit of a cuddle on the sofa with David. I haven't half missed him.

I'm still torn by the fact that David knows nothing about mine and Oli's sideline. I'm gonna be his wife in a few weeks and I've told him nothing about it. The only people that know're me and Oli, obviously, and Sapphire – and that's only cos she's done a bit of work for us. She's been quite good really, in the last year, and business has certainly been good for us. Can I actually carry this on when I'm married, though? I haven't said anything to Oli but I know he'd be gutted if we had to stop. He loves it. Plus I know in me heart I'm destined to be more than just a wife. It's been in the back of my mind for a while, now, but I've tried not to think about it too much. Oli hasn't asked if I'm gonna tell David, I just think he thinks I won't. I don't know how David would feel about it. Anyway, I can't tell him really. I'm sure he would keep quiet and not blow our cover but his opinion of me might change an' I can't risk losing him.

He'll be here in a bit, he's bringing the takeaway with him, so I'd best get meself all glammed up...

Shirley closed her diary ensured the lock was securely in place and put it in her bag.

She walked through to the bathroom and turned the shower on. Within a few minutes she was engulfed in the floral aroma of jasmine and rose shower gel.

Ten minutes later she was out, hair dried and ready to add the finishing touches, when her mobile phone rang. She held the phone between her ear and chin, simultaneously pulling the straighteners through her hair. It was David.

'Hey, babe, you ok?' Shirley asked cheerfully.

'Yeah, just running a bit late… Is the Indian just for you and me or the whole tribe?'

'The whole tribe, babe, but the kids are going out later and so is Oli I think, so we will get a bit of time to ourselves.'

'Great. I want to know all about the move and how you lot managed, I would've loved to be a fly on the wall watching all the action.' He giggled.

'We did miss you but we managed ok. Listen, babe, I'll tell you all about it after. I need to finish off me hair now. I wanna look all beautiful for you,' Shirley assured him, struggling to still straighten her hair and hold the phone at the same time. She finished the conversation dropped her phone down into her bag on top of her little pink diary.

Fifteen minutes later, Shirley walked downstairs wearing blue jeans, a yellow long sleeved T-shirt and beige Ugg boots. She was greeted by Oli who held out an Indian beer.

'Cheers, babe,' he said clunking his bottle against hers. 'You look gorge,' he added, planting a kiss on her forehead.

'Ta, hon'.'

Fiona was flat out on the sofa and Jason was stretched out on the white fluffy rug in front of the telly.

'What time's the grub coming, Mum?' Jason asked before taking a sip out of his bottle of beer. 'I'm starving.'

'David's on his way now, just running a bit late.

'What you lot up to tonight then?' Shirley inquired sheepishly.

'Oh we're all staying in tonight, babe,' Oli announced. 'I've got a few mates coming round and I think Digo and Shaz are due in a bit. We had to fight her off when she knew your David was coming over with an Indian.'

Shirley's heart sank.

'Oh look at her face.' Fi laughed.

'What's up, Mum?' Jason asked smiling.

'Aww we mustn't be tight… I'm off out, babe, after me grub, so don't you be worrying and I'm staying over at Marc's tonight,' Oli trilled.

'Marc with a c, again… Ooh are things getting a bit serious, Oli?' Fi asked, eager for any gossip.

'Hey you, mind your nose,' Oli replied quickly.

'Has he had that new tattoo yet?' Shirley asked.

'Not sure. I'll have a look tonight.' Oli giggled.

'Please…' Jason protested.

'Sorry, babe.' Oli raised his eyebrows at Shirley and quickly pulled tongues at Jason behind his back.

'I'm staying over in Shaz's an' all,' Fi announced.

'And I'm staying in Digo's,' Jason added turning round.

'So you've got the place to yourselves all night long kid. David can stay if he likes, may as well, it'll save driving home and he can have a few drinks…'

'Well make sure you change the flamin' sheets before I get back in that bed,' Fi said, alarmed.

'Course I will.' Shirley blushed, pleased at the good news but a little shame-faced that they'd all guessed what was on her mind. It was more than a bit embarrassing sharing with your teenaged daughter. Kids just didn't want to know that their parents had sex lives – especially with one of their teachers…

Half an hour later the door bell rang. Shirley leapt out of the chair and quickly opened the front door. David stood there balancing a large cardboard box full of the Indian supper on his knee and right arm while he rang the door bell with his left hand.

'Hope you're hungry,' he said as he struggled through the front door.

10.30pm

Aww, we've had a lovely night. The rabble buggered off after the food and I'm sat up in bed waiting for David to emerge from the bathroom. I can't wait and to think I waited all them months without sex and now it's like anytime I like!! Hope it carries on like this when we're married. You hear all these stories don't you about how once you're married it all goes downhill in the bedroom department. Well, I'm gonna make sure that it doesn't happen in my house, no flamin' way. I've waited too long for it to go downhill once we can do it morning noon and night!!! Oh hell, I can hear the flush go, he'll be here in a min smelling all gorgie, I'd best put a bit of scent on me an' all.

Shirley quickly locked up her diary and threw it into her bag, which was open beside the bed. She reached into her bedside drawer and having picked up her treasured perfume gave a generous squirt to her neck, chest and wrists, then lifting the duvet gave a squirt inside the bed for good luck. She was already for action when her sexy David walked through the door.

'All ready lover boy,' she said peeling back the duvet to reveal herself in a sexy black and pink brand new matching bra and pants set.

David looked at her and raised half a smile.

'Oh Shirley, you look gorgeous but I'm afraid I'm not up for anything love, my stomach's killing me. I've got the runs after all that curry. I'm just gonna make myself some warm milk then I'll be up, but I don't think I'll be up for it tonight.'

'Oh no, poor you...'

'You smell nice so does the room, just as well...' David grimaced. 'I wouldn't go into the bathroom in a hurry, though.' Noting Shirley's horror, he said, 'Sorry.' And he limped out of the bedroom and down the stairs.

Saturday, April 14th
8.30 am

Well bit of a disappointing end to the night really. Poor old David had the shites after the curry and he was letting rip so much in his sleep that I've used nearly all of me scent trying to get rid of the smell. I did give him a few kicks but that seemed to make him worse. It was like sleeping with a friggin' brass band. Anyway, I'm sitting up in bed looking at him sleeping like a baby, now, and he looks so bloody gorgeous all is forgiven. I'm gonna go down now and make him some hot sweet tea and some scrambled eggs, see if that get's him a bit perkier.

Shirley carried the tray of scrambled eggs, toast and two mugs of hot sweet tea up the stairs. She found David had just got out of the shower and was looking even more perky than she had hoped for sitting on the bed with just a towel to cover his modesty.

'Brought you some brekkie,' she announced cheerfully.

'Lovely, just what I need, but didn't you know I prefer my scrambled egg cold.' He took the tray gently from her and pulled her firmly onto the bed.

Oli , Fi and Jason left the happy couple in peace for most of the day, all returning late afternoon. Oli only to have a bit of a sleep, shower and change before heading back out to see Marc, with a c, for the second night in a row.

'Hey, we're not kicking you out are we?' Shirley asked when her mate woke up from his beauty sleep.

'Nah, it makes a nice change. I get waited on in someone else's house, they have to make the brekkie. Probably stay there tonight an' all kid,' Oli said excitedly.

'Oh. You getting on well with this Marc fella then?' David butted in.

'Marc with a c,' Shirley said smiling.

'I bet it looks dead good when you have to write it down, Marc with a c, you know on a card or summat,' Oli suggested smiling dreamily.

'What about the tattoo?' Shirley asked.

'Oh he's had another one. He's got a load…on his back, chest, arms and this new one a Celtic sign on the back of his neck. Looks dead good it does,' Oli went on. 'Just like Beckham.'

'Hey you'll be getting them next.'

'No way, not me. I'm too scared. Oh God, no way. I can't stand the pain, don't you remember I nearly fainted when I got me belly button pierced last year. Oh, no ta, tattoos are not for me. They look dead good on him though.'

'Oh if it isn't the fab four,' Shirley said as Jason, Fiona, Digo and Shaz walked into the living room.

'Hiya,' sang the chorus of voices.

'Hi, Mr Wilmore,' Shaz said trying to pretend she was prim and proper.

'Shaz,' David said nodding.

'Can you sponsor me, sir? And you Ols and Shirl…' Shaz said, searching her bag for her sponsor form.

Fiona Jason and Digo all went to find comfy seats to watch Shaz negotiate a good deal from her targets.

'Yeah, what you doing, love?' Shirley asked.

'I'm doing a mini-marathon, Shirl. You know, one of them charity runs, raising money for a good cause,' Shaz reported proudly. 'Running five k.'

'Are you kid?' Oli asked shocked.

'Well done you,' Shirley said. 'Course we'll all sponsor you.' She nudged David, who was glued to the TV.

'Eh?'

'You'll sponsor Shaz won't you? She's doing a mini-marathon, a run for charity.' Shirley took the sponsorship form from Shaz and passed it to him.

'Oh yes, of course Shaz, put me down for a tenner.'

Digo raised his eyebrows at Jason who looked equally impressed.

'I'll give you a fiver,' Shirley said writing it down on the sponsorship form.

'Put me down for a fiver an' all, babe,' Oli called over.

'Ah, Shaz, your mam's given you a fiver an' all, fair do's,' Shirley noted.

'Nah, Shirl, that's what I thought at first but if you look closely you'll find it's 50p made to look on a first glance like a fiver,' Shaz said matter of factly.

They all looked at each other feeling really rather sorry for Shaz – fancy having such a spoilsport for a mother.

'She's dead tight, even the three of us have given more than her,' Fi pointed out.

'So, you started preparing for this marathon yet, then, hon'?' Oli asked brightly, in an effort to put Shaz out of her misery.

'Oh, aye, yeah, I have. I'm up to six minutes now,' Shaz announced proudly.

'Six minutes? You'll have to up the ante kid, you should be doing at least half an hour by now,' Oli recommended.

'Don't think I'll go more than eight,' Shaz sighed. 'I'll burn to a crisp otherwise.'

'Eh? Burn on an exercise machine; surely you're not going that fast that you'll set the place on fire?' Oli asked, confused.

Everyone else looked on not sure where the conversation was leading.

'What you on about? I'm not going on no exercise machine. I'm up to six minutes on the sun bed. Wanna look me best for all the press and the fellas on the run, don't I?' Shaz explained cheerfully.

'Eh?' Oli inquired.

'Well…me prep for the race is getting me sun bed sessions in. I know I've used me fake tan before but I didn't want it to go all streaky and start to come off with me sweating in the race, so I thought I'd better get prepared properly.'

Everyone looked at Shaz in puzzlement. Fi looked at her mother and shrugged her shoulders.

'Why aren't you doing this marathon, kid?' Oli asked Fiona, who was slumped in an armchair picking off her nail varnish.

'She was gonna, weren't you babe? But I've got her to be me pacer 'cause she's a dead good runner isn't she, sir?' Shaz explained.

'Pacer? What the bleedin 'ell's one of them?' Oli inquired.

David just looked at Shaz unsure why she'd thought he know anything about Fi's talents as a runner, after all he wasn't their sports master.

'Well, 'cause Fi is a good runner and I'm crap I've chosen her as me pacer. All these top runners in the London marathon and that have 'em. She's gonna run alongside me giving me encouragement and maybe she'll have to give me a bit of a drag an' all.'

'So, Fi, you still have to do the race, but you don't get you get any sponsors so you don't raise the money?' Shirley asked.

'Yeah,' Fiona replied, still picking off her nail varnish, but since she was in Oli's home ensured it ended up in a neat pile on the arm of the chair rather than flicking it all over the place as she would have done in the comfort of her own home... Shirley made a mental note to make sure their new house was treated with the same respect as Oli's. No more hoovering up nail varnish confetti in her new life.

'Sounds like a crap job to me,' Digo muttered.

'It's a very important job; I may be the pacer for a few more,' Fi objected.

'Ah well, it'll save us forking out on more sponsor money I suppose,' Oli said with relief. 'Anyway I'm off out. See you losers later,' he said, teasing them, and got up to leave the room.

'Oh, where you off, Oli?' Shaz asked eager to get any gossip she could on Oli's latest conquest.

'Takin' me old auntie out the bingo…' Oli said winking and, blowing them all a kiss, shut the door behind him.

'Let's go to mine, love. We've got a lot to sort out for the wedding and most of the paperwork's there,' David pointed out.

'Oh yeah, I want you to look at some pics of cakes,' Shirley said as she shot off upstairs to look for the pictures Lynda had given her.

'Don't worry about us four, we've got a pizza being delivered and a good film to watch, have a good time.' Jason grunted as Shirley and David got ready to leave. Looking at wedding cakes definitely wasn't his idea of a fun night in and he reckoned they were best off out of it.

<u>11pm</u>
Well we've picked the cake. It's gonna be a three tier chocolate one with a cute icing bride and groom on the top. Angie's mate from the factory is making it. I texted her earlier to tell her the one we want. I just wanted David to agree with me although bless him he said it was up to me. I know it's a bit mad relying on Angie's mate to do the cake, but she is good. She's the one who made Angie's cake when she was due to marry

27

that no hoper last year. She'd finished it before the whole thing was called off so Angie brought it into the factory and we all had a piece. It was bloody lovely, so I knew I'd have her to do it just as soon as David asked me to marry him.

It's a load of work this wedding even though we're only having a small one. The two of us, obviously, the kids – his as well as mine. Jason is giving me away. Oli is me male maid of honour and Fi me bridesmaid. Me mum, Auntie Dilys, David's mum and dad, his brother who's the best man and his brother's wife and their two kids: so only the sixteen of us for the wedding in a lovely little church near our new home. It's so pretty and the vicar is dead chuffed that we've chosen her church to get married in. We're having the reception for sixteen in the little pub over the road from the church. It's one of them country pubs in the middle of nowhere – really lovely. It's got a thatched roof, the whole building's painted white and it's got pink roses around the door frame. We only wanted a very small intimate wedding with just our nearest and dearest. Then the following week on the Saturday we're gonna go for it and have a massive party in one of the hotels in town. We've got about 200 coming: all me mates, clients, factory girls, old and new neighbours, the rest of the family and they are all gonna mix in with David's lot and most of the teachers from David's school. It'll be a right laugh. Digo and Shaz, obviously, are coming an' all. They're almost part of the family, now. We're in for a hell of a night. We couldn't do anything much else really as there is so many people who would feel left out, specially since we haven't asked them to the actual ceremony. That's why we were both determined to have the actual wedding day a nice, quiet close family thing. I think we've definitely made the right choice. We've ordered lovely food for the reception. Cos there's only sixteen of us we've gone for the best of everything. Beautiful menu, real Champagne, fine wines it'll be friggin' lovely. We're not bad for the party as we call it but I'm afraid even on David's fab wages it'll be Cava for the 200 on the Saturday! We've still put on a buffet – a nice one – but they can have a glass of bubbly then pay for their own drinks the rest of the night.

Got a fitting for me dress next week. It's lovely. A tight-fitted, strapless one. The type of dress I've always wanted but could never afford first time around (plus I was preggers so I couldn't fit into it!). Fi is me bridesmaid in a beautiful blue silky, spaghetti-strapped, fitted, long dress and Oli is gonna wear the same colour suit. I've seen it on him and he looks friggin' fab. Only he could get away with it.

Anyway, I've got lists as long as me arm for this wedding, plus work, the move and mine and Oli's sideline that we really need to talk about in the morning. Me head's buzzing so I really do need to try and relax now and get some sleep.

Shirley locked her diary and switching the light off drifted off to sleep with the sound of the fab four still laughing and enjoying them selves downstairs.

<u>Saturday, April 15th</u>
9am
I woke up in the night thinking of all the stuff I need to do. I know the main day is sorted, apart from the flowers, but it's this party... There are so many people I hope it will turn out ok. I've got me hen night an' all, Oli's in charge. And there's David's stag do. They're going to Amsterdam for the weekend two weeks before the big day. I've been told it's an activities weekend but I'm not sure what kind of activities. Paint-balling, I hope!!

Oli said that's the weekend we'll do the hen night, so I won't spend the weekend moping about David being away! He said it's all organised and we are going away for the weekend, me, him Fi and Shaz and the factory girls. All Oli's told me is that we're all taking a half day on the Friday and meeting for tapas to get us in the mood at lunch time, with me mum and Auntie Dilys so they don't feel left out, then we're leaving them and the real hen weekend starts. The hen party know all about it but they've been sworn to secrecy cos Oli wants to make sure it's a complete surprise for me. Fair do's, David's asked Jason and Digo to go on the stag night and his own boys. Least I know he'll behave even if Jason and Digo don't!!

I'll have to have a chat with Oli today about our latest job an' all. It's been going on a few weeks now and we're none the wiser. We'll have to try and get a result soon or risk a disappointed client. Our first. And I don't want that to happen.

Shirley pulled on her dressing gown pushed her feet into her slippers and smiled as she looked over at Fiona who was still sound asleep with just her head peeking out from under the duvet.

Oli was already downstairs and sitting at the kitchen table drinking coffee from his 'What Happens in Vegas Stays in Vegas' mug, a prized keepsake from his weekend trip there with a gang of lads three years ago.

'Morning. Coffee?' he asked, getting up and putting the kettle on.

'Lovely, Oli,' Shirley answered heading for the toaster and putting in four slices of wholemeal bread.

'I've not long got in, can't even be arsed going to bed,' Oli said.

'You're having toast, yeah?' Shirley asked.

'Yeah, go on then. I didn't wait around for brekkie. I didn't sleep that well. Marc had a few mates over, so you never sleep the same do you. I made my excuses and left them to it. I couldn't be arsed with all the chatting over the toast and Marmite this morning. Too many wines last night.'

'How's it going with him?' Shirley asked warmly.

'Oh he's a laugh and all that but, I dunno, he's a party animal and I think I'm getting ready to settle down now, babe. I want more than just a bit of fun.' Oli was serious this time.

'Bloody hell. Really?' Shirley handed him a plate with two slices of toast buttered thickly and with a generous helping of strawberry jam.

'Yeah. I must be getting old.' Oli, squeezed Shirley's hand and smiled.

'Hey, listen,' Shirley said, squeezing his hand back. 'Now it's just the two of us we really need to talk about this latest job.'

'Aye, I know, kid, we've had such a lot on haven't we? But she's gonna start whinging if we don't come up with any thing soon.'

'It doesn't help that he's at it with lots of different women and he's bloody good at covering his tracks an' all.'

'Well we've been at it a few months now and we're no better off than his missus. We've got such a great track record, there is no way I'm gonna let this bastard ruin it,' Oli said determinedly.

'Good on you, babe. Apparently he's meant to be out on Friday and she knows where he's going, so we could go as well if you fancy it. I'll tell David we're planning the hen night.' Shirley took a sip of her coffee.

'You not gonna tell David then after you're married? About this detective work an' all…'

'I have been wondering, to be honest with you, and for now I think this thing we've got works 'cause only you and me know about it – and Sapphire, of course,' Shirley said deep in thought.

'You sure, babe? You know, starting off your married life with secrets…'

'Don't make me feel worse than I do already kid. I'm not doing anything bad to him am I? I think it works ok like this.' Shirley looked guilty.

'I know babe, you're probably doing the right thing keeping it just between us three. Easier to keep things under wraps.'

Still not really convinced Shirley carried on eating her toast and let her mind wander. Not always a good idea as her mind tended to make mountains out of molehills.

'Ok, we'll go to his local on Friday then follow him on to wherever he goes after nine,' Oli suggested.

'Aye, ok, let's see if we can get this one in the bag this week, 'cause I really need to be concentrating on this wedding.'

Monday, April 16th
6pm
Back to work today. It feels weird going to work from Oli's place. I had an extra ten minutes in bed this morning cos I didn't have to go and pick him up.

I had a phone call from Jan this morning asking for an update on the hard to catch at it Des case we're working on. I told her we're hoping for a result on Friday. She sounded a bit pissed off. I do feel sorry for her, but what can we do? This has been going on for a few months now. Basically, Jan, who's in her late thirties, is convinced her fella, Des, is at it with lots of different women every week. Oli and I just can't get any evidence. He's definitely a man's man, we've seen him loads of times in the pub without her and all gobby with his mates. We've tried to trail him and we get so far then we just lose him. We've never seen him chatting to other women, not once. We just can't get any thing on him. He seems to be able to cover his tracks or drop a tail without breaking a sweat. Jan said he's really secretive about his whereabouts in the week, goes out to the pub every Friday with his mates, but when she's asked the bar maid who also works in her local paper shop she's said he only stays in the pub till nine. But he's not home till after midnight and always stinking of women's perfume. I think I've managed to pacify her, for a bit. She knows what a git he is, but wants evidence - she just wants a result at the end of the day, so she's going to keep us on for a couple more weeks.

I kept Oli up to date on it all and he's really up for getting this Des. I think he sees it as a challenge cos he's been so hard to get hold of. We started off calling this one Des the hard man now we're calling it Des the hard to find man!

We worked together all today and it made the day go a whole lot quicker, cos we could have a gossip as well. I told Oli about the wedding cake and he thinks it sounds lovely. He's gonna come with me tomorrow night for my dress fitting, too. He wants to try on his suit and Fi will try on her dress and Jason his suit, so we'll see the full Monty!!

Determined not to take advantage of Oli's hospitality, Shirley had been to the supermarket and stocked up on all all the essentials from Pot Noodles to ready meals of all kinds especially slimming ready meals, because she was determined to lose a few pounds before her big day. She had even signed up to a gym and tried her best to get there a couple of times a week. She was beginning to like the new shape her body was taking… She'd bought three pizzas for the kids and Oli (there was no way she could burn them even with her lack of cookery GCSE), a bag of ready prepared salad and three French sticks. Not the best meal for her new regime but she couldn't give everyone microwaveable slimming meals.

'Hey, babe, this looks lovely.' Oli said happily sitting down at the table.

'No chips?' Jason asked disappointedly.

'No, not tonight, love, let's all try and be a bit healthy, eh?' Shirley said smiling.

'Oh, aye, yeah, kids, we don't want to look like sumo wrestlers going down that aisle, do we?' Oli said taking huge portions of salad.

'There's nothing of you Oli.' Fi said looking disgustedly at the salad she had put on her plate.

'Well, it's only for a bit, anyway. We've got the fitting tomorrow, haven't we?' Shirley said pouring on some low calorie dressing to try and liven up the limp leaves in the salad bowl.

'Oh, I can't wait for that I really wanna see it,' Fi said chasing some cucumber round her plate.

'What me in me dress?' Shirley asked smiling at her daughter.

'No me in mine,' came the reply.
'Do you know what I like about you Fi?'
'What Mum?'
'Absolutely nothing…'

TWO

<u>Tuesday, April 17th</u>
8.30am
Busy day today. I've got me dress fitting this afternoon. We're all meeting in the shop in town at half four. David will drop Fi and Jason there after school. He'll go straight home, though, I won't even see him. Don't want him to get even a sniff of me dress. It has to be a complete surprise. I want to see his face when I come through the church door!

Oli's gonna do me hair for me this afternoon. I've already got me tiara at home so he'll put that in ready so we can see the whole lot. Fi hasn't seen the 'ensemble' (that's what the girls in Beautiful Brides call it – well posh) yet, well not all together anyway.

Shirley and Oli arrived at the first client of the day: Sapphire. They had long got used to her neighbourhood. It wasn't the most pleasant place to be, but at least now Oli managed to walk up the stairs in a straight line not jumping from side to side as he used to – they say practice makes perfect and at least he didn't scuttle back to the car at the sight of anything in a hoodie now. He was even getting used to the bull terriers though his walk still speeded up to a mince the minute he spotted one.

'Hiya, kids,' Sapphire said opening the door to them attired in her dressing gown.

'Hiya, babe. Never fear, the rescue squad's here to sort out your big wiry mop,' Oli said barging his way past her and into the living room with his bag of tools.

'Good job I friggin' love you.' Sapphire said looking mildly wounded as she stepped to the side letting Shirley trail in behind.

'So…what the latest word on the street?' Oli asked trying to drag a brush through Sapphire's matted hair.

'Well, I've got a bit of exciting news kids. I'm thinking of setting up an escort agency.'

Shirley and Oli looked at each other and Oli raised a neatly tweezed eyebrow.

'Friggin' 'ell, love, got any punters on your books, yet?' Oli asked.

'Well, I was thinking that's where you come in,' Sapphire said excitedly.

'How d'ya mean?' Shirley asked.

'Well, I was thinking I could take on some of yours, you know, from your sideline. Any of the leftovers who've been dumped and are looking for love… We could even do it as a joint thing.'

'Oh I don't know about that, love, all our work is confidential, that's how come we get so much of it.' Shirley went on, unsure of the direction the conversation was taking.

'Aye, Sapphire it is. Mind you, you could always get a bit of info out of it for us. You know…tell us who's shagging who,' Oli mused.

Shirley didn't look at all convinced. 'Let us have a think, eh, babe. To be honest I'm not too keen on the idea but we'll have a chat about it, eh, Oli?' She promised looking at her pal.

'You had any nights out since last week, then, hon'?' Shirley asked eager to change the subject.

'Yeah we went out last weekend. Had a bloody good time an all. Went in Louise's over the road. She's just come back from two weeks all inclusive in Tenerife and wanted to show off her tan,' Sapphire giggled.

'Get a good one did she?' Oli asked.

'A hell of a tan it is, she looks like an old mahogany side board, it's great. The only white mark she's got's on her arm – you know where they put that band on you for all the free drinks.'

'Oh, aye, yeah. The band of shame – remember? We had that didn't we, when we went to Faliraki last year?' Oli said laughing.

'"Band of shame", what d'ya mean? I think they're bloody great,' Sapphire protested.

'Anyway, great tan then?' Shirley said for the second time in as many minutes trying to change the subject and avoid another potential conversational minefield. Oli seemed determined on picking something guaranteed to send Sapphire off on one. She'd be feeding him to the terrier wielding hoodies before long. Wouldn't they just love a gay scouser in pink to play with…

'Well good. She looks like a set of traffic lights now, though, after our night out. Red and orange from the tan and green from the bruises 'cause she fell on her face when she was pissed.' Sapphire laughed. 'You should get her on your hairdressing books, you know, her hair is like a brillo pad. Especially after her holiday.'

'What, worse than yours?' Oli asked teasing.

'Come on then, love, let's get going. We've got a lot on, an' we want to be finished for at least four.' Shirley sensed hoodies coming over the horizon – there's only so far you can push a girl like Sapphire.

'Oh, got a job on?' Sapphire inquired.

'We have: still that Hard Des. We can't get to the bottom of him. But it's not that…we're going to get a fitting for the wedding,' Shirley said excitedly.

'Oh lovely. I can't get anything on that Des either, I've tried to make a few discreet inquiries like you said, but sweet FA. He's bloody good if there is anything – I'll give him that,' Sapphire went on.

'Anyway we'll be in touch,' Oli said packing up the tools of his trade.

The day went by in a haze of colour and cut and before they knew it they were both in the entrance of Beautiful Brides, Shirley's dream dress awaiting them inside.

'Oh, I'm so excited me heart is racing,' Shirley said clutching her best mate's arm tightly. 'I hardly dare go in…'

'Welcome you two; we've been waiting for you. Your son and daughter are upstairs, Shirley.' A tiny woman of about fifty greeted them once they'd summoned up the courage to cross the threshold.

'Oh, great…' Shirley said following the tiny woman up the stairs.

'I'm Maj. I know you've seen my sister before but she's away in the Caribbean and I'm standing in for her. Glass of wine?' She said handing Shirley and Oli a glass of chilled white.

'Oh my God, you look beautiful…' Shirley said taking the glass of wine and spotting Fiona standing in front of a row of white dresses in her perfectly fitted bridesmaid's dress.

'Isn't she adorable? Fits like a dream,' Maj agreed, brushing out imaginary creases from the front of the dress.

'I love it Mum, really love it.' Fi said almost in tears.

'Bloody 'ell, Fi, you look amazing,' Oli said. 'Can't wait to get my clobber on can I?' He was taking his coat and shoes off in a whirl of expectation.

'And what about this handsome young man?' Maj asked as Jason stepped out of the dressing room.

'Wow Jase you look friggin' gorgeous,' Shirley exclaimed bursting with maternal pride, what prize kids she'd got – their dad had been good for one thing at least: he'd given her these two stars.

Jason did a few model style poses as everyone cheered and smiled. Fi linked arms with him and then, not to be outdone, Oli emerged like the star of the show in all his finery and struck a pose.

'Aww… I'm so proud of you three, you look like…absolutely amazing,' Shirley said wiping the tears from her eyes.

'Right, then, you three: time to put them outfits back now and sit back with a glass of wine and wait for the star of the show,' Maj said looking over at Shirley.

Maj busily tidied away the stunning blue dress and suits and, as if it was the centrepiece of the crown jewels, carefully carried out Shirley's magnificent wedding gown.

Ten minutes later, while Oli, Jason and Fi were chatting excitedly and enjoying their drinks, Shirley entered looking the room looking every bit the perfect bride.

'Mum you look fantastic,' Fi said standing up in appreciation.

'Wow,' was all Jason could manage.

'You look like something from Hollywood, babe,' Oli sniffled taking a tissue from the embroidered box on the nearby table.

Shirley made her way to the mirror and took a look at herself in all her glory for the first time: hair, tiara the lot. 'Oh my God, is that really me?' she gasped. 'I love it, the whole lot, absolutely love it'. She laughed shyly.

'Mr Wilmore's a very lucky man,' Jason said hugging his mum. 'Especially for a teacher!'

'He certainly is,' Fi added.

Then it was tears and tissues all-round (all except Jason, of course, who just muttered under his breath about big girls' blouses), until the glamorous frock was in danger of staining and

Maj put a stop to the little mutual admiration party by putting it back under it's protective covers and ushered them out.

<u>11pm</u>
The dress fitting went really well. The three of them looked really great. I'm so proud to have such beautiful kids and Oli looked as gorgy as ever. Even though I say it meself I looked fab an' all. I didn't hardly recognise meself. The dress fits like a glove. I can't put an inch on, but I don't need to lose anymore either or it will hang on me and that's the best bit; it's so fitted across me boobs and tum it makes me look really slim. I love it and I know David will an' all. He's getting his suit and the boy's suits from the same place so everything is coordinated. I think they've got a fitting soon an' all.

Anyway, it's all coming together on the wedding front. I just wish we could sort out Hard Des.

<u>Wednesday, April 18th</u>
<u>8.30am</u>
We've got the factory girls this afternoon. They asked to swap from their usual Friday this week cos Comb-over is away on business and is due to make an appearance in the office Friday afternoon with a new girl. Angie texted me an' said she's got loads of gossip and will tell us all about it later. Can't wait to find out!

Shirley still in her PJs waltzed into the kitchen to find Shaz sat at the table eating toast.

'Oh, hiya love. Bit out of the way for you kid, what you doing here?' Shirley inquired.

'Got me mum's taxi to drop me off here, didn't I.'

'Your mum's taxi?' Shirley quizzed.

'Yeah, it was free so thought I'd get 'em to drop me off here so's I could go into Strangeways with Fi,' Shaz said grimly tucking into the toast.

'Mo's gonna be on telly, she's gone this morning to Leeds by train to do the filming,' Fi said excitedly.

'Telly, Shaz, bloody hell. What on? ' Shirley asked shocked.

'She's goin' on that Tanya show; you know…the thing that's on every morning.'

'What the one with the no-hopers sleeping with their long lost mother and crap like that?' Jason asked. He'd come in mid-conversation.

'Yeah that's the one. Boss innit?' Shaz said, laughing.

'Oh my God, babe, what's the one your mum's one about?' Oli asked standing in the doorway.

'It's called "I'm addicted to younger men",' Shaz announced mouth full of white sliced.

'Oh my God, babe, I can't believe it! She's gonna go on national telly and tell everyone that?' Oli said alarmed.

'Why not, everyone round here knows it,' Jason put in.

'Oh, aye, yeah, Jase. Remember when she tried it on with you and you were shitting yourself you couldn't perform.' Shaz giggled.

'Do one will ya,' Jason barked and walked out of the room with his bowl of cereals.

'Have they contacted him, I wonder? They do that, don't they – get the other person on and then they have a hell of a friggin' scrap live on air. It's great innit?' Oli said with a mischievous smile.

'Don't be daft, he's in his school uniform anyway.' Shirley answered looking slightly worried. 'I'll kill that Mo if she names him. No offence Shaz.'

'None taken. Don't think she'll mention Jase, Shirl, she's got a list as long as your arm. All the ones she's had success with, she's not gonna mention one she couldn't get is she?' Shaz reassured her.

They all looked at each other. Four minds worked as one: 'Digo!!'

Shirley and Oli arrived at Henshaw's just before lunch time. The factory girls were all sat round tucking into their various lunches. Kelly and Jeanette were tucking into chicken and mushroom Pot Noodle; Jeanette was dipping a bread roll into hers. Susan and Angie had both been over the road to the greasy spoon and had brought back burger and chips. Ali was tucking away from her plastic container – it looked to Shirley like corned beef on white but she couldn't be sure and Gail, who was in charge while Comb-over was away, was just taking the last bite of her tuna on granary.

'Friggin' 'ell it's like a chimp's tea party here, kids…' Oli said, cheerfully, looking around at the girls munching away.

'All right for some… I'm starving,' Shirley said taking her slimming micro' meal from her bag and popping it into the machine. 'Any one for a cuppa?'

'No ta, Gail's sorted us out, you have your dinner and we can tell you all the goss,' Angie said excitedly.

Within a few minutes Shirley was enjoying her slimmer's version of spaghetti Bolognese and Oli a supermarket ready prepared prawn and pasta salad.

'Well, what's been going on? I've been on pins waiting to find out.' Shirley was agog.

'Aye, come on, Angie, dish the dirt, love,' Oli instructed her.

'Well you know Comb-over's been away and our Gail's been in charge?'

'Hope you've cracked the whip,' Oli said teasing.

'Oh, aye, yeah, we've had a great week, a right laugh,' Kelly said happily munching her way through the Pot Noodle.

'Sod that, tell them,' Susan complained. 'You'll wet yourselves when you hear.'

'Ok, ok, well…you know Comb-over's been away in Thailand? Well he's back on Friday and he's bringing a new girl here,' Angie babbled.

'He's gone and bought a mail order bride…' Susan said portentously, stealing Angie's thunder.

'Hey, you!' Angie was annoyed that she'd been outdone.

'Never?' Shirley said, nearly chocking on her spaghetti Bolognaise.

'Yeah. Gail's been checking his emails while he's been away and she found loads from this woman: May Sing. Got all the info, didn't you, queen?' Angie continued, determined to finish the story before Susan butted in again.

'Oh my God, is she gonna work here with you lot?' Oli looked genuinely shocked.

'Well, it said in her emails that she's looking forward to seeing his factory and working for him,' Gail announced.

'How old is she? You hear about it don't you…years younger and all that?' Shirley asked.

'Twenty-three,' said Ali, who was still wading her way through her pile of corned beef on white.

'He always had a fetish for Orientals…' Jeanette said grimly.

'How do you know that?' Susan asked suspiciously.

Oli darted Shirley a panicked look that she immediately returned before giving Jeanette the same look.

'Oh he told me once; he was perving over an oriental page three girl when I took his coffee into him once. Ages ago like…' Jeanette said relieved to have thought so quickly on her feet. Oli and Shirley were the only ones in on the secret of her ill-fated affair with the boss. Something Jeanette was trying to forget and which they'd stumbled on whilst on an earlier sleuthing job.

'And you reckon she's gonna be put in here, to work with you lot?' Oli said shaking his head.

'Why would he put her to work?' Shirley asked.

'Well we don't know that she *is* gonna work here, yet, do we? She's just said she's willing to do so for free. I reckon it's just so as he brings her over,' Ali said ever the pessimist.

'So he's never met her then?' Shirley asked.

'No but she did send a pic of herself. She's really beautiful,' Gail said.

'Friggin' 'ell, has he sent her a pic of him?' Oli asked horrified.

'Yeah he has, but it's one of him about twenty years ago. He's got a head full of hair and not a comb-over in sight,' Gail reported.

'I bet he didn't look that much better, did he?' Oli asked disgusted.

'Nah, not really,' Gail muttered, taking a sip out of her supervisor's mug.

'You'd have to be absolutely friggin' desperate to shag that minger,' Angie moaned.

'Desperate? I'd rather cut off me own leg and shove it up me arse.' Susan laughed almost spitting out her lunch.

'That's a bit extreme, queen.' Oli giggled.' I know what you mean, though, he has gorra face for radio hasn't he?'

'If he was the last person on earth, I wouldn't shag him,' Ali added her tuppence' worth.

Noting Jeanette's unease Shirley decided to change the subject. 'Anyway, I've sorted out me cake, Angie, love. You're mate, Lynda, is all set to do it. Picked it out the other night,' she said brightly.

'Aww…she's a good un, makes lovely cakes…' Angie said, pleased that her recommendation had been acted on.

'Who's that, Shirl?' Gail asked.

'You know, lanky Lynda, works in the pet shop. She makes lovely cakes,' Angie replied.

'Oh yeah, I know her, me sister had a cake from her once for me nephew's birthday. The cake looked lovely an' all that, but I'm sure she'd ran out of chocolate buttons and added a few dog ones, they didn't taste quite the same as the others…'

'Oh great…' Shirley sighed.

'You'll be all right so long as you're not having a chocolate one,' Gail commented.

'I am,' Shirley said grimly.

<u>8pm</u>

I've just texted Lanky Lynda about me cake and told her we've had second thoughts about the choccie buttons and I've asked her to pipe some fondant icing around it instead! She can't use her doggie buttons on it then. I was gonna cancel her completely, but I'd have felt too tight and, like Oli said, Angie's cake was a nice one and she's cheap an' all – not that that has anything to do with it cos on this wedding we're splashing out.

I still can't get over old Comb-over and his mail order bride. Well, if that's what it is. Oh… I've just realised how're we gonna get in next week to do the girls hair if he's got his bird sitting there doing the work?? Nevermind, the girls will have thought of something or maybe we'll have to give her a freebie and tell her to keep her gob shut or summat.

Old Comb-over must have been looking for love for a bit now, especially since his wife left him after the swinging parties. She's got some new fella now an' all, I heard. I'm glad. Still, can't believe Comb-over's cheating was one of our early detective jobs an' I still remember it well. Jeanette from the factory hasn't gone anywhere near him since, I think she was well put off with the swingers – the old perv – and now he's bringing some poor cow over from Thailand. I can't believe the cheek of him. Surely May Sing will see sense but I remember watching a programme about it

46

and the brides seem to worship the old mingers that bring them over. Oh well, we'll have a good look at her and a chat see if we can talk her round.

Be next Friday, though, for me and Oli unless one of the girls texts us with some major goss and an excuse for us to drop in for a nosy!

Gonna have to go to the gym tomorrow an' all, haven't been since the move. Not long to go now...just need to keep the weight off till the wedding, then I can ease off a bit. I don't wanna put it all back on like but it's friggin' killing me not having me Kit-Kat with me coffee of a morning and afternoon tea break. It's not quite the same, coffee and an apple!!

I'm still thinking about that old tart Mo an' all. I wonder if she'll name Digo on the telly. That morning's show is one not to be missed that's for sure.

Anyway 100 sit ups now before me no added sugar hot choccie – tastes friggin' awful but at least it's sweet – then an early night for me. Stops me thinking of food!

<u>Thursday, April 19th</u>
<u>8.30pm</u>
Packed me gym bag ready... I'm gonna try and do a bit there this dinner. I have to make sure I'm all trim; no good just cutting down I wanna be toned up an all. I've been going now for a few months. Can't be arsed half the time but once I'm there I'm ok. I've got this monthly membership so I can go anytime I like. It costs a bit, thirty quid a month, but I think that's a good thing cos it makes me go, you know, cos I've paid for it like. It'd be a hell of a waste of money otherwise.

Bit like when them in the factory were doing that slimming lark and eating and drinking the same old crap after the meetings. No, I'm determined to keep it up. I may go for a swim today see what Oli feels like. Oh, aye, yeah, he's joined an' all, not that he needs to lose weight or anything – he's just joined to keep me company and check out the fit lads pumping iron.

Shirley closed her diary threw it into her large brown fake designer label handbag and made her way downstairs.

'Hey soft lad, don't forget your gym stuff today…we're going dinner time, gonna do an hour. And put your Speedos in an' all, I fancy a few lengths.' Shirley doled out the day's instructions as she poured herself an orange juice.

'Aye, ok, babe, so long as we can have a bit of time in the jacuzzi after just to have a relax and an unwind,' Oli said happily.

'Oh, yeah. No probs, we've got a couple of hours' break in between calls today.'

'Oh good. I hope we can finish early an' all, I've got an appointment and I was hoping you'd come with me,' Oli said grabbing Shirley's arm excitedly.

'Oh, aye, yeah…what you got planned? Am I getting a look at this gorgeous Marc with a c, then?' Shirley asked equally excited.

'No, babe, even more exciting than that. I'm going to see this gorgeous creature,' Oli announced holding out a picture.

'Oh…my…God,' Shirley giggled.

Facing her was a picture of the most adorable chihuahua in the local newspaper.

'That's Trixi, the mum, she's had three pups and they're ready next week. I'm really keen babe, I've phoned and they sound gorgeous. Two little girls and one little boy. So I've said we'll call in at half four just phoned her now only just seen the ad in the

paper. Even the name, babe, Trixi – it's fate brought her to me…'
Oli went on, thrilled at the prospect of being a 'dad' again.

'Well, she is cute, Oli, but are have you really thought this through. I mean this is the first I've heard of you wanting a dog. Are you sure you're ready you know after…' Shirley tailed off.

Looking upset and fighting back the tears Oli said, 'Aye, babe, I know what you mean but I've got to move on. It's been nearly a year and the counsellor in the doctor's said it may take a while but one day I would feel ready to love again.'

Giving Oli a big hug, Shirley remembered the pain he had gone through when his beloved cat Mixie had accidentally got out and been run over by the milk float. He'd cried for months solid, blaming himself. Shirley had been very patient with him but even her patience wore thin when Oli refused to have anything to do with any milk products or fresh orange juice for the following six months. Eventually, she had persuaded him to have a little chat with his doctor who after four weeks of Oli visiting him with the same story had referred him to the surgery's counsellor.

How Mixie'd got out no one knew but it was on a day that Digo had gone round to Oli's to pick up some hair dye that he'd left in his kitchen. It wasn't the wisest move asking Digo but Jason was ill in bed and Fi was over at her nan's doing a job for her and Auntie Dilys so there was no choice. Shirley and Oli had been all set up in a client's house ready to do the hair and Digo and his scooter were available. To this day Digo swears he was in and out in no time, he just picked up the spare key, which Oli always hides in the back under a plant pot, picked up the hair dye from the kitchen worktop and left; he said he never even saw Mixie. Poor Oli arrived home to find Mixie lying on top of a milk crate and three pints of milk, a tray of toffee yogurts and two bottle of fresh orange on his step with a note from Bob the milkman saying sorry.

Oli had a proper funeral for Mixie and the cat was buried in the pet graveyard. Jason was the bearer and carried the specially built pet coffin that Oli had bought from the internet. There were flowers and speeches and after the private burial (it was only Oli, Shirley, Jason and Fiona) they went out for tea and a few drinks to celebrate the good times they'd all shared with Mixie. Shirley struggled to think of any good times, as each time she had any contact with Mixie the cat had either scratched her or given her a menacing look, but for Oli's sake she smiled thoughtfully as he asked them all to remember Mixie in their own way.

'Well, Oli, if you're sure you're ready hon' then ok, we'll go after work,' Shirley said looking at the newspaper again smiling.

'Come on you two, you giving us a lift or what?' Jason butted in, taking the newspaper from Shirley's hands.

'Yeah, come on, we were waiting for you. Where's Fi?' Shirley asked.

'Trying to do something with her hair – it looks like a Brillo pad.'

'We've no time for that,' Shirley said looking for her keys in the lucky dip that was her handbag.

'Fi…hurry up kid we've gorra go,' Oli shouted up the stairs as they all made their way to the hall.

'What's this rat you're looking at?' Jason asked looking at the page with Trixi's photo on it.

'Hey, you…' Oli snatched the paper from Jason. 'That may be the mum of your new little cousin.'

'Eh?' Jason said looking totally confused.

Meanwhile there were screams and bangs from upstairs as Fi tried to tame her locks.

'What the hell are you doing?' Shirley shouted up the stairs.

'I've had a disaster with them Velcro rollers, me hair's gone all frizzy,' Fi shouted back.

'Come here, babe, I'll put it up for you,' Oli said marching up the stairs.

'What's with this rat, then, Mum?' Jason asked Shirley still looking at the paper.

'Oh it's Oli's new baby...well maybe. We're going to look at Trixi's pups after work. Hurry up you two.' Shirley yelled up the stairs, trying to have two conversations simultaneously.

Within minutes Oli and Fi walked down the stairs with Fiona sporting a glamorous up 'do'.

'Wow, lovely.' Shirley was impressed. 'That's why I have you, Oli, work miracles you can.' She planted a kiss on Oli's cheek.

'Can we go, then, eh?' Jason asked looking pointedly at his watch. Anyone'd think he actually wanted to go to school...

Half an hour later with the kids dropped off, Shirley and Oli were engrossed in their first clients of the day, Shirley thinking of her gym work out and Oli thinking of his new baby and wondering what he or she might look like.

The morning went by in a whirl of curlers, straighteners and hair dye. Before they knew it, it was two o'clock.

'Hey it's a late dinner for us today, babe, what's gone wrong?' Oli asked feeling and looking shattered.

'Well, I thought we'd go for it this morning and ease up this afternoon. We've only got a cut and blow in Baker Street on the way to see the pups.'

'Ok then, we'll have a butty then go the gym, quick swim and jacuzzi then do Pearl and her mother's cut and blows and go have a look at me babies,' Oli said clapping his hands in excitement.

9pm

What is it with people that go the gym? I was looking at them this afta. They are either skinny as hell and don't need to go or they are great big fat things that can't do anything. There are hardly any normal sized people that go there. What's that all about? The fella on the reception, oh my God I can't believe him. He's a massive great big thing – you'd think they'd employ someone who looks the part. The laugh of it was that Oli was trying to use this machine for his waist and he couldn't do it properly, well to me he looked as if he was doing it properly but there was this like clunking noise while he was doing it, then the big fat fella came over and had the cheek to tell Oli he was doing it wrong. Oli felt dead embarrassed cos a few people cottoned on. I told him not to worry just carry on next time doing it the way he wants to, what does that big fat fella know about it anyway?!! Friggin' cheek.

Oli had a relax though in the jacuzzi; we didn't bother with the swim, we couldn't be arsed, so we just sat in the jacuzzi and looked at all the old women doing the aquarobics class, bless 'em. Had a quick five minutes in the steam room, cos Oli said he needed a bit of a facial then made our way out. But the really exciting news is that on our way out who did we see in the gym but Hard Des – we couldn't believe it, he was with a couple of fellas going for it in the weights section, that's near the way you go in and out of the gym so we had a good look, it was definitely him. So he's keen on his keeping fit then, an' wants to look good. It gave Oli a chance to have a good look at him anyway, cos he said he wasn't sure if he'd got the right person before!! Friggin' 'ell.

We're out tomoz trying to get something on him. Nothing suspicious today, just him and a group of his mates but you can tell he's a right poser...he was there checking himself out in the mirror big time. Dick head.

I'm up in me room getting away from Oli for a bit;

he's driving me mad over that dog! We went to see Trixi and her puppies this afta, they were absolutely gorgeous I must say: two little girls and one boy, one was all fawn, a little girl and the other two were mostly fawn with little bits of white on them. Since we got back Oli's been on the internet getting as much info as he can on the friggin' breed. He's found out they are nosy and love to investigate, so he thinks he can bring it out with us on the job!!

Anyway, after spending over an hour at the house he's going for the fawn little girl and cos the breeder said she's got the perfect apple shaped head he's gonna call her...you guessed it Apple!!

We're going next week to pick her up. She won't weigh more than 4 to 5 lbs when she's fully grown and will only be about 6 or 7 inches tall. I think Jason was right she is a rat!

Didn't see David tonight. He's got a load of marking to do, so I thought I'd better leave him to it. Won't see him tomorrow night either, cos we're going to try and see if we can get anything on old Hard Des. Really miss David when I don't see him. Can't wait till we're married. Anyway, I'm gonna get an early night tonight cos we've got them factory girls tomorrow so we can catch up on Comb-over's mail order bride. I had a text from Angie earlier on tonight saying it's ok for us to call in tomorrow. We weren't meant to like, cos we only went on Wednesday, but Angie said there's been a change of plan in the factory and Comb-over is calling in the morning and taking the afternoon off like usual. We're gonna go in late afternoon though just in case, none of them need their hair doing so it's just a coffee and a chat. Then it's a late night catching out Hard Des.

Shirley pulled on her pyjamas and went down stairs to join Jason and Fiona who were engrossed in a film about secret agents. Oli was still sat with his laptop on his knee researching chihuahuas.

'Oh, hiya, babe, where've you been?' he asked momentarily looking up from his laptop.

'Oh, just getting changed and taking me make-up off.'

'You don't fancy making a brew?' Fi asked with a fake smile and batting her eyelashes. 'Pleeease?'

'Aye, ok, nothing much else going on is there?' Shirley complained looking at the TV and Oli still engrossed in the laptop.

'I could murder a bit of toast an' all,' Jason suggested not even looking away from the screen.

'None for me, babe, no point after the gym is there…' Oli said then, in the next breath, 'Oh, sod it, I'll have a piece but can you make mine brown.' He reached out to squeeze Shirley's hand.

Shirley smiled at him, she didn't mind really – how could she complain when Oli was putting her and the kids up for so long and all for nothing?

Walking through into the kitchen, Shirley put the radio on and flicked the switch for the kettle. She pulled out of the cupboard her fat free hot chocolate and a slimmer's cereal bar, determined to keep the weight off till after the wedding at least. She popped four slices of white bread into the toaster and picked up her mobile phone that she had left to charge on the kitchen counter. A little envelope indicated a message. It was from David and had only just been sent. She seemed to be able to sense when he'd sent her a message, just had a feeling somehow. Excitedly she opened the message: *Missing you so much, love you lots xxxxxx.*

Smiling she replied, *Miss you 2 gorgeous can't wait to c u xxxxxxxxx*

'Shirl, quick babe, come here.' She was brought back to reality by Oli's scream.

'What is it?' Shirley asked rushing in to find out what was so urgent.

'Oh my God, I have to have them,' Oli trilled turning his laptop to face the intrigued Shirley.

She came face to face with a page full of chihuahua and toy dog accessories. A bag to carry the dog in, a diamond studded collar, a shocking pink doggy t-shirt with *Top Bitch* written in pink glittery writing, a doggy head band, you name it, it was there.

'Oh lovely,' Shirley said, horrified at the very thought. It was bad enough that Mixie had similar regalia but at least Mixie rarely saw the light of day, Mixie had been a house cat. The thought that Oli might, and she knew he would, parade that poor little Apple around the place dressed like that depressed her more than a bit. Poor flippin' dog.

'I've put an order in already, won't be long and they'll be here,' Oli said clapping his hands in delight.

'You haven't even got the dog, yet, babe.'

'I want them all here for when my little Apple arrives and as a welcome to your new home pressie I've ordered this,' he said, smugly, pointing at a tiny diamond tiara.

'That's dead tight, that,' Fiona announced, walking up to the computer to see what all the commotion was about.

'What do you mean, it's friggin' lovely. My Apple will want for nothing.' Oli looked wounded.

'I think that maybe a tiara is a little bit OTT, babe,' Shirley said gently.

'Don't be such spoilsports you two, what do you think Jase?' Oli called, turning the laptop to face Jason who was sitting on the floor with his back against the sofa.

'Oh my God, they look like right tits,' Jason laughed.

Feeling very hurt Oli, quickly pulled the top down on the laptop and said, 'Well get used to it, I'm getting them.'

Quickly changing the subject Shirley turned back towards the kitchen, 'Best check on that toast eh?'

Half an hour later, all was forgiven and the four had got together an order for the new arrival. Well Jason had nodded and grunted in the appropriate places, which was enough to satisfy Oli.

THREE

Still excited at the prospect of all his new purchases Oli was up early and had made a full cooked breakfast for the four of them when they came down.

'Come on kids, sit yourselves down, I didn't sleep a wink last night I was so excited about me doggie treats.' He put a pile of toast down on the table.

'Hey I could get used to this.' Jason said tucking into the plate of fried eggs, bacon, sausage, beans and mushrooms.

'I've done you a slimming version, babes.' Oli told Shirley who looked a little concerned that all her hard work at the gym and supermarket was about to go to waste.

'Aww thanks kid.'

They had their usual Friday morning appointments booked and the pair had Sapphire to look forward to, she'd phoned earlier on asking for an extra this week as she had a night out booked and needed to look extra special. So, fifteen minutes after the last plate was emptied, they made their way through the barrage of supermarket trolleys, old prams and rusty bikes outside Sapphire's block of flats.

'Hiya, kids, how you doing?' Sapphire asked.

'Fine, ta. So what's the hurry? We were only here on Tuesday…' Oli asked eager as ever to get the updates on any gossip.

'Oh, I'm off out on the town tonight. Hey…you two had a chance to think about me offer on the escort front?'

'Oh, damn, no we haven't.' Shirley had genuinely forgotten about it what with the dress fitting and the puppies and everything.

'Oh no, kid, soz, we've had a lot on this week,' Oli added.

'Oh, what the old detective work?' Sapphire said eyes widening.

'Nah, Shirley's wedding fitting, but even more exciting than that I'm getting a pup!' Oli announced getting out his mobile phone to show Sapphire the pictures and video he's taken of Trixi and her brood.

'Urgh you're not getting one of them rats are you?' Sapphire pulled a face.

'Yeah, I am, so do one or I'll give you a friggin' scalping,' Oli said roughly dragging Sapphire's matted mass of hair with the brush.

'All right, all right, keep your thong on,' Sapphire protested, pulling away in pain.

'I should think so…' Oli eased off only slightly with his brush.

'Think on though, kids. If you want to come in on this escort lark it could be great for all of us,' Sapphire said with great enthusiasm, trying to overcome the pain she felt from her still tingling scalp.

'We'll have a think, eh, girl. Our work is dead confidential, we don't want to shaft any of our loyal vulnerable customers,' Oli said, nearing the end of his tether with her matted hair.

Noticing his agitation Shirley took over and tried teasing the tangled locks with a tail comb.

'Aye, ok, kids, but if you've got one who's been done over, bit fragile, send them over to me, and I'll have them back in the saddle again in no time.'

Friday, April 20<u>th</u>
2pm
Just having our dinner break. We had that loony Sapphire this morning, she's still after us passing customers on to her, you know, the ones who've had the dirty done to them. She wants a mix of women and the fellas. Wants to have a range of clientele. She said she'll sort out the fragile ones, more like push 'em over the edge! Anyway, we keep changing the subject – hopefully she'll get the message.

I could see Oli was pissed off with her this morning, he was bit rough with her an' all. Just as well it was only Sapphire, anyone else might've sued. He's gone over the road to get a bar of chocolate to keep him going, said it's his nerves waiting for Apple to arrive! Factory girls in a bit, just for a goss and a coffee, then we've got our night out to look forward to...that friggin' Des to catch at it.

Shirley could see Oli half walking, half running across the road in a sort of camp skip; she hid her diary in her bag and took out her make-up bag for a quick touch up before they set off again.
Carefully applying her lip liner she listened to Oli chirp away about his chocolate bar and the special offer they had on chocolate chip cookies.
'…so I bought a couple of packs to cheer up those miserable cows in the factory this afternoon.'

'Mmm.' was all Shirley could manage as she carefully traced the outline of her already perfect lips with the lip liner.

'It suits you that, babe, is it a new one?' Oli inquired.

'Yeah, got it to try out for the wedding,' Shirley replied handing over the pencil to Oli for closer inspection.

'Oh nice, it's a good one an' all, cost a bit I daresay, but you do want your lips to look kissable don't you, babe? A nice lip gloss with that I'll friggin' kiss you meself.' Oli laughed as he popped the lip liner back in her make-up bag.

A couple of hours later and the pair were parked up outside Henshaw's. They made sure that the coast was clear regarding Comb-over's car.

'I'll just give Angie a ring to double check,' Oli insisted. He picked up his blue crystal studded mobile from the glove box and dialled Angie's mobile.

'Ok babe coast is clear and, better still, the kettles on,' he said, snapping the mobile shut and getting out of the car.

They were warmly greeted by the gang who had packed in the work for the day, determined to enjoy their last hour just chatting and drinking coffee.

'Gail's made a sponge,' Kelly announced, bringing the cake to the table with a roll of industrial blue tissue to serve as napkins.

'Oh lovely, seeing as you made it, Gail, love, I'll have a piece…just a small one mind,' Shirley said unable to resist temptation.

'So, come on you lot, what's the goss, has the wanderer returned?' Oli asked, settling down to his milky coffee with two sugars and a slice of Gail's sponge.

'Oh, aye, yeah, come back earlier then expected,' Angie said eager to dish the dirt.

'He's only brought that woman here this morning, no more than a kid, couldn't speak a word of English—' Ali butted in, to Angie's disgust.

'Hey…I'll tell 'em,' Angie said sharply.

Ali rolled her eyes: 'Go on then, queen.'

'Well…she's here for a few weeks holiday and apparently her two sisters are joining her soon,' Angie began.

'We reckon he's gonna gerr'em to work here as slave labour, like,' Ali said unable to contain herself. Angie shot her an angry look.

'Never? Oh…my…God!' Oli said alarmed.

'He wouldn't, would he?' Shirley said, looking over at Jeanette who knew Comb-over more intimately than the others.

'What you looking at me for? How should I know?' Jeanette objected, turning slightly pink.

Fortunately no one seemed to have noticed Shirley's slip, they were too concerned over the fact that their boss may be some kind of slave trader.

'Well, it's a case of watch this space girls, I reckon,' Oli said taking a careful sip of his piping hot coffee.

They munched their way through Gail's sponge and Oli's two packets of chocolate chip cookies in a haze of chit chat, speculation and laughter.

'So… What's the plan for tonight, then, you gorgeous beauties?' Oli asked.

'Oh we're off out, just a few of us like…me, Susan, Kelly, Jeanette and Gail, and Ali's been given parole for good behaviour an' all,' Angie said mischievously, smiling at Ali now she had been given priority in the Comb-over slave trader story.

'Why don't you two come with us?' Kelly asked cheerfully.

'Well we're off out tonight, anyway, just a quiet drink mind.'

'Oh, don't worry we'll sort that out, don't be worrying 'bout a quiet drink, you can join us. We're having a wild night out, there's a foam party going on in the Water Fall Club. We're going to Susan's to start the night off with a few wines and a few shots then we're heading to the club about half ten,' Angie said keen to entice the duo along.

'Oh, hell, no chance… I'm not up for that kind of night. I'd need to build up to that one.' Shirley laughed remembering they were actually working for Jan that night trying to nail Hard Des.

Shirley looked over at Oli who was grinning away at the prospect of a night on the town with the girls. They were always guaranteed a laugh.

'We're going to the George and Dragon, just for a quiet one,' Shirley insisted.

'Oh, aye, yeah, we are sorry, kids,' Oli said looking disappointed.

'Oh you boring sods, no way. You're coming with us it'll be boss,' Susan insisted.

'Well… Maybe after a few in Susan's we could all go over to the George and Dragon then onto the foam party?' Oli suggested looking hangdog at Shirley.

'What's with this wanting to go to the George and Dragon?' Angie said confused. 'It's not your usual kind of boozer.'

'Oh they've got a new chef and everyone said he makes a cracking steak and ale pie, talk of half our regulars. Been promising ourselves all week,' Oli piped up quickly trying to cover himself and his big mouth.

Looking impressed with his quick response, Shirley gave in and slowly smiling nodded her head.

'Oh, great, eh girls – home made steak and ale pie, that'll line our stomachs up a treat, you're on,' Ali said warmly. The sentiment was echoed by the rest of the girls who set about discussing their favourite meals and where they'd eaten the best ones, warming up for a night of food, drink and frolics in the foam.

6pm
Well I can't believe that we're going on such a wild night out tonight. Don't know how the hell I got roped into it. If I'm honest, though, I can't wait. It's been

ages since I really let me hair down. Shaz and Digo have arrived and the four kids have ordered a pizza delivery so I know they'll be ok. Apparently Shaz's mum did that telly show and it's gonna be aired next week, on Monday in fact so we have to remember to watch that.

Anyway, I'm gonna try and beat Oli into the shower now cos we've gorra be in Susan's by seven, taxi's due here at quarter to, so I'd best get me skates on.

Engulfed in the aroma of her energizing shower gel Shirley got lost for a while in her own little world. Her thoughts drifted to her forthcoming wedding, not to mention the stag and hen parties. She was abruptly bought back to reality by a frantic knock on the door.

'Hurry up, babe, we're gonna be late,' Oli shouted from the other side of the door.

'Coming,' Shirley answered, turning off the steaming shower. Wrapped in a towel she opened the door.

'Hey, I've just phoned the George and Dragon and they have got steak and ale pie on the menu, thank frig' for that,' Oli said starting to undress.

'Eh?' Shirley asked looking confused.

'Well we said that's why we're going there, hon, for the friggin' pie. We'd look a right couple of tits if there was no pie on the menu after this afta, so I just phoned up to make sure.' Oli now stood just inside the door in nothing but his tight jersey boxers.

'Very impressive, all this detective work has given you ideas, very good love,' Shirley said brightly.

Oli smiled proudly.

'So what would you have done if they didn't do the pie?' Shirley inquired.

Oli just pulled a face, shrugged and started to pull down his pants. Quickly Shirley nipped out past him and pulled the door closed behind her before she saw any more than she wanted to, best pal or not. She had her limits.

Shirley looked through her array of clothes and decided on a red pencil skirt, black chiffon blouse with a plain black bra underneath and a pair of high black sandals. Her toe nails and finger nails were painted red anyway so she wouldn't have to waste time doing that. She smoothed on moisturizer with a hint of fake tan all over her body. This had been a nightly ritual for weeks to build up a decent tan for the big day. She decided to pull her hair up into a scruffy but very flattering bun, with bit of wispy hair gently framing her face. Make-up done it was only a case of a squirt of her favourite perfume and she was good to go.

'Hiya, Shirl, you look nice, like your shoes,' Shaz said as Shirley walked into the living room to wait for Oli.

'Ta Shaz. All right Digo?'

Digo was texting away on his mobile sat on the sofa. 'All right,' he said, momentarily looking up.

'So…big night out?' Shaz asked always eager to know what everyone was up to, just in case there was an opportunity for mayhem she couldn't miss.

Knowing full well Shaz's game, Shirley replied, 'Aye, yeah, just a girly thing. Hey, tell me, love, how did yer mum get on with that telly thing?'

Digo suddenly took a great interest in the conversation and the texting he was so determined on came to a sudden halt.

'Oh she had a boss time. It's gonna be on the telly on Monday, I think. She had a lovely spread an' all that, you know, behind the scenes,' Shaz said relishing the fact that her mum had had her fifteen minutes of fame.

'Ooh, well, did she get a good reception, you know, from the audience?' Shirley asked.

'They booed her off stage, but she wasn't arsed 'cause there was this dead fit seventeen year old on an' all, he was addicted to the older woman, like. Well, anyway, he stuck up for her and I think they hit it off.'

'Oh my God.'

Digo and Jason looked from Shirley to Shaz and simultaneously shook their heads.

'So is she seeing him now then?' Fiona asked her mate.

'Oh, nah, she just had a bit of a sesh with him in the pub and a bit of…' Shaz tailed off.

Complete silence swallowed up the room. They all knew exactly what Mo was like there was no need to finish Shaz's sentence for her.

'So when's the mini-marathon?' Shirley asked breaking the silence.

'Sunday,' Shaz said smugly.

'So make sure you're all free to cheer her on,' Fiona said proudly.

'And you an' all, Fi, you're the pacemaker, aren't you?' Shirley said.

'Oh no I'm not doing that anymore we've checked the rules and I'm not allowed, have to run the whole 5k and, to be honest, I can't be arsed. Come an' see you though, babe.' She said to Shaz, warmly squeezing her friend's arm.

'Ta,' Shaz smiled back. 'Not sure how far I'll go, but I'm gonna go for it after all this training.'

'What, on the sun bed?' Jason laughed.

'Yeah. And I have put a bit of special training in,' Shaz giggled in reply. 'Don't you lot worry I'll be all right, no danger. It's gonna be brill, you'll all be dead impressed.'

'Tadaaaa.' Oli announced standing in the doorway dressed in white skinny jeans with a silver and white studded belt, a tight white t-shirt and white and silver trainers.

'Gorgeous,' Shirley assured him.

'And just in time. Taxi's here,' Oli said looking over his shoulder down the hall.

Blowing kisses to the teenagers, Shirley and Oli giggled their way to the waiting taxi ready for their fabulously foamy night out.

'We have *got* to watch that show on Monday,' Shirley said already touching up her lippy in the back of the cab.

'I know…it'll be dead good to see that Mo getting booed off stage. We'll have to Sky-plus it an' all for the kids, eh? Watch it again with them, with our tea.'

'Ok, kids, behave yourselves,' Bill the taxi driver said, as he pulled up outside Susan's two-up two-down.

'As if…' Oli giggled, handing Bill the fare.

Susan stood in the open doorway with a drink each for the newly arrived pair: a wine glass full of a blue liquid with a few frilly bits hanging over the sides.

'Hiya, queens, we've made a start, hope you don't mind, and we booked a minibus, hon', so you can have your steak and ale pie all right,' she said to Oli handing him his drink then pinching his bum as he made his way into the house.

An hour raced by in a sea of laughter and screams and the gang were already well on their way to a Saturday morning hangover when they pulled up outside the George and Dragon.

'Hey, I could eat a scabby horse between two mankey mattresses,' Angie said as they all sat down eager to enjoy the best steak and ale pie in Liverpool.

'Hey, eyes left, eyes left…' Oli muttered under his breath as he noticed Hard Des walk in, all dressed in black with his black hair slicked back and his top half decorated with a mountain of gold jewellery.

'Hey you two, who you got your eye on now?' Angie asked not missing a trick.

'Never you mind,' Oli said, tucking into his middle of the road, if he was perfectly honest, steak and ale pie.

'Not that minger over there?' Susan asked looking over at Hard Des.

'Nah, we were just saying look at the state of him, with all that gold he looks like he's been with DI Gene stuck in the eighties,' Shirley suggested eager to get the factory girls off the trail.

It must have done the trick as Angie piped up, 'I love the music of the eighties me.'

'I'm gonna text Marc, see if he fancies meeting up with us in the foam, that ok?' Oli asked Shirley.

'Course it is, the more the merrier…'

'And I need a private word with you lot at some point an' all, to let you in on the latest for the hen night,' Oli added.

'Oh, aye, yeah, what is going on then? I've been given the date and sod all else.' Shirley inquired.

'That's all you need to know, babe, all you need to know.' Oli smiled squeezing her hand.

'Yeah, but it's next week, I need to know what to pack an' all that,' Shirley protested.

'What's your fella doing, hon'?' Susan asked trying to distract her from interrogating them about the secret destination for the about to be legendary hen weekend. There was no way she'd guess where they were going to take her. Not in a million years! The rest of the girls giggled amongst themselves at Shirley's frustration.

'Away on one of them activity weekends with the lads from work, and our boys, it's in Amsterdam though so I'm not sure what activities they'll be doing. He did ask Oli an' all,' Shirley went on looking at Oli smiling.

'Very kind, but not my scene getting all covered in mud and playing action man. It's all above board though babe, don't you be worrying.' Oli assured her. 'Far rather rough it with you load of old tarts,' he said, laughing and lifting his wine glass in a toast to the girls.

Plates all cleaned up, the gang made their way from the pub

onto the club. As they left they passed Hard Des who was standing in a corner alone nursing his pint.

'Fancy getting soaped up with a group of gorgeous girls?' Angie winked and tried to snuggle up to him.

'You're all right, ta,' Hard Des said pushing her back with one gold-ringed hand. 'Got things to do.' Putting his pint down on the bar and checking his watch, he headed out the pub door leaving the usually cocky Angie lost for words.

Looking put out, Angie took her pint of lager and downed it in one. It was expertly done, she managed not to spill even a drop on her red and black print dress. Slamming the beer glass down on the bar top, she patted down her large bushy and slightly frizzy brown hair that was held in place with a large red floral clip. Shirley was puzzled, even Angie's ample bosom trying to escape from the low cut dress wasn't tempting enough for the supposedly womanising Hard Des. So just what was he up to?

'The brush off from a minger!' Oli announced. 'The cheek!'

Two hours later the girls were dancing the night away in the foam party along with Oli and Marc with a c.

Kelly was centre stage, hair in a half-beehive, half-bun and a sequined band across her forehead, with her clutch bag under one arm and the occasional whoo coming from her mouth she made a few heads turn. With her husband working away, Kelly made every opportunity to strut her stuff count.

'I don't know why I'm dancing to this, it's shit,' Kelly said, struggling in her four inch heels over to where the rest of the gang were sitting.

'Hey, best sit here now, the foam's getting switched on in a bit, don't want to get your hair messed up,' Susan said to Kelly. 'We'll watch all the action from here.

The rest of the night was spent trying to avoid the foam in the foam party that they had decided to go to and the gang were soon in a minibus taxi on their way home, with the added addition of Marc with a c who was wedged somewhat uncomfortably between Susan and Angie all the way home. The night hadn't been that eventful detection-wise although Shirley and Oli had established that Hard Des wouldn't look at Angie but he was obviously on his way to something more important than a pint in the pub, but what exactly that was the duo had to get working on and quick.

Saturday, April 21st
11am

I'm still in bed, going over last night in me head. Not very eventful on the old detective front, which let's face it was the only reason we went out, but we had a hell of a laugh anyway. Angie was well away. I thought Susan was going to batter her she was trying it on with so many, and poor Ali couldn't take the heat, every time I looked at her she was fanning herself with a soggy beer mat.

There was no news either on the Comb-over front, the mail order bride hasn't been seen. Apparently Gail overheard Comb-over talking to her on the phone and it sounded like he's got her doing jobs around the house, cleaning and ironing and that. There was talk, though, that she's be working part time in the factory and the rest in his house. Like a friggin' slave poor cow.

Marc with a c is here – he came back with us last night. Aww he's lovely, gorgeous and so into Oli you can see it a mile off. He sat through an hour of Oli showing him stuff he's got for Apple, the new pup; he even thought the tiara was cute so gained a few more brownie points.

I was really missing David when I got back and was

up for ages talking to him on the phone. I really wanted him over but at the last minute his boys landed on him, so he had to spend the night with then. They're meeting us in town today for a bit of shopping then we're going out for an Indian tonight. I've met them a few times over this last year but I still get nervous because I want them to like me. The kids get on well with them and Shaz; well she fancies the pair of them, surprise, surprise. They are good looking, mind, just like their dad, Ben he's 19 and Josh he's 16. Josh is an emo, long floppy dark hair, black skinny jeans you know the type. Shaz will try and get in on today but I'm gonna make sure it's just us: me, David and the kids. It'll give Oli and Marc with a c the whole day to themselves. They look like they'd appreciate a bit of privacy. I'm meeting everyone in town at one so I'd best get me skates on.

Shirley was greeted by Marc, who was busy in the kitchen making breakfast. Oli sat proudly at the table looking over lovingly at Marc every now and then. Even Fi and Jason were up and ready.

'Good God, you lot all up?' Shirley said with surprise.

'Well, Ben texted me last night and said we were meeting up in town…don't want to be late,' Jason said.

'That means we've got the day to ourselves as well then.' Oli smiled.

'And night, we're out for a curry later…' Fi said raising her eyebrows.

'Nice one,' grinned Marc.

After breakfast the kids went to get ready and Marc carried on in the kitchen clearing all the breakfast things away.

'Hey babe, I need a word with you about work,' Oli lowered his voice to a discreet mumble. 'We've had a new request. Got a phone call this morning, from a woman saying her girlfriend is cheating on her with a fella,' Oli whispered.

'Oh God we've got such a lot on, what with the wedding, house move an' that and we still haven't sorted out Hard Des have we?' Shirley said looking concerned.

'Well, I did think that at first but can we afford to say no, after all we have got a reputation to keep up?'

'Ok then, if you think we can manage…' Shirley wasn't entirely convinced.

Breaking into the unease Fiona shouted from upstairs. 'Mum, Shaz wanted to meet us in town today, but I've put her off so long as we can take the boys to watch her in the mini-marathon tomorrow. That ok?'

Oli's face broke out into a huge smile and Shirley giggled. 'Aye, ok, love.'.

'And tell her, kid, I'll bring Marc with us an' all to cheer her on,' Oli said with a mischievous smile.

'Aww, great, she'll be made up,' Fiona said walking down the stairs.

'We all set?' Jason asked making his way to the door.

Minutes later they were in the Cuts and Curls van heading for town and the three hunky fellas waiting for them, leaving Oli with only his own gorgeous man to think about for once.

11pm

Aww, we've had a brilliant day with the boys, and we decided to go back to David's for the night. The kids have said they'll crash out on the sofas but Ben's gonna give up his bed for Fiona – bless him – and the lads will sleep down stairs. We're gonna go back now and have a few beers before we hit the sack and have a good old chat. The lads wanna talk stag nights cos Jason's going with them for this activities thingie. Only hope we get up in time for Shaz, cos she'll be gutted if we miss it. Sounds like she's put loads of effort in. She did say she's put a bit extra in this last week an' all.

<u>Sunday, April 22nd</u>
<u>11am</u>

We're gonna be late if we don't hurry up she's on the starting line at 12 midday.

Shirley frantically hooted her horn outside Oli's house and waited for Oli and Marc who came racing out of the house – Oli with only one shoe on and the other in his hand. 'Hiya kids, we late?'

'Not late enough, unfortunately,' David said grimly, from the driver's seat.

'Hey what's up with you, you look about as excited to be here as Bernard Matthews' pet turkey at Crimbo,' Oli announced putting his seat belt on.

'Know how you feel mate,' Marc said knowingly looking at David.

'Oh, get into the swing of it boys it'll be fun. Ben taking the kids?' Oli asked.

'Aye, and picking up Digo on the way. He said he's only coming for a laugh though,' Shirley explained.

They arrived to a crowd of runners and spectators and joined Shaz's fan club of Fiona, Jason, Ben, Josh, Digo, and Mo, Shaz's mum who had at least turned up to watch her 50p being earned! Digo looked uncomfortable, but Mo obviously had her sights on something far more superior to Digo, who was yesterday's news, now she had star quality Ben and Josh to have a go at.

Noting Mo's interest Oli announced, 'Hey, lads, our Mo is on the telly tomorrow on that Tanya show: "I'm addicted to younger men".'

'Aye, lads, so make sure you watch it, I'm good, dead good,' Mo screeched.

Quickly changing the subject a cringing Shirley stepped in: 'Hey, there's a good crowd here isn't there?'

Around three thousand people had gathered in the park ready to watch the thousand runners who had agreed heroically to run walk or jog the five kilometre circular route. Part of the journey was on the road so bollards and police were strategically placed along the route. The runners gathered to listen to the commentator and Shirley watched as some started warming up, jumping and stretching and jogging on the spot.

'Hey this lot are keen,' Oli said raising his eyebrows at a group of women warming up in a synchronised routine.

'Yeah, I hope Shaz is doing a bit of warm up. Where is she, anyway? She should be here now with this lot,' Shirley pointed out looking out for Shaz.

'She's probably trying to get a last bit of sun,' Oli said pushing his sunglasses back on his nose. 'Hey, hope it's like this for the wedding, eh?'

'Oh God, me too,' Shirley groaned.' It's gorgeous today isn't it?' she said looking up at the cloudless blue sky.

'I hope we get a few that pass out in this heat,' Digo sniggered. 'Should get a laugh out of it, looking at 'em all rolling around like dying flies!'

'Behave,' Shirley scoulded looking round to make sure no one had heard him.

'Hey, I hope those get a moooooooooove on.' Digo yelled at a group of five girls strolling past dressed in black and white cow costumes.

'God, I bet they're hot.' Oli sighed.

'Aww, that's good innit, fancy dress. Shaz should have thought of that,' Shirley said.

'She doesn't need one of them cow outfits,' Mo said flatly. 'She's enough of a donkey as it is.'

Oli and Shirley looked at her quite disgusted.

'Shaz is all right,' Shirley protested.

Suddenly a loud scream could be heard over the crowd. 'Hiya! Over there Tony. Hey, watch me legs.'

Shaz came galloping towards them, hair and make-up perfect, wearing the tiniest white shorts, white knee high socks, perfect white trainers and a white vest top with the number 666 on it. And she was mounted on the back of a man who looked about ready to meet his maker. Shaz was on top form ready for the race of her life.

'Hey, what's with this piggy back thing? What you doing, you soft mare?' Oli asked horrified.

'Great innit, couldn't believe me luck, Tony say hiya,' Shaz said instructing the seven stone old man to introduce himself.

'Hhhhiya.' Tony managed to get out, staggering slightly under Shaz's size fourteen and a bit.

'What's going on?' Fi demanded.

'Well when I got here this morning, Tone was looking for someone to give a piggy back to for the mini-marathon, that's what he's said he'll do, see, a sponsored piggy back for the home he's in,' Shaz explained. 'You're so fit, mind, Tone, can't believe you're in an 'ome.'

'Dodgy cow...' Digo muttered.

Jumping off her mount Shaz, giggled at their gaping mouths. 'I'm only joking! Ta, Tone,' she said erupting into a throaty laugh.

'Ok love, see you at the end,' Tony the OAP joker said waving and jogged off.

'God, you had me going there, babe!' Fi exclaimed.

'You should have seen your faces then. I wouldn't do that to the poor old fella, but he was game for a laugh when I asked him to wind you lot up.'

'Shaz, you ready?' A deep voice came from a fit looking crowd of male runners.

'Oh, hiya, babe. I was wondering where you got to,' Shaz said to a seventeen year old would-befire fighter, and then she climbed onto the brawny young man's back.

'What the...' Oli said gobsmacked.

'I told you didn't I that I'd made a special effort last few weeks.' Shaz giggled. 'Took me a while to get him to agree. Got there in the end though didn't I. You didn't really think I was gonna run all that way did you?' She asked her astonished supporters. 'Come on Matty, giddy up, we've gorra make our way to the start line. See you lot later and Fi, be sure to get me plenty of water for the finish, I'll be dead thirsty...especially in this heat.'

'Hey, have you made any progress on your uncle getting me in with Blue Watch yet?' The gullible boy asked.

'What friggin' uncle?' Mo mumbled.

'So she's pulled another fast one...' Jason said shaking his head.

'Good on ya, Shaz,' Fi giggled.

Shaz's now somewhat unenthusiastic fan club watched the pair fight their way through the crowd to gain pole position.

Almost two hours later, Shaz and and Matty still hadn't crossed the finish line. Mo had long gone to the pub to wait. Only Fi, Shirley, Oli and David were left to cheer in the scamming duo.

'Well done, queen,' Oli said patting her on the back as Shaz single-handedly crossed the finish line. 'Hey, where's Matty?'

'Who? That git? He just dropped me, nearly on me arse an' all,' Shaz panted.

'He's just gone with the St John's Ambulance, I've just seen him,' Shirley announced. 'They said he'll be ok, though, once he's had a good rest and some water.'

'What have you done to him?' Oli asked.

'Well, to be honest, he only took me half way round. We saw me mum sitting outside the pub on the way, so we thought we'd have a rest and a quick one. Once me mum got her claws in, well I couldn't get him to leave so I left them to it…' Shaz informed them flatly.

'Hiya.' Mo appeared from behind the trees. 'Did I miss anything?' she added innocently.

They all glared at her.

'What?' she asked, shrugging her shoulders.

'You'd have been better sticking with Tony, babe,' Oli said putting his arm around Shaz.

'Hey, don't be saying that. Chin up kid it's an achievement and you did half of it by yourself,' Shirley said trying to cheer up the young girl. 'Hey, did you get your medal babe they've been giving them out to all the finishers.'

'Oh, aye, yeah, and a little goody bag. I'm dying to know what's in 'em,' Oli added enthusiastically.

'And look… All that training paid off, no streaks from the fake tan.' Fi laughed.

Admiring her legs and with a newfound pride, a contented Shaz happily made her way to pick up her medal and goody bag before they made their way out of the now near empty park.

'So what's in the bag?' Oli asked as they headed back towards the cars.

Shaz opened the pink goody bag and pulled out a herbal boiled sweet, cereal bar and a mini body spray. She gave her armpits a quick squirt before putting the body spray back in her pink bag.

'There you go, babe, feel better now, eh?' Oli smiled at her.

'Spray on sweat! Nice.' Fi teased and put her arm around her mate.

'Hey, the sight of all that running gear's got me in the mood, I'm gonna go to the gym tonight Oli, you coming?' Shirley asked brightly.

'Aye, ok, babe, we'll go for an hour. I need to talk to you about something, anyway,' he muttered.

'Come on Shaz, we'll give you a lift home hon',' Shirley said giving the delighted girl a hug.

After their work out which for Oli consisted of five exhausting minutes on level 1 of the exercise bike, five minutes on the ski machine and two minutes on the cross trainer finished off by forty five minutes lying on the mat pretending to do abdominal exercises, he and Shirley went and had a coffee in the gym's café.

'Now then, we've got two cases on the go. Hard Des: ongoing, serial shagger – we think, married to Jan and out regular up to no good, but we can't get anything on him.' Oli looked through his note book. 'I have been thinking about this one a bit. I was thinking maybe I should try and get pals with him, well at least try and get to know him a bit better. You know…lads together an' that, he might get all loose lips on me and reveal all.'

'Lads together? Come on, babe, surely even you can see that won't work…' Shirley said gently, looking at Oli who sat legs crossed in tight white skinny jeans, white pumps, bright pink t shirt and his sunglasses sat on the top of his head.

'Ok, ok, I know I'm not a man's man, but what about Marc?' Oli asked.

'Do you really want to get him involved hon'? Plus he doesn't even know what we've got going here, does he?' Shirley asked keen to keep their detective sideline confidential.

'I know, I know. Ok, then, what about Sapphire?' Oli asked enthusiastically, swinging his legs over. 'I know we have mentioned Des to her, but I mean actually get her to set him up somehow.'

'Oh come on, babe, let's try a bit harder ourselves first, eh? She's a last resort, 'cause we don't know he'd go for her, do we? I mean I know there's not much in it, but Angie is a bit better catch than Sapphire and that was a no go.'

'Yeah you're right, let's get cracking on it. What do we know about him, again, then.' Oli said checking his note book one more time.

'Jan said he was in the army for years, so we don't want to mess with him do we? He won't go with anyone, though, we know that from the other night,' Shirley said adding her bit to the equation.

'Aye, he looks a tough sort but he must be at it with someone, why all the secrecy otherwise?' Oli said. 'And now we've got "Mrs and Mrs" as I've named the case.'

'Well what's the story with these then?' Shirley asked taking a sip out of her skinny latte.

'This woman called called Bernie phoned and said we'd been recommended – apparently a few months ago we helped her mate out. You remember…those two lesbians from near Sefton Park?'

'Oh, aye, yeah, the ginger one was having it off with that vicar's wife?' Shirley said recalling the events.

'That's the one. Well this Bernie thinks her partner of five years, Val, is trying to get off with Bernie's ex-husband Lenny,' Oli explained.

'Go 'way. How's all this come about?' Shirley asked eager to know more.

'Well, when Bernie comes home from work Lenny's always there. Says he's there to see the kids but the kids are always in school or at their mates an' that. Anyroad, look at these...' Oli instructed getting out a selection of photographs from a large brown envelope.

'Wish we had this much info on all our cases.' Shirley said flicking through the photographs of Bernie, Val, Lenny and their cars – complete with visible number plates.

'Well I think this one will be a piece of piss,' Oli announced. 'In the bag, no danger.'

'Wish we could say the same for Hard Des, though.'

'Come on kid, let's get going. We've got Mo on the telly

tomorrow to look forward to, a bit of light relief, like!' Oli said picking up his and Shirley's gym bags and heading towards the fresh air.

FOUR

Monday, April 23rd
9am
Well the day has finally arrived: mad Mo is on the telly. We've set the Sky Plus so we can watch it later an' all. It's on at half nine then we're going into work. Made a later start time today. Got a text this morning from Angie asking us to call in, Comb-over's going home early to take his mail order bride home, he's got her working in the factory this morning making him brews and that.

Anyway, Oli's got the kettle on here, now, so we can have a brew together watching Mo!!

Engrossed in the tacky television show even the hard to shock Oli was amazed at Mo's confessions and Shirley thanked the lord that her Jason had had a lucky escape. Mo did mention Digo, but in fairness to him she didn't name and shame him. However, it was obvious from the way she described the lanky lad that it was him she was talking about. Anyone who knew him was going to have no doubt about that. Soft sod wasn't going to be able to show his face on the street for weeks without getting the ribbing of his life.

The giggly couple sat perched at the edge of their seats unable to even take a sip out of their mugs of coffee they were so excited.

'I can't bear this.' Shirley said holding a cushion on her knee as she watched a particularly toe curling moment.

'What the hell made her do such a thing?' Oli added as they watched Mo revealing all dressed in a turquoise glittery micro mini dress and white stilettos and perched provocatively on one of Tanya's stools.

'Oh this is bad. She looks such a tart,' Shirley went on. 'And look how she's flirting with the other guests, she's unbelievable. Oh thank God Jason didn't go anywhere near her.'

'Aye, at least she didn't get her grubby little claws into him kid,' Oli said reassuringly.

They listened to Mo as she gave away all the havoc of her eventful love life and squirmed as she flirted suggestively with other guests on the show.

'How long is this on for? I don't think I can take much more…' Oli asked pressing the remote control button on the television and checking the time.

'I know. I'm in a hot sweat here,' Shirley confessed. 'And she doesn't give a shite.'

'Oh good, that's it.' Oli announced relieved the ordeal had come to an end as Tanya thanked her guest for being so open about her unfortunate compulsion to date men half her age.

'Well she's got balls, I'll give her that.' Shirley muttered.

'Yeah, an' unfortunately she's always got her hands on someone else's son's!' Oli replied grimly.

The morning raced by and it seemed Mo was the talk of most of their clients, even the ones that didn't know her. Oli took great pleasure in revealing that she was well known to both Oli and Shirley.

In the company of their pals, the factory girls, Oli and Shirley could relax and catch up with all the gossip.

'Ask me how I am, go on ask me how I am?' Ali said looking in as much need of a makeover as ever.

'How are you, Ali, queen?' Oli asked brightly.

'Don't friggin' ask.'

'Aye, don't bother asking, kids, we've been hearing all about her woes all friggin' morning, from her fella's athletes foot to her Vera's bowels and her own wild shites. So don't bother babes, we've heard it all before. Here, I've put the kettle on, let me tell you all about the mail order bride,' Angie squawked.

'Ooh, poor Ali, no sympathy, eh, queen? You've gorra sharpe tongue, Angie, babe. It's a wonder you don't get arrested for carrying a dangerous weapon when you're out,' Oli joked.

'So what about this girl of old Comb-over's then? What's she like?' Shirley asked.

'Well, she can't speak a word of English, well, a bit she can but very little, but he's got her knowing how to put the kettle on. All she's been doing is making brews, massaging his friggin' shoulders and fannying around in his office.' Angie was disgusted.

'Aww, poor cow. Got her slaving has he, like with you lot?' Oli said winking at Shirley. 'Mind you it is disgusting, getting a minging old fella like him after a young girl like that. How old d'ya reckon she is?'

'Only looks about twenty, maybe younger,' Susan announced.

'Er, and he's taken her off home now then?' Shirley asked.

'Aye. Said she'd got jet lag and needs a lie down…' Gail said raising an eyebrow.

'He needs one an' all I'll bet,' Oli said.

'So how was that old tart Mo?' Susan asked, changing the subject.

82

'Well from one minger to another, her and Comb-over, well she was a disgrace, I tell ya, friggin' disgrace.' Oli answered. 'We did have a hell of a laugh though didn't we Shirl?'

'Aye we did, well sort of… I felt dead embarrassed for her and I feel sorry for poor old Shaz having a mum like her.'

'Heard she's a chip off the old block, though, isn't she?' Angie sniffed.

'Well she's ok; she hasn't had a good role model has she? Our Shirl is more like a mum to her.' Oli said thoughtfully.

Shirley smiled at Oli, she liked being thought of that way.

'Well I'm glad that Mo's nowhere near any of my sons from what you pair have told us.' Ali said flatly.

'Friggin' hell Ali, queen, your Paul and Jamie would friggin' crush that Mo; have they even got it in them?' Angie asked.

Ali's nineteen year old twins had taken after her not only in their lack of dress sense and hygiene issues but also their colossal size.

'My boys have got girls queueing up for them. Just very picky they are,' Ali objected.

An hour passed with Mo and Comb-over's mail order bride prime topics for discussion, in addition to which Oli tried to bring the new puppy, Apple, into the conversation whenever he could. The hen night was brushed upon briefly, but still keen to keep the destination secret from the bride-to-be they all just aired their excitement.

'Come on then, queen, we'd best get on our way if we're gonna watch Mo in action again with the kids tonight. We'll need to get some crap to eat with it, ya know crisps, dips, choccies an' that,' Oli said standing up and putting his man bag over his shoulder.

'Hell! I thought you were me mate… I can't be eating that sort of crap so close to the wedding, me dress won't go on,' Shirley exclaimed.

'Behave, yer sad cow, there's not a pick on yer. One night of eating crap won't do yer any harm,' Angie announced.

'Aye. It's taken us lot a lifetime of nights like that to get to this size…' Susan laughed.

Driving away from the factory Shirley got lost in day dreams of the wedding, how she would look in the dress and her future life with David. She became so engrossed in it that she even managed to block out Oli's chit chat, something she had become accustomed to doing over the years, still managing to nod and say yes and no at mostly appropriate times. Oli didn't seem to notice he was far too involved in his own fantasies.

'Oh my God!' Oli shouted bringing Shirley back to reality.

'What?' she screamed back, slamming the brakes on, her nerves shredded.

'Look over there. It's that Val's car…it is, quick, follow it.' Oli yelled instructions whilst frantically waving his arms. Drama queen wasn't in it…

'You sure? We haven't got the paper work with us, the photies. We don't *know* it's them,' Shirley pointed out, getting used to his melodramatics.

'It's them; follow them they're going down towards the car park by the park.'

'Ok friggin' hell, have we even got the camera?' Shirley asked, reluctant to embark on something she totally sure about.

'Never mind that now, let's just take a look.' Oli was insistent.

'Ok, ok. Oh look they've parked up; it does look a bit like her and granted the car's the same. Give me them binoculars from the glove box,' Shirley told Oli, starting to get excited that they may actually be onto something. Pity it wasn't Hard Des with Val, though! That way they could have got two birds with one stone…

'It's gorra be them, why else would they pull up here. It's a bit secluded isn't it?' Oli said with a mischievous smile.

Shirley looked at him and smiled. It did seem a bit secluded for anything else. It was a car park at the back of a recently closed down supermarket; hardly the place for a country stroll and too far from any shops to be out for some retail therapy. Maybe Oli was right and they could get this one in the bag quickly.

'I can't really get a good view from here can you?'

'Not really but it looks like...erm....' Oli said neck stretched as far as he could. 'Hey, hey...looks like they're having a snog... Quick he's leaned over... Friggin hell...' He went on, frantically slapping Shirley's thigh with each phrase.

'Ouch, hey watch it, soft lad, that hurts,' Shirley objected giving him a shove.

Engrossed in the action in the car Oli didn't notice his pal's reprimand he was far too busy looking at the couple engaged in a full on snog.

'We need a closer look, babe, to be properly sure...' Shirley announced.

'Aye you're right. I'm sure that we could make our way to that bush over there before they notice us.'

'What, hide like a couple of perves in the bushes?' Shirley asked looking horrified.

'Come on hon', it'll be ok, they won't notice I tell yer they're too into each other.'

Tentatively Shirley got out of the car, carefully closing the door and wincing quietly when it gave out a slight bang; she looked over at Oli who pulled a bit of a face. Taking Oli's lead – he was pointing frantically at the overgrown area at the far end of the car park closer to the suspects' car – they both made their way Pink Panther cartoon style to the safety of the bushes.

'Ouch! Friggin' hell...' Shirley complained, scratching her arms on the out of control brambles.

'Shh...'

Crushing cider cans and cigarette packets and God knew what else under their feet, they managed to cram themselves into a space with a very good view of the car.

'If I get rabies from this, I'll friggin' kill you, Oli,' Shirley moaned.

'Behave…you won't be able to do a thing to me.'

'Wanna bet?' Shirley said nearly losing her balance and falling against an old worn out supermarket trolley.

'Well you wouldn't be able to shout with rabies would you? You'd be frothing at the mouth. Hey maybe we should give a dose to them factory girls, eh?' He laughed.

Unable to resist the vision of the Henshaw's production line struck dumb, Shirley's face broke into a grin.

'There you go… I can always make you laugh, even in the most dangerous of situations. Now, come head, I'll see if I can get anything on me mobie,' Oli said, struggling to get his mobile phone from the pocket of his sprayed on blue jeans.

'Hey look he's got in the back and she's climbing in after him. Oh my God.' Oli pointed out positioning his mobile to take the incriminating evidence.

'What's the pics like, then?' Shirley asked looking through the binoculars. 'Don't want us to be here wasting our time, we need evidence.' Shirley transferred her weight from one foot to the other.

'Aye good, well not bad, you can make out the car and the clothes.' Oli checked his phone. 'Hey, she's getting on top of him now, friggin' hell.' He went on clicking, eager to capture all the action.

'Well snap away, babe, so we can get going, these brambles are playing havoc with me arse,' Shirley complained.

'Hey, someone is walking over to the car, oh my God, maybe it's the ex's other half caught them in the act.'

'Someone's walking this way an' all, I'm sure there is, I can hear summat,' Shirley said, horrified.

'Ok, you two, out you come.' An unfamiliar voice spoke.

'Oh friggin' hell,' Oli said, 'what now?'

'Shite...who is it? Lenny's mates?' Shirley said starting to tremble – this wasn't the kind of place to be cornered by strangers with only a pink T-shirted, nine stone weakling on your side.

'Don't think so, babe, unless they're in fancy dress and on their way to the policeman's secret ball.'

'Eh?' Shirley said moving to get a better look. 'Oh, fer f....'

'Think we've just been caught doggin', babe,' Oli said grimly, his fuschia pink shoulder gripped by one of the Liverpool Constabulary's finest.

7pm

Oh my God, what an afternoon. Can't believe what we've been through. We've just got back from the friggin' police station. On our way home from the factory Oli, bright spark, thought he saw that Val we're trying to catch out. It was the same make of car we'd be shown a photie of, so off we went, only trouble is we weren't the only ones watching the pair, the bizzies were as well. So we've just been released with a caution and told never to go anywhere near the Super Stores car park again. I feel so ashamed. We had this right sour faced woman interview us, we did say it wasn't what it looked liked and Oli tried to explain what we were really doing there, about the detective case an' all, but they weren't having any of it, didn't believe us one little bit.

Apparently they've been watching that place for weeks and only cos they haven't seen our car there before they've let us off, but that woman pc...what a complete bitch she was, said our behaviour was disgusting...the cow. I feel so ashamed I really do. Oli got so wound up I thought he was going to pass out. Last time I saw him that cross was when someone grabbed the last pair of black skinny jeans he'd had his eye on out from under his nose in H+M. He was livid, face like a Ribena berry, and he wasn't much different today. He nearly got done for a breach of the peace, so I had to just listen, accept what they said so I could have time with Oli to calm him down. I can't believe what a bitch that woman copper was though. Looked at me like I was worse than them performing in the car...

Anyway, back home safe now. The thing was, we didn't even get to nail those cheats cos it wasn't even them. We were way off. So it's back to the drawing board for that one an' all, never mind the invisible Hard Des.

Shirley closed her diary locked it and put it safely in the bedside drawer. She made her way downstairs to have her tea with a very sheepish Oli.

'Friggin' 'ell, babe…' Oli said slowly moving his ham salad around the plate.

'I know, I don't think I can eat much, it's put me off me food,' Shirley said looking grimly at the plate.

'Behave… There's nothing in that, it's only crunchy water. Come head. I don't feel like it either but we've gorra eat. To be honest with ya, girl, I'm more mad than anything. They just wouldn't believe us would they? The bastards…' Oli said trying to get enthusiastic about his plate of crunchy water.

'I'm so glad the kids weren't in, aren't you? I'm sure they'd notice something was up with us. Listen let's just keep it to ourselves, eh? Don't tell Marc will ya?' Shirley pleaded.

'Course not Shirl, he doesn't know about our sideline does he? If I told him about the caution I'd have to spill the beans, otherwise he'd think I'm a perv. Hey this is hard to swallow isn't it?' he said gesturing at a small pile of grated carrot. 'Bet it'd go down better with a glass of rosé.' Oli put his plate down and headed for the fridge.

'Aye, yeah, that would go down a treat… Oh, text,' Shirley said, picking up her mobile from the table. She took one look at the little screen, smiled and kissed her phone.

'David?' Oli asked, walking in with a bottle of ice-cold wine and two really pretty thin stemmed black wine glasses.

'Yeah. He's in a year seven parents evening. The head's just asked us to go round to his tomorrow night for a meal and a few drinks. He's asked the other deputy and her fella an' all,' Shirley said taking a large sip of the ice cold wine. 'Mmm lovely…'

'Ooh, very nice…' Oli said sipping and settling down to the now more appetizing tea of crunchy water and glass of rosé.

'Well, I've met him, the head, before. He's a bit posh, mind. Oh it'll be ok, I'm sure, can't be worse than this afternoon, eh?'

Tuesday, April 24th
9am

We ended up laughing about our little brush with the law last night. Well, after two bottles of rosé and a few bags of crisps, we did!! I know, I know…and I'm meant to be watching the weight, but we were both starving after that friggin' salad, the wine had given us the munchies. The kids got back and Oli kept saying 'evening all' and we both ended up in fits of giggles. The kids got so pissed off with me telling 'em private joke that they both buggered off early to bed leaving me and Oli time to polish off the wine in between us both texting our gorgeous fellas. Marc was working late in the shop, he's a piercer and wants to get into tattooing. Jason has told Oli if he wants he can have a practice on him. I'm not so keen though.

Anyway, Sapphire this morning, let's see what the old trollop has to say for herself today then...

'I hope she doesn't mention us joining forces again, it's a right pain in the arse,' Oli complained to Shirley, dragging himself up the flight of stairs to her flat.

'I know, but I've been thinking about your idea of using her again. Maybe we should, see if we can get anywhere with Hard Des, that case's driving me mad.'

'Well, yeah, that's why I said it. Plus it would keep her off our backs for a bit. Let's see what she says then, eh?' Oli said knocking on the front door and walking straight in.

'Hello?' Sapphire said from the living room.

'Only us babe...put him down,' Oli laughed walking through into the living room.

'Hiya, kids, I've just brewed up. Fancy a cuppa?' Sapphire got up from her stretched out position on the sofa.

'Go on, I'll have a coffee,' Shirley said.

'Nothing for me ta, got me water,' Oli announced, still put off by Sapphire's chipped mugs.

Sapphire handed a cracked Princess Diana mug of weak coffee to Shirley: 'So what's the goss, then, kids?'

'Ermm, not much really, we're struggling a bit with a case we're working on. You know, that Des, we've mentioned him before,' Shirley said tentatively.

'Oh, aye, yeah. Struggling are you? You kids need a hand?' Sapphire asked eagerly. 'Mind you, I did make a few enquiries about that one before and didn't get very far.'

'Well, have you got the time? I mean you might be too busy now with your new business an' all?' Oli asked.

'Well, to be honest with ya, I've knocked that one on the head, babe, too much like hard work. I've started me own home business. Fit's in with me doing the benefit forms…' Sapphire explained cheerfully.

'Oh aye. What's that, then?' Shirley asked.

'Well I've made a start, I was at it when you two walked in,' Sapphire giggled.

'You were horizontal on that couch, queen, and watching the telly at that,' Oli screeched in derision.

'I've started on the sex phone lines… It's friggin' brilliant. I get to lie on me couch all day long, watching Jeremy Kyle, the lot, talking dirty and I get paid for it and I don't even have to meet them. It's great.'

'You never are?' Oli said shocked.

'Flamin' 'ell Sapphire, you gorrit all worked out, haven't you, babe? Hey, and by the look of them tiny knickers on your radiator you're getting into the swing of it all right,' Shirley pointed out.

'Aye, they're lovely aren't they?' Sapphire said walking over and picking up the tiny, black, lacy briefs. 'I couldn't believe me luck when Denise from next door gave 'em me.'

'Aww bless. Pressie were they?' Shirley asked.

'Hey, I thought one of your fellas had got them for you, not the woman next door…' Oli teased.

'Oh no, not a pressie, well not really… Denise has started in that new gym in town, goes there after work, an' she found 'em on the side; some daft cow had got changed and left 'em there. They didn't fit Denise, bless her, they cut into her. Well, she has got a humungous arse.'

'You what? You're wearing some poor cow who's left her trollies in the gym's knickers?' Oli gasped.

'Couldn't believe me luck. They're a good make, an' all,' Sapphire said proudly showing them the label.

Oli just shook his head.

'Well, don't look a gift horse an' all that… Anyway, get cracking on me hair and tell me all about this job you've got for me.'

So, Shirley and Oli got to work on Sapphire's unruly mop and explained how she might help them find out just what it was Hard Des was getting up to after nine at night… When they'd finished, she was back on the subject of her latest enterprise.

'Tell us some of your chat up lines, then. I'm dying to know what you say to them old farts on the phone lines,' Oli said all agog to hear the worst.

Back in the car, Shirley and Oli went over the last hour's chat.

'She get's worse doesn't she, eh?' Oli laughed.

'Well, it sounds like she's gonna give us a hand with Hard Des. Can't believe he calls into her local and watches her sing. Same night every week an' all,' Shirley said excitedly.

'Let's see what she comes up with, eh, after she's had a go at flirting with him. Up to now he's just been watching her. She has got a great voice, you know. Mind you, like you said, she's not much better than them factory girls in the looks department is she? In fact she's a whole lot worse, and he turned his nose up at Angie, didn't he. We're panicking, really clutching at straws with him, aren't we?'

'Positive thoughts babe, positive thoughts… It makes me feel a bit better; at least we're doing something a bit extra to try and nail him.'

'Ohh…text…' Oli said excitedly as his mobile phone vibrated in the pocket of his jeans.

'Who is it? Marc?' Shirley inquired, starting the engine and driving off.

'No it's Angie in the factory. Oh my God, I don't believe it. That young girl – the May Sing – one she's gone, she's friggin' gone, and a new one has arrived in her place. There's been no mention of the two sisters that were meant to be joining her. But this new one's arrived. Comb-over's got her working in the factory. Oh my God, what do you think to that then?' Oli said staring at his phone and reading the message again.

'Never! What's he up to? Maybe she wasn't what he thought she'd be.'

'What d'ya mean? He can't just get one then send her back. It's not the friggin' catalogue, you know…if it doesn't fit back it goes…' Oli informed her.

Shirley looked at her best friend and laughed. 'I know, love, we'll catch up with all the latest goss when we see them and we'll be able to clock this new one an' all.' Shirley informed him. 'I just want to pop into town, me mum's asked me to pick up a few things for Auntie Dilys.'

'Oh, how is the old crow?' Oli asked still looking at his phone.

'Same as ever, me mum can't do as much for her now, though. Well she still does, but I mean carrying heavy shopping from town an' stuff.'

'Shall we go out for lunch, then, seeing as we're in town?' Oli asked.

'Yeah, why not? Not too much for me, though, I'm out for me meal tonight, remember. What should I wear, d'ya reckon?' Shirley asked her favourite fashion guru.

'Smart but casual, I think. Maybe those nice white linen trousers and that nice green blouse you got and your white dolly shoes.'

'What would I do without you, eh?' Shirley said warmly.

David's just phoned to say he's on his way. Haven't long got in after dropping off all Auntie Dilys's shopping and listening to her and me mum's ailments. All that hearing about who's had what operation and what's been taken in as a pressie for them – from grapes to a trifle to the word search – my God, me ears were ringing afterwards. Anyway Oli mentioned to them about meeting up with us all in town for a few bevvies and tapas on the day of me hen weekend. They soon forgot all about their ailments then. All excited they were. I don't know what they'll make of the factory girls but, hell, they have to meet them sometime I suppose, they'll all be at me wedding party anyway. They girls shouldn't get too leathered in the time me mum and Auntie Dilys will be there for. Oli said he's gonna pile them up with sangria and a taxi home so they'll be sorted. In a strange kind of way I'm glad that he's included them, makes them feel part of it. Mind you, I wouldn't want them for the whole weekend. The mind boggles...

Me mum showed me Auntie Dilys's outfit and shoes for the wedding. Bless... She got them from the catalogue and they look – nice; she won't let the side down, put it that way. Me mum's outfit's been long bought; months ago Fi and I trailed every shop in Liverpool to get the right thing for her. (I knew she would be really fussy and say she wasn't!!! so I wanted that stress out the way long ago so that I could concentrate on me own stuff). So it has been hanging in the wardrobe in her front bedroom for months, covered in a big plastic sheet for some reason, maybe she wants to keep it a secret from the window cleaner!!

All in like a coffee and copper colour, she'll be, with a great big hat, I have to say she looks a treat in it, mind.

Anyway, better get me outfit on for this meal. The kids said they're not gonna tell anyone that their mum is off to the head's house for tea!! Oli's got Marc coming over for tea here; I hope Jason doesn't get talking to him about his tattooing!

Best get me skates on David'll be here in a bit.

'Hey, now, just you behave yourself d'ya hear?' Oli teased Shirley as she took a large sip of his wine.

'Bit of Dutch courage,' she said as he tried to grab the glass back.

'He's not that bad, Shirl,' David said reassuringly.

'Isn't he?' Shirley asked, unconvinced, as Marc handed her her own glass of wine.

'Here you go, babe,' he smiled.

'Wish I was stopping here with you lot.' Shirley looked around at the familiar faces of Fiona, Jason, Oli and Marc.

'We've got a cosy night in with James Bond, a pizza and a few of these,' Oli announced holding up his black thin stemmed wine glass.

Shirley sighed wishing that she was about to enjoy a night in with her nearest and dearest instead of facing the nerve wracking ordeal she was no doubt about to endure. She just didn't want to let David down in front of the people he had to work with…

'Come on, get that down your neck, we don't want to be late,' David said standing up and looking at this watch.

Shirley drained the glass before putting it down on the coffee table rolling her eyes and pulling down her blouse neatly over the waistband of her trousers.

Once in David's car, Shirley pulled down the sun visor and checked out her perfect make-up.

'You look gorgeous – you always do.' David smiled at her noting her anxiety and wanting her to relax a bit before they got to the head's house.

'Mmm, just don't want to show you up,' Shirley said rubbing imaginary smudges from her face.

Half an hour later, they turned into the gravelled driveway of a large detached property in a leafy suburb.

'Friggin' 'ell, this is a bit of all right, isn't it.' Shirley was impressed by her surroundings.

'Nice isn't it. We could have something like this in the not too dim and distant future…if I aim high,' David said equally impressed.

'It is lovely but money isn't everything, is it…' Shirley was concerned that her husband to be might be getting a bit carried away with himself.

'I know, but look at the place, Shirl, wouldn't you just love something like this?'

'We've got a lovely place. Where we're moving into, it's like a palace to me.'

'I know, love, just saying… Come on then, you ready?' he asked opening the car door and getting out.

Nervously, Shirley crunched her way towards the front door, thankful that she had listened to Oli and worn her flat white dolly shoes.

'David… Welcome,' John, the headmaster, said standing in the huge doorway. 'And this must be the beautiful Shirley. Welcome, come on in, I've heard so much about you.' He kissed the overwhelmed Shirley on both cheeks.

John was a large man, balding with a dark moustache, looked a bit like a farmer Shirley thought, rather than a head teacher, not that she'd noticed it before. He led the way into the neat and orderly sitting room.

'Please, take a seat.' John ushered them to sit on the deep red coloured leather settee. 'Wine, Shirley?'

'Lovely.'

'Angela won't be long, just in the kitchen— Oh, that must be Sally and Andy, won't be a sec', make yourselves at home,' John instructed as he went off to answer the ringing doorbell.

'You ok?' David asked Shirley, thoughtfully.

'Aye... I'll be even better after a few of these, though. Come head and fill me up.' Shirley told him polishing off her glass of wine in record time and holding her glass out for David to refill. Raising his eyebrows he obliged.

'Here we are Sally and Andy... Please make yourselves comfortable and I'll check on Angela,' John said as he ushered in the rest of the guests and then he left the four to it.

Half an hour later there had been no sign of John or Angela, apart from the odd head round the door from John to make sure the four were ok, and Sally and Shirley had polished off another bottle between them and were getting on like a house on fire.

'Hey, what's keeping them, eh?' Sally said with just a hint of a native scouse accent.

'God knows...' Shirley laughed, but I'm glad they're taking their time, it's given me a chance to calm me nerves.'

'Well *she's* a bit of a cow, that's why I said Andy had to drive; I need a few to stand up to her,' Sally said taking another large sip of red wine. 'He may be the head of school but he's like a little boy with her, she's definitely the head of this house. Come to think of it, it was like this last time we came, wasn't it Andy? And we walked in to a banquet with everything just so.'

David and Andy were sat nursing their Cokes in a lull in the conversation, when once again John's head poked around the door. 'Okey dokey, folks, dinner is served.'

A little wobbly from all the wine she'd drunk on an empty

stomach, Shirley got up and followed the rest of the group through to the lavishly set dining room.

'Oh, it looks gorgeous,' Shirley said cheerily.

'And the star of the show, my very own Delia, let me introduce to you my darling wife Angela. Angela…Shirley,' John announced proudly.

Angela stood at the head of the large dining table looking immaculate in a jade green silk dress, which set off her silky, coppery red hair wonderfully. Shirley almost froze on the spot. She'd seen this woman before.

'I think you've met everyone, here, darling, except of course for David's better half, the beautiful Shirley,' John said brightly.

Angela held out her hand to shake with Shirley, who, fervently hoping she hadn't been recognised, held out her hand in turn.

'Pleased to meet you. Are you sure we haven't met before?' Angela asked quizzically.

'Nuh…no, I don't think so… Hey, you've been to lots of trouble, Angela, haven't you? It looks gorgeous…' Shirley babbled sitting down hurriedly.

'Well, come on everyone, please take a seat,' John instructed as he went around the table pouring yet more wine as they looked at each other over the soup bowls…

Shirley made an uncomfortable start on her chilled watercress soup wondering if it was really meant to be cold – probably was judging from the ice cube floating in the middle, but she didn't really fancy the idea.

'Mmm lovely, this soup is delicious,' David said obviously not fazed by it. So Shirley thought she better get on with it and tucked in regardless.

'Bread roll, Shirley,' Angela asked scanning her face rather more than the offer of a piece of bread warranted.

'Thank you.' Shirley responded, avoiding making eye contact.

'You really do have a very familiar face, Shirley,' Angela continued. 'Where do you work?'

'I'm a mobile hairdresser,' Shirley muttered, anxious to avoid becoming the centre of attention.

'Hey, Shirl, you couldn't give me a bit of a restyle could ya?' Sally asked. Having loosened up with the wine she'd drunk, her earlier subtle scouse accent had relaxed into something much broader and more like Shirley's usual brogue.

Angela gave Sally a disgusted look and asked, pointedly, 'The wine to your liking, Sally?'

Remembering where she was Sally reined in her native tongue and answered in a more acceptable if not more patronising tone, 'Marvellous, Angela, just marvellous.' Shirley was just relieved to be let out from under Angela's piercing gaze even if it meant poor Sally was getting it in the neck.

Drinking more and more wine in the hope it might make her somehow invisible Shirley finished off yet another bottle. By this time David was kicking her under the table every time she filled up. She just looked over at him and smiled. Sally was oblivious to it all, and just carried on tucking into her second course of salmon en croute, baby new potatoes, green beans and carrots.

'Dessert, now...if you've all had sufficient? Angela announced. 'I've made my grandmother's secret recipe apple cobbler.'

'Well, I wouldn't say no...you really are a marvellous cook,' David insisted. 'Wonderful, in fact. You're a very lucky man, John,' He went on, smiling fleetingly at Shirley as he did so. Well aware of her own distinct lack of culinary skills, she wondered if she was going to have to compete with the likes of Angela, and cook for David's guests. If so, she was going to have to put her skates on and get some lessons from that Gordon effing Ramsey, pretty friggin' sharpish...

'Well, I find it very relaxing – especially after the kind of work

I do and the people I have to deal with.' Angela went on.

'My darling wife is a police officer you see, Shirley, deals with criminals and the dregs of society all day every day.' John looked lovingly at his wife, 'She's very brave and I'm extremely proud of her.'

As if a light had been switched on, Angela looked at Shirley and Shirley realising that she had been clocked took another huge sip of white wine and interrupted quickly, eager to change the subject, 'Oh that's great. Anyway, let's be having the apple cobbler, I'm a sucker for sweets.'

'Cobbler, nearly same as copper...' Sally giggled, drunkenly, then quickly straightened her face when she realised her gag had dropped echoing into the silence.

Angela stared at Shirley, obviously now remembering that the last time she had seen her dinner guest she was hiding in the bushes behind Super Stores with Oli queen of the camp perving over a courting couple in a parked car. There was no hole big enough for Shirley to crawl into this side of the Mersey...

'Yes I am a police officer, and in the course of my duty I see all kinds of lewd behaviour. You'd be surprised what I see in a day, Shirley...' Angela said smugly handing a bowl of apple cobbler to her. 'Or maybe you wouldn't. Cream?'

'Erm, best not, I'm trying to be good...' Shirley muttered submissively, hoping David hadn't noticed Angela's remark. But she wasn't out of the woods, yet. Angela wasn't letting her go that easily.

'Really – are you?' Angela asked.

'Yes she's gorgeous, doesn't need to lose an inch. Mad isn't she?' David butted in.

Shirley managed to get through the rest of dessert and coffee without any more interrogation from PC Delia and thankfully, noting her alcohol intake and feeling exhausted himself, David suggested they make their way home just after eleven.

'I'll just use the loo, if I may?' Shirley asked as the others left the table and headed for the front door.

Waiting outside the bathroom for Shirley was her hostess. 'Don't think I haven't realised who you are. I won't say a word, it's more than my job's worth and I am all for the accused protection until proven guilty in court...'

'Hey lady, I'm no criminal...' Shirley protested.

Angela closed her eyes and held both hands out palms facing Shirley. 'Let's hear no more of it. It's a condition; I've done research on it. A disgusting, disgraceful, lurid condition, but a condition nonetheless. I wish you – and David – luck in challenging your demons and hope never ever to see you again during work hours.'

'Hey you went for it tonight, sweetheart. You ok?' David asked the by now slumped Shirley who was fighting back the tears as she dragged the seatbelt across her chest.

'Aye...too much of the vino with that Sally. Sorry babe, hope I didn't show you up,' Shirley sighed.

'No way... You let yourself go a bit, but it was cool. John's ok, he won't have noticed. His missus is a bit of a stickler, though, isn't she?'

'You can say that again,' Shirley muttered under her breath.

David dropped Shirley off at Oli's, made sure she was ok and safely in through the front door then left her to it after a quick goodbye kiss. Every one was up and wanted to know all the nitty gritty.

'Sorry kids, I'm too pissed and too tired. I'll tell you tomorrow,' Shirley announced and carefully made her way up the stairs. She peeled her clothes off, left them in a pile on the floor and climbed into the bed in just her bra and pants hoping she'd have forgotten all about it when she woke up in the morning...some hope.

FIVE

<u>Wednesday, April 25th</u>
<u>8.30am</u>
Me head is pounding after all that wine last night. I just wanna go back to bed. I've got to tell Oli about that old witch Angela. I still can't believe it. What's the chances of that, eh? Of all the coppers in Liverpool to get done by I end up going to her house next day for a meal!! God knows what she must think of me...some perv that's for sure. Mind you, probably better that she thinks that I'm a dogger than the competition, least it didn't blow our cover. Perhaps it was lucky she didn't believe Oli when he told her the truth. That's dedication isn't it eh? Protecting me clients... Hope to God she doesn't tell her John, he might tell David and he still doesn't know about Oli and me's sideline!

Anyway I can hear the kids getting ready to get out so I'd best make a move; I can tell them all about it on the way to school and work.

'So, come head, girl, we've been in suspenders all night wondering how you got on last night.' Oli was eager to know what had happened once Shirley had washed, breakfasted and got them all into the car.

'Don't friggin' ask,' Shirley answered rubbing her head.

'Hey… You're not still over the limit are ya, Ma?' Jason asked, noting that Shirley's driving wasn't quite up to it's usual high standard.

'No I'm fine, just gorra bit of a hangover,' Shirley complained, crunching the gears as they got to a roundabout. 'It was ok, really, that Sally's all right.'

'Aye, she's a laugh,' Fiona agreed.

'Yeah, she's sound her. What about the head? What a plonker he is…' Jason added.

'He was ok, but his wife's a right cow, she is, and fussy as hell. She definitely wears the trousers.'

'I heard he's all talk in school but like a little boy at home,' Fi said, looking out of the window.

'Right, here we are, your stop.' Shirley pulled up outside the school gates where Shaz, frantically chewing gum, was standing waiting with two other orange skinned girls.

'Oh… So no goss, then, babe,' Oli said disappointedly as Shirley pulled away from school.

'No goss, no friggin' goss! I nearly died Oli; the friggin' head's wife was that copper who did us for doggin',' Shirley shouted.

'What? No never?'

'Aye, I couldn't friggin' believe it.' Shirley momentarily forgot about her headache.

'Did she recognise you, babe?'

'Of course she did, by the end. I had to get arseholed just to get through the humiliation. She said at when I was going that I was disgusting and she never wanted to see me again.' Shirley blushed remembering the previous night's events.

'Well yer never gonna forget her, babe. But you might never have to see her again.'

'They've been invited to the wedding night party,' Shirley pointed out.

'Oh,' came Oli's grim reply.

'Anyway, never mind that now, I just wanna try and forget it, to be honest with ya. Listen now, what's happening this weekend. It's the hen do, remember, and I know nothing except the tapas bit then that we're off somewhere till Sunday. Plus, have you forgotten we're picking Apple up in the morning?'

'All sorted kid, don't worry about a thing. Marc is coming to stay in mine for the weekend…gonna look after the house and look after me baby, Apple. I do feel dead tight leaving her after only one night, but it's early days for her so she won't have had time to get used to me, will she, before I go. It'll be okay, I think,' Oli explained.

'Well I suppose that'll be ok. She can get used to the house and that can't she?'

'True, babe, and with a bit of luck I'm hoping Marc will have made a bit of progress on the potty training front before I get back.'

Shirley looked at him surprised. 'It takes ages, you know, to train a dog. Are you sure you've thought this all through?'

'Yeah, yeah, don't be worrying.'

'And what about the hen night? What's happening?' Shirley persevered in getting her answer.

'We're gonna have a great time, don't be worrying. All you have to think of is no clients to be booked in on Friday.'

'I know…you told me that ages ago. I haven't booked any in and I'm still none the wiser am I?' Shirley complained.

But Oli wasn't giving anything up. Still in the dark about her hen night-come-hen weekend, Shirley got on with the day's work and decided a trip to the gym was in order on the way home just to be sure she was at her best by the end of the week.

7pm

That flamin' Hard Des was in the gym tonight; well, we saw him walking out, check his watch, then get in his car. Still no more than that. It's terrible really we just can't get a grip with this one. Haven't done any more on Val and Bernie, or Mrs and Mrs as Oli has codenamed the job, either. It's not looking good. I really want them out the way before my big day. Sapphire texted an' all, saying she'd tried it on with him and he'd just said no thanks he's a happily married man. But he does like her singing!! So, God knows what the hell's going on there.

Still none the wiser on me hen night, either, which is starting to stress me out. Fi is having a half day an' all on Friday. I've said she's got a dentist appointment. David knows like, but he's not gonna say anything is he? Jason's going home from school with him at the usual time and they're flying out to Amsterdam on the 8.30 flight from Liverpool. They've got this activities thing booked, a brewery tour, karting and shooting or something. I know more about the friggin' stag night than I do about me own hen night, daft innit…

Think I'll go over and see David tonight; just on me own, just the two of us. It's been dead hard getting *him to meself since the move. It'll give us a chance to go over a few things in peace.*

Shirley lay in bed enjoying the last few moments before she knew she really had to make a move.

She went over in her head the details of the wedding, now more or less finalised, and smiled happily that she was well on her way to being Mrs Wilmore. She couldn't remember when she had ever felt as happy.

Quickly bringing her out of her day dream her mobile made a noise indicating a text message. 'David,' she said out loud, picking up her phone from her bedside table. She looked at the phone and read *Oli. Today's the day babe my baby girl is coming home!!!*

Shirley laughed and shouted loudly, so Oli could hear downstairs: 'I know, you friggin' nutter.'

'No need to shout, I'm only here.' Oli smiled poking his head round the door. 'Yer decent? Not waiting for a reply he skipped into the bedroom and plonked himself on Shirley's bed.

'Friggin' 'ell! I take it you're excited then?' Shirley asked moving along the bed to give him room.

'Oh I can't wait. Can we go at two, is that ok?' Oli pleaded rubbing his hands together.

'Aye, ok, then I'll drop you two off here and leave you to it, yeah?' Shirley winked.

'What? I'll need yer here, won't I…just for a bit,' Oli protested.

'Well, I have taken it as a half day an' all but that's more to get meself sorted out for me hen night, not to mind your friggin' dog!' Shirley informed him.

Looking wounded Oli threw a fluffy cushion at her.

'Come head… Out the way I need to get going now.' Shirley laughed throwing the cushion back at him and an hour later they were both up to their armpits in shampoo and sets in the Bay Tree Nursing Home.

Well, we just got back from picking up little Apple and I have to say she's the cutest thing ever. She's tiny: really, really tiny, and the most gorgeous fawn colour. She's a toy size so when she's fully grown the woman said will only be six to nine inches and only weigh four to five pounds. How cute is that, eh? And thankfully she'll live 14 to 18 years so I've gorra while before I have to deal with Oli's moping about her kicking the bucket – well, so long as he doesn't let her near any milk floats that is!!

Anyway, Oli's down stairs messing about with her now and we've got a little welcome tea party arranged for her when everyone comes in from school an' work. The kids, and Shaz and Digo (if you please!!), David and Marc are all coming. We called off in the shops on the way home to get proper party food. Oli got the lot little fairy cakes, sausage rolls, little sausages and I'm in charge of making the butties in a bit!!! Then I really have to get cracking with the packing for me hen night. I've had to make sure all mine, Fi and Jason's stuff is ready an' all cos what with Jason going with David and Fi coming with me I had to. Shaz is coming an' all!! I know, I know... I don't know what came over me, but one night after one or two glasses of rosé I asked her. Oli's face was a picture, but Fi and Shaz were made up. Apparently her gran's paid for it all as a pressie for putting up with her mum all this time. Digo did want to go with the lads to Amsterdam but he's got a job in the carpet shop in town and they wouldn't give him the time off. He was going to throw a sicky but he's on a warning, any more sickies and he's out. He's saving for a new car, so he's on his best behaviour and won't be going. I 'm glad in a way, it'll give my lads a chance to get on and get to know each other better.

We can have a chance to all catch up on the weekend an' all with everyone here. I feel a bit sorry for Marc; he's gonna be left here with Apple. He wasn't really on the scene, mind, when David arranged the stag do so that's why he's not going. He said he would have gone, though. According to Oli he would have loved it. He has to work in the piercing shop for a couple of hours, anyway, on Saturday morning so it would have meant taking holiday. Oli said he has to take Apple in with him to the shop in that designer bag, don't know what the customers will make of that!

I can't see Marc liking the activities an' that, he's nothing like Oli at all, nowhere near as camp, in fact if he wasn't gay and I wasn't engaged to the most gorgeous man alive... Only messing!!

Anyway best get on with them butties, they'll all start arriving by four.

Shirley locked up her little pink diary and put it back safely in her bedside drawer. She had started to get a few things together for her weekend and had piled them neatly on the bed along with two small holdalls, one for her the other for Fi. Shirley had a sneaky suspicion that they would be flying somewhere like Barcelona, which was meant to be good for hen nights or so she'd read in a magazine.

She could hear a commotion from downstairs: Oli excitedly calling Apple. Poking her head around the living room door before embarking on the mountain of sandwiches Oli had instructed her to do Shirley smiled, 'Awww…how's she getting on? Looks like you're getting on ok together, anyway.'

'She's brilliant, we're getting on like a house on fire, I think she knows I'm her mum bless her.' Oli looked quite the proud parent. 'She's looking forward to her party an' all, aren't you babe?'

'Best get on with the butties then eh?' Shirley said, trying to build up some enthusiasm for the doggy welcome do.

'Ah, ta, babe,' Oli said still dancing around the living room with Apple jumping at his feet, like something off *Strictly Ballroom*.

Shirley put some eggs on to boil; if she was going to have a party for a four inch high dog, of all things, then she was going to have the kind of fillings she enjoyed and stuff the rest of them.

With the party table all set up with food and drinks by four the guests started to arrive. Fiona and Shaz were the first through the door.

'Oh my God, she's gorgeous…' Fiona said brightly.

'It's dead…small,' was all Shaz could muster.

Digo and Jason sneaked in behind them. Digo laughed. 'Hey is that the rat?'

'Hey, you, remember why you're here,' Oli scolded.

'Ah sorry Oli, I'm only messing.' Digo bent down and attempted to stroke the dog, trying to make amends. But every time he patted it, the poor little thing ended up flat on the floor legs akimbo. But his efforts seemed to please Oli who looked on smiling, though he did ask Digo to be a bit gentler if he could.

Marc and David arrived, finally, at about half four and the party got underway.

'I can't believe the size of her,' Shaz said tucking into an egg sandwich.

'She'll only grow as big as 6 to 9 inches,' Oli informed her keen to show off his superior knowledge of the breed.

'Hey, Shaz, d'ya know how big that is?' Jason laughed.

'Yeah, I do. Heard you don't though,' came the quick reply and everyone roared with laughter.

'Now then, time for the pressies...' Oli announced.

'Me and Shaz have got her this,' Fiona said brightly, handing Oli a silver bag.

Inside was a little pink doggie T-shirt with *Gorgeous* written in silver glitter on the front.

'Aww, ta, girls. Look, she loves it,' Oli said dangling the pink and silver glittery top in front of the little dog's nose.

'This is from us, me and David,' Shirley said cheerily, handing Oli a gift bag with a similar looking chihuahua puppy on it.

'Aww, look, Apple, it's just like you,' Oli fawned. He opened up the bag to find a silver frame with a little dog on the side of it snuggled within a nest of pink tissue with bones printed on in silver.

'Thought you could put a pic of you two in it.' Shirley smiled.

Jason and Digo looked at each other and shrugged their shoulders uneasy because they had forgotten to buy the new arrival a welcome to your new home gift.

Showing a bit of quick thinking Digo reached into his pocket and took out chocolate bar, looking at Jason who once again shrugged, and handed it to Oli.

'Ermm...and this is from us,' Digo muttered, handing over the ever so slightly flattened chocolate bar.

'Oh, ta, lads. It's a lovely thought, but I've read up on it and ordinary chocolate can kill dogs and I don't want any of that going on, you know after Mixie an' all.' Oli said trying getting his point across to Digo but also trying not to be rude. 'They're only allowed special doggie chox.'

'Oh, aye, yeah, I forgot,' Digo said taking back the chocolate and taking a big bite out of it.

Jason just shrugged his shoulders again – universal teenage boy language.

'I didn't get anything for Apple, but I got these for the new parent...' Marc handed Oli a dozen red roses.

'Ah... They're beautiful, babe,' Oli announced planting a kiss on

Marc's lips.

'Ah, isn't that nice, eh? Everyone getting her a little something…' Shirley said jollying everyone along – she was eager to get to her egg mayonnaise and cress.

The party continued full swing and Apple enjoyed it to the full by having little accidents all over the living room.

'Aww, bless… It's 'cause she's excited.' Oli excused her.

'Great,' Marc said, raising an eyebrow. 'I'll be in for a busy weekend then.'

'I'll give you an' 'and mate,' Digo said enthusiastically.

'Well…' Marc said looking at Oli.

'Ah, er, ta very much, but I think it's best if it's just Marc, babe. I don't want Apple getting used to too many people before me,' Oli said, remembering the last time Digo had any contact with one of his pets.

'So, what's going on tomorrow, then, Shirl, you all ready for your hen weekend?' Shaz asked. 'I'm dead excited me.'

'Aye, I think so. I haven't got a clue what's happening though, any clues Shaz?'

'More than me life's worth, Shirl. I do have a bit of good news for ya, though.'

'Oh, aye…'

'Managed to make sure me mum doesn't turn up. She was trying ya know, but I told her that Susan was coming, her from the factory, and she can't stand her and her sister Trace, so you'll be ok.' Shaz smiled.

'Oh…great.'

'I didn't know she was even invited,' Shirley whispered to Oli, threateningly.

'She wasn't,' Oli said sternly, looking daggers at Shaz.

Shaz just looked over smiling at them both, unaware she was the topic of conversation. Shirley smiled back.

Finally we're all packed, all four of us. We managed to get rid of Shaz by telling Digo she needed to get home and pack and Digo, being the gentleman, offered to give her a lift so it worked out fine. Marc is still here, he's in residence now for the weekend's dog sitting. Oli wants Apple to get used to him. David went about an hour ago to get his stuff sorted. That's the last time we'll see each other till after the hen and stag weekend. I feel really happy though, there isn't on bit of doubt in my mind that he'll behave himself. It's a lovely feeling knowing I can trust him so much, and he feels the same way bout me, he's told me so loads of times.

Jason's got all his stuff in a rucksack, it'll be easier for him to carry to school an' that, so I don't have to worry about him. He's going home with David; they're meeting Ben and Josh at David's then the four of them are getting on the minibus all the lads have sorted out to get them to and from the airport. They'll be back around nine on Sunday, apparently.

Me and Fi are all sorted now. It's gonna be somewhere with cooler weather. I know that from what Fi has packed, and told me to pack, so that will be something a bit different. I hope we are going abroad...and it's not somewhere in this country, you never know with this lot what they'll tell you to throw you off the scent. Good job I've been putting a bit of fake tan and having the odd sun bed before the wedding, anyway. I was gonna book a spray tan for the wedding itself, but after the colour Shaz goes with her fake tan, I'll stick to me own fakes and the sun bed, may have a few more sunbeds I think if we're not going somewhere hot. We've got our stuff in two small holdalls – that should be enough, it is only a weekend after all.

Oli's busy doing his packing; he's putting his stuff in a medium sized suitcase on wheels. I'm very impressed, to be honest, I thought he'd have taken a great big suitcase.

So that's it, we're all set, just a couple of clients each in the morning then we're meeting the factory girls, me mum and Auntie Dilys, and Fi and Shaz in the tapas bar in town at one o'clock. I'm getting really excited. I hope it's nice, nothing too tacky, to be honest. I like to think I'm a bit more classy than Angie at least, her hen night was way too tacky for my liking.

'What'ya doing, Mum?' Fi walked in on Shirley coming to the end of her diary entry.

'Oh...just writing a few bits down for the wedding, stuff I need to remember.' Shirley didn't like lying, but she didn't want anyone to know about her little pink diary and the secrets it held. Not even Oli knew what she wrote in it.

'I'm dead excited Mum about this weekend, it's gonna be boss. I'm dead chuffed an' all that you said Shaz could come. I know she's mad but we'll have such a laugh.' Fi sat down on the double bed. She had changed into pretty pink pyjamas, she'd bought especially for the weekend.

'Well, so long as she behaves herself...' Shirley said worriedly.

'Well she won't, probably, but at least we haven't got her mad mum with us, eh?'

'I know, she was never invited, what was Shaz on about?' Shirley asked shaking her head.

'God knows...that's Shaz for ya,' Fi said laughing.

'Hey girls, Marc's going down to make hot choccies, d'ya fancy one?' Oli said standing in the doorway in a black silk dressing gown.

'Ooh, lovely...'

'I'll have one an' all, ta,' Jason said from the hall way.

'Okey dokey, hot choccies all round, babe...' Oli shouted down the stairs to Marc, who was already working on them with Apple yapping and jumping around his feet.

Friday, April 27th
10am

Well, we're well on our way now, just another hour or so of clients then I'm heading to the tapas bar to meet everyone. I can't wait to finally find out where we're going. I'm dead excited. Oli had a little cry this morning about leaving Apple – it was Marc, though, who looked more in need of a good weep. Apparently they'd both been up most of the night with Apple crying for her real mum. They'd had her in bed with them in the end, sleeping between the pair of them. Marc's eyes looked like two pissholes in the snow, God love him. He's got it all himself for the next two nights. Let's just say it didn't look like he was looking forward to it very much.

We've got all our stuff in the hall ready, we need to be back in the house by 12 cos we've got a taxi picking us up at 12.30 from the house to take us bag and baggage to the tapas bar. We picked up Shaz's huge suitcase on the way to school this morning, to save them carrying their stuff around all morning and then on the bus to the tapas bar. That mad Mo came to the front gate, while we were there.

'Sorry I can't make it Shirley, love, just that I can't

114

stand some of your mates so I'll have to give it a miss. Be thinking of ya though,' she said and wiggled her way back up the path in her leopard skin skirt, laddered black tights, high heel, black, knee-high plastic boots and a skin tight red low cut top.

Oli was about to tell her she hadn't ever been invited but she didn't wait, just said her bit and buggered off, leaving Shaz to struggle down the path with a huge pink suitcase and matching hand luggage that her gran had bought for the occasion. I had to get out and give her a hand with it. Oli was still sobbing from having to say ta ta to Apple and Fi was too busy listening to her iPod to care. 'Ta for that.' I said when I got in the car, but none of them battered so much as an eyelid and Shaz left me to it an' all and climbed in the car taking one of Fi's ear pieces out and listening to Fi's iPod with her.

Anyway, I'm on the countdown now, getting really, really excited. Oli must have texted Marc about 20 times about Apple. He's even phoned so he could talk to Apple, so that she doesn't forget the sound of his voice. Marc must have the patience of a saint, I tell yer. I've warned Oli to stop moping cos I don't want him with a long face on me hen weekend. He's promised to cheer up and get into the spirit of it, thank God. When he gets with them factory girls, mind, he'll be well away anyway. He's got a photo of him and Apple wearing her tiara as his screen saver on his mobile. I ask you. Anyway, got to get on, not long to go now!!!

Shirley and Oli's arrangements came together and after being picked up at home, having collected all the luggage, they were soon being greeted by Shirley's mother and Auntie Dilys who must have been in the tapas bar quite some time, given the condition they were in.

'At last! What's kept you?' Shirley's mum giggled holding up a glass of sangria.

'Oh, so you got here all right then…' Shirley noted.

'Oh yeah, we had a lovely taxi driver, brought us right inside the place,' Auntie Dilys said.

'Hey, where did he put the taxi, not that much space in here, is there, what with all the tables and chairs?' Oli teased looking around the room.

'Behave,' Auntie Dilys giggled. 'What's he like, eh?'

Next to arrive were Fi and Shaz.

'Awww, come here, love, and give your Auntie Dilys a kiss. I hardly get to see you nowadays, too busy with boys are you?' Auntie Dilys said to Fi with a slight slur.

Reluctantly Fiona obliged and gave her great aunt a peck on the cheek.

'Awww, bless you. Come here, love,' her grandmother said, not to be outdone by her own sister.

Fiona gave her gran a huge hug. She thought the world of her grandmother, even if she was more than a bit fussy at times.

Shirley and Oli returned from the bar with more glasses and two large jugs of sangria for the growing party. Just as they put the drinks down, the factory girls arrived compete with their luggage.

'Way hay!' Angie shouted excitedly. 'We're here and ready for action.'

The gang comprised of Angie, who was joint ring leader with Susan. Angie was twenty-nine, a larger than life character and always up for a laugh. Famed for her skimpy outfits, which hugged her size eighteen figure, Angie was always on the look out for a man. Infamous for her marital close call of the previous year, Angie was determined to always have the best nights out ever, even if she struggled to remember them the next morning.

Susan, who was best pals with Angie, was slightly older at thirty-five, and unlike Angie Susan had been married before and was now a divorced mum of twin boys – Shane Junior and Bobby Junior – now seventeen. She divided her time between partying with her mates, working with the same mates in the factory and accompanying Shane Junior and Bobby Junior to their regular court appearances. Susan was famed for her love of slogan T-shirts, which she wore proudly stretched over her ample bosom.

Always bickering, but the best of friends, Susan and Angie led the pack and both fought to be top dog in the factory.

Kelly was the young slim attractive one of the gang. Married to Kev, a thug who worked away installing satellite television, Kelly was yet to start a family. Feeling lonely with her husband away so often, she had been taken under Susan's wing. It would be fair to say that though Kelly may have been first in the queue for looks, unfortunately she had taken a back seat when the brains were dished out.

Gail was thought to be well over fifty, although she told everyone she was only forty-eight. Slim and attractive for her age, Gail was Henshaw's nosy supervisor. Crawling to Comb-over to his face, but pulling him apart with her mates. Gail was the factory mole. She just couldn't keep her mouth shut and was the perfect informer for the girls on the ins and outs of the internal factory workings.

Jeanette was still the new girl, although she had been at the factory over a year now. In her late forties and married, (her husband was continually in and out of prison for various crimes including GBH) she had been the one-time mistress of old Comb-over. This titbit was only known by Shirley and Oli and they were both sworn to secrecy.

Finally there was Ali. Ali was seventeen stone and all woman. Although only forty-four, Ali could easily pass for fifty-four. Famed for her mish-mash (or mismatched) wardrobe and ever complaining attitude, Ali was part of the gang whether the rest of them liked it or not. She had been living with Ray for the past twenty years and he was just the same; moaning about everything they were like two peas in a pod.

Shirley's mum and Auntie Dilys looked at the gang, then at each other, laughed and took huge gulps from their sangria.

Oli took charge of ordering the food while Shirley waited eagerly to be told where they were going.

'Please tell me now I've been so good waiting…' Shirley pleaded. 'Is this a clue, us being in the tapas bar?'

'Ok, guess,' Oli instructed her popping an olive into his mouth.

'Ok then. Barcelona?' Shirley crossed her fingers.

'Uh uh.' Oli shook his head. 'Try again.'

'Oh, I don't know. Benidorm?' Shirley replied, trying to hide her disappointment. She really had hoped for a city break in Barcelona.

'Where did she say?' Ali asked confused.

'Barcelona,' Gail informed her.

'Oh nice, where is that?' Ali asked still confused.

Gail just looked at Ali and shook her head.

'Come on, tell her.' Fiona pleaded.

'Ok…ok…' Oli promised clapping his hands excitedly.

Shirley sat at the edge of her seat waiting in anticipation.

'We're going on your hen night to…Iceland!' he shouted.

All the girls shouted excitedly. Shirley was a little taken aback, she wouldn't have guessed at that even though Fi had said to pack some woollies and a mack, but she eventually smiled. She wasn't quite sure it was where she wanted to spend her hen weekend, though.

Realising how excited up all the rest of the gang was about the trip she relaxed into the idea and after a few sangrias started to look forward to it.

'Hey, I hope there's none of this crap in Iceland,' Angie protested looking at the array of tapas with disgust.

'Don't be worrying, queen, there's none of that there. Fish chips and burgers, I reckon, you'll be ok. Fish fingers for sure, I go there every week. It's great,' Auntie Dilys said smugly.

'Eh?' Angie asked.

'That Iceland, I go there every week. The shop, you know…' Auntie Dilys said slightly drunk and unable to hear the full story with all the factory girls chatting at the same time.

'No, no, it's Iceland we're going to for the hen weekend,' Oli explained.

'Why you gong to the shop for her hen weekend?' Shirley's mum asked equally confused.

'No, Mum, it's the country Iceland.' Shirley tried to clear up the confusion.

'Eww… Iceland, why on earth are you going to that place? Hope you've packed your thermals.'

'Hey, we haven't got much time, now, drink up,' Susan pointed out looking at her diamante watch.

'Hey, Mum, what time's your taxi?' Shirley asked concerned that her tiddly mother and auntie would be abandoned.

'Don't you be worrying about us; Fiona's phoned our taxi and changed the time. He's coming in a couple of hours. We're having a great time here, so we're going to stay for another then go over the road for some food. Sorry love, don't mention it to Oli in case it upsets him but we're not that keen on the food here.'

'Yeah, bless him, don't say a word after he's gone to all this trouble but the chippy over the road has a place out in the back to sit down in. After a few more of these we'll go there, eh, love?' Auntie Dilys said.

Delighted that they had enjoyed themselves and a little bit tipsy from the sangria Shirley became a little emotional when it was time to say good bye.

'Thanks for coming, you two...' she blubbered, kissing them on the cheek and hugging them. 'It means a lot to me.'

'Get on with it, go on and leave us to it,' Auntie Dilys said trying to diffuse Shirley's emotion.

'Come on Mum, the minibus is here,' Fiona said pulling her mother's arm.

'Bye, bye.' Shirley struggled with her own holdall, sniffing and wiping her eyes, and picked up Shaz's huge suitcase.

'Come on now girl get a grip,' Susan said rubbing Shirley on the back as she continued to cry.

'What's she crying for?' Shaz asked confused.

'Just emotional aren't yer, babe, lots of bride to be's get like this. I read it in a magazine,' Susan went on.

'Well what's his excuse?' Ali asked looking over at Oli, who, looking at his mobile phone and the picture of Apple, had started crying too.

'Hey… You said this would be a laugh. We'll have a boss time… Well it was ok in there but it's going downhill now isn't it?' Shaz said grimly looking at Shirley and Oli who were still crying like babies.

'I know…' Fiona answered flatly, looking over at the factory girls for a bit of light at the what could turn out to be a dark tunnel.

Noting the young girls' concern Susan announced loudly to the whole the minibus: 'Hey, you two, we forgot to tell yer both, can't believe we did… You know that second girl from Thailand that Comb-over had in the factory, well she's gone an' all. He's brought in a Russian girl this morning.'

Having brought the cry babies to just a curious sniffle, Susan smiled and winked at Fiona who returned the smile.

'Oh my God. Really?' Oli asked.

'What's he playing at? That's the third one, now,' Shirley said.

'I know, I think he must be looking for a bride; he tried the two Thai girls but they couldn't speak much English at all, this one can a bit can't she girls?' Angie said.

Oli now recovered from his little tearful outburst suddenly exclaimed, 'Right girl, it's yer hen weekend, so we're gonna have fun. We're emotional, I know, but let's put that to one side, now, we're gonna have a great weekend.'

Taking a tissue out of her bag, blowing her nose and taking a look at her make-up in a compact mirror, Shirley said, 'Right you're on, let the fun begin...'

'Nice one...' Shaz said smiling.

The trip to the airport was filled with the usual factory girl banter, much to Fiona and Shaz's satisfaction. They were delighted hearing Angie's tales of alcohol-fuelled nights out.

'Hey, I think we are in for a good time, that Angie's mad isn't she,' Shaz said to Fiona as they stood in the queue to check in.

The afternoon's drinking session seemed to have caught up with the hen party and the four hour plane journey to Iceland passed in a cloud of sleep. Even the usually constant complainer, Ali, hibernated all the way. As they were still comatose on arrival in Iceland, a member of the cabin crew who had to wake up the hen party.

'Oh my God. Thought we'd never get here. Haven't been able to sleep a wink,' Ali groaned.

'What? You were snoring like a pig,' Angie complained. 'I had to ask for a double brandy to help me get off.'

'Come on, you lot, we're the last on the plane. Let's get off now,' Shaz suggested looking around the empty plane.

An hour later the hen party were charging on to the transport to their apartment.

'Hey, looks like we got on the ugly bus,' Oli muttered looking around.

'Aye, you look like a super model Ali, compared to this lot, queen.' Angie laughed, pushing herself into her undersized seat.

Shirley looked around the other clientele on the bus and came to her own conclusions as to the type of people who would be sharing her accommodation for the weekend.

Sitting behind them was a middle-aged couple clutching tourist books and maps of Iceland. Both were thin and scrawny and the woman had very short black hair and very pointed features. She was dressed in a multicoloured jumper over a high collared white blouse and navy blue cords covering her obviously skinny legs. Her husband was nearly as thin and small as she was. Glasses sat on the end of his nose, his head buried in tales of the Vikings and the history of Iceland. He was dressed almost identically to his wife, same sort of jumper, white shirt and beige cord trousers.

'All set then, kids?' Oli smiled.

'Oh, yes, we're thrilled. We can't wait to go to the blue lagoon, it's meant to take your breath away,' the woman said, excitedly.

'Blue lagoon... Oh, aye, yeah, we're doing that an' all,' Oli replied.

'Are we, babe? Hey that sounds a bit of all right. Sounds a bit cheeky – hope it is.' Angie giggled.

The couple looked slightly uncomfortable.

'It has therapeutic properties,' the man explained, pushing his glasses back on his face and twitching slightly.

'So it is a bit rude, then. That's what we like to hear.' Susan had plonked herself behind the tourist couple.

Monopolising the whole of the back seat was a family of five. The mother was in her late forties replete with fake tan, bleached blonde hair and in top of the range ski wear from head to toe.

'Come on Miles, get your arse into gear,' the blonde woman instructed her husband, who was struggling to get to them while holding a large bag in one hand and a small boy in the other.

'Well, if you helped out a bit Virginia...' he said, in an accent that wouldn't have been out of place in Buckingham Palace.

'Oh, stop moaning, what are you a man or a mouse?'

Settled in their seats the family looked like clones in their coloured ski wear.

'Oh, don't you all look the part,' Angie commented.

'Oh, yah, we're ski bunnies.' Virginia guffawed. 'We've been all over the world skiing. Never been to Iceland though. Thought we'd come dressed for the weather. Ready for a bit of snow mobiling.'

'Hey, are we doing that an' all?' Ali asked Oli.

'Well, I don't think we could get you on one of them, queen. No offence like…'

'They look like they've got a few bob,' Shirley whispered to Oli.

'Well that's as may be, but we're gonna be the best looking ones in the place for sure,' Oli said smugly. 'Look out blue lagoon.'

'Aye, we'll have a laugh anyway. You ok now?' Shirley asked warmly.

'Aye, I was being daft, a drama queen. Are you ok? You're more important, it's your weekend,' Oli squeezed his best friend's hand tightly.

'Yeah… I don't know what came over me, I was so chuffed that me mum and Auntie Dilys had come and they had a lovely time. I think it's just everything you know, the wedding, the house move. I just got a bit emotional,' Shirley said resting her head on Oli's shoulder.

About fifteen minutes later, the bus pulled up out side the hen party's hotel.

'Here we go,' Oli announced brightly.

'Lucky we made it at all,' Ali said grimly.

'Why's that, love?' Shirley asked.

'Well, not one to grass, but I was sat in front of your Fiona and that mad mate of hers,' Ali said quietly.

'And…?' Oli asked, irritated that Ali may be about to stir things up.

'Well, I heard that Shaz say she was worried about the sniffer

123

dogs, you know, them ones that sniff out drugs,' Ali said raising her eyebrows.

'What? I'll batter her,' Shirley said charging off towards Shaz and Fiona, who were sat on the pavement waiting for the others to sort themselves out.

'She wouldn't…' Oli protested, following Shirley to where the girls sat chatting.

'What's this about you bringing drugs?' Shirley demanded.

'Eh?' Shaz asked.

'What? No way!' Fiona came to her defence.

'I heard ya,' Ali stated defiantly.

'Oh god, no, I've never taken anything in me life, it's just that I was shitting meself when we got to the airport.'

'Why – if you'd not done anything?' Shirley asked.

'Well, me mum had a party last night and me case was in the living room where they were smoking pot. And I had some of me clothes out, so I was worried you could smell it. Then when I heard about them sniffer dog, well I was really shitting meself,' Shaz explained.

'Oh, is that all, then?' Shirley was heartily relieved, though she'd thought as much, otherwise how on earth would they have made it through two lots of Customs?

Oli walked passed Ali and shook his head.

'Well, I wasn't to know, was I?' Ali protested.

'Hey, come head. Let's check out our rooms. Come on we haven't gorra lot of time,' Kelly shouted, making her way up the hotel steps. ''S funny, though, I thought there'd be snow everywhere.'

'Aye, I did an' all Kelly babe. I've gorra brand new pair of moon boots an' all off the internet! Anyway, let's rock, we've got a hen night to get into.' Oli skipped up towards the steps.

'Come on, you two. I'm sorry, Shaz, I didn't think you would've, really. Just had to be sure,' Shirley said getting back to her conversation and looking suitably apologetic.

'It's ok, Shirl. Me mum did flick some ash on me jacket an' all, look, burnt a hole right through it.' Shaz showed Shirley the burn hole.

'Never mind, babe, first round's on me.' And with that they went in to have a look at their base for the weekend.

6pm

Well, we're here. All made it in one piece. We're in chilly Iceland! Not quite where I'd hoped for but I think we'll be in for some fun. Just texted David to tell him where we are. He said he was quite jealous! He said he'd love to be in Iceland for all the Viking stuff and something about some monks that lived here!! Once a teacher always a teacher! I had a text from Jason, too, saying they were having a fantastic time. Sounds as if their do is a bit more upmarket. Mind you they haven't got Shaz and the factory girls with them have they! It sounds like a nice hotel. This one we're in isn't too bad. I'm in a room with Oli. Shaz and Fi are together. Susan, Angie and Kelly are in one triple room and Ali, Jeanette and Gail in another. They decided that it wouldn't be fair for someone to have a room with just them and Ali so that's why they did the two triples!!

Had a lovely day, so far. I did get emotional after the tapas bar – think it was the sangria and having me mum and auntie Dilys there. I know I whinge about them a bit, but I think the world of them, it just got a bit much that's all. My life is gonna change in a few days, I've been on me own now for so long, managed the kids meself, I think it just all got to me and I had to have a cry. Felt much better after, though. Oli started an' all: he was crying about Apple, though, which was bit over the top I suppose, but you know when someone you care about starts crying, well it sets you off doesn't it and Oli is dead sensitive like that. Not sure what the plans are for the weekend but we haven't gorra lot of time, so I think we may get an early start. Shaz and Fi are already downstairs in the bar. They came in dumped their stuff and said they were getting in as much party time as they could, bless 'em. Shaz hasn't really come dressed for the weather, mind. I don't know what she was expecting but she's still wearing the stuff she would at home and, let's face it, she wasn't dressed for the weather there!! I think Fi may have a few spare things for her to wear, though, if she's too cold.

Anyway, think I'll have a quick shower now. Freshen up and get me in the mood for tonight. Oli's already in there. Gonna let me hair down this weekend, really enjoy it. In a way I'm chuffed it is Iceland, I mean it is something totally different isn't it. I can't believe we got here for the price an' all!!

Shirley opened her holdall and unpacked the few things she had brought along with her. Oli emerged from the bathroom wearing nothing but a tiny white towel wrapped around his waist.

'Ooh, that's better, it is friggin' freezing though, isn't it babe?'

'I'm going in now. It is quite cold, yeah, isn't it? You know, for the time of year, I didn't expect it to be quite this chilly,' Shirley said getting her towel and clean underwear out of her bag.

'I know. Colder than I thought, an' all. Wish there was snow, though. Are you ok with it here, babe? You're not disappointed are ya?' Oli asked looking concerned. 'Did you want to be in a sunny place?'

'Nah, of course I'm not, it's gonna be great.'

'Ah, great. I wanted to have something different for ya,' he said planting a kiss on her forehead. 'Now, come head an' get in that shower ya minger.'

'I know, I do feel I need to freshen up. I wonder when them kids will come back.'

'Oh gerron with it, they won't be long. I'll text Fi an' ask them what they're doing.'

Engulfed in the aroma of refreshing zingy lemon and lime shower gel, Shirley savoured every second of the warm water and began to feel energised. In the background she heard a door slam and the familiar voice of her daughter and she smiled happily, beginning to hum a little bit of Kylie to get herself in the party mood.

'Come on, Mum,' Fiona said banging on the bathroom door.

'Ok, ok...'

Shirley stepped out of the shower, wrapped herself in the remaining bath towel and went through to see what Fiona and Shaz had been up to.

'Hiya, Mum,' Fiona said happily. 'Hey that pool is quite cold.'

'Oh, you've been in the pool. I thought you and Shaz were partying in the bar.' Shirley said, impressed by their devotion to the holiday spirit, in the light of the sub-20°C temperatures.

'Well I did have to bribe Shaz. I told her there were some good looking lifeguards down there. I thought we'd have enough of booze all night,' Fi sighed.

'Oh, you're not your mother's daughter are you kid?' Oli winked.

'Well done you, babe. It's not the be all and end all, booze, is it.' Shirley smiled. 'Now you'd better get in that shower, we're wasting valuable drinking time.

Laughing, Fi left them to it.

'Well, I'll have a dip in the morning just to say I've been. I put me cossie in 'cause I thought there'd be a pool inside the hotel,' Shirley said happily.

'Oh, aye, yeah. I put me Speedos in an' all.'

'What? Those budgie smugglers? Oli, can't you get something a bit more, well, you know…?'

'Hey what d'ya mean? I love me Speedos, me.'

'Well, I just think they're a bit dated now. I bet Marc doesn't wear them. I bet he's got some board shorts, you know, those trendy surfy type things, baggy to his knees.'

'When you've got it, flaunt it.' Oli giggled dropping his towel and presenting himself in a tiny pair of white designer briefs.

'Aye, all right, then.' Shirley fell back on the bed laughing hysterically at the dinky drawers.

Half an hour later the toothsome twosome were ready for their first night on the town in Iceland.

'Let's go and see if Fi and that mad Shaz are ready yet.' Oli got the room card and put it into the pocket of his skin tight jeans.

They found Shaz sitting in her wet bikini and towel on the bed.

'Hey, love, you've got to sleep on that tonight ya know,' Shirley informed her.

'Oh, have I? Thought it was Fi's bed,' Shaz replied matter of factly.

'Ta a bunch, mate,' Fiona grumbled.

Oli looked at Shirley and shook his head. Shaz had her head buried in her camera.

'Ok, no probs,' she said, still not looking up. 'Hey I've already taken a load of pics of me and Fi. Gonna have 'em on Bebo by Monday morning.'

Shirley went to sit next to Shaz. 'Let's have a look then.' Shirley held her hand out for the camera.

'Oh, they're great,' Shirley smiled as she flicked through the pictures. 'Where are you here, Shaz? That's not today is it?' Shirley asked still scrolling through the pictures.

'Let's see?' Shaz asked looking over. 'Oh, nah, that's the party in ours last night. Look at the state of me mum.'

Oli, not too interested in seeing a couple of teenage girls by the pool, had a sudden surge of interest in Mo and her party.

'Oh, let's have a look, love...' he asked, almost running over. 'That's a good one of yer mum, Shaz, love. She could put that one on the mantlepiece an' keep the kids away from the fire, eh, love? He laughed.

'Just look at her! That's some fella she's after,' Shaz said, passing a running commentary on the snaps.

'Hey, that's—' Shirley stopped mid sentence.

'Oh, that's some woman, Val I think her name is, and that's her again with her fella, Lenny. He used to work with me mum in the pub that's how she knows him,' Shaz volunteered.

Shirley looked at Oli and he looked at the camera shocked.

'Let's see?' Oli said taking the camera from Shirley.

'I think there's a picture of the old mingers snogging, somewhere,' Shaz said with a shudder.

'Well, you've got some great pics there, babe. Just make sure you don't delete them while you're away.' Shirley was concerned that they may lose the vital evidence they'd been trying to secure for the past couple of months if Shaz got a bit woozy and erased them by mistake.

'Maybe we should take a look an' see if there's a place we can print them off for yer, before we go home?' Oli suggested.

'Oh, nah, it's ok, they're only some mingers in a party at ours God knows why she' taken them. I'll dump 'em anyway if I run out of shots. Anyway, gonna get me shower now. Shirl, you ready for the night of your life?' Shaz said, excitedly making a start on her own transformation.

'All yours, Shaz. Hurry up though, yeah? You can't be taking ages 'cause we're meeting the girls downstairs in less than half an hour.' Fiona informed her friend as she emerged from the bathroom.

'Listen, Fi, you hang on here for Shaz. I think I may have left me straighteners on. Oli come with me – you've got the key.' Shirley's mind was on the case not her hen night.

She tucked Shaz's camera into her handbag while Fi's back was turned and then hustled Oli into a hasty exit from the bedroom.

Once outside in the corridor Shirley whispered, 'Listen. We have to get these pics printed off ASAP.'

'Aye, I know that, kid, but where can we at this time of day? We can't even speak the language,' Oli flapped.

'Well, we'll have to take a walk up the street or ask in reception, they all speak English,' Shirley insisted.

'I know, I'll go and ask, but just in case how about I try and take pictures of the pictures with my phone? Let's get back to the room for a min' and try that.'

'Ok, babe.'

Closing the bedroom door Oli said, full of drama, 'Come on get them pics up again and I'll try with me phone.'

Slumping onto one of the twin beds Shirley frantically looked through the camera for the incriminating pictures. 'Can you believe it? Actually solving a case by chance like this? Without even doing that much. What a break!'

'Well I wouldn't say that, we friggin' deserve it, don't forget the trouble with the bizzies in that Super Stores car park,' Oli reminded her, looking at the picture he'd taken on his mobile.

'Oh, aye, yeah, how could I forget that?' Shirley pulled a face thinking of the sour-faced headmaster's wife.

'Not bad. I think they'll do as a back up,' Oli said thoughtfully before showing the picture to Shirley.

'Oh, yeah, not bad at all, babe. Brilliant idea.'

'Well, we can't let her delete them photies. We'll have to offer to pay for the lot as a holiday pressie. Put the weekend's photies in an album for her maybe and keep the ones we need to show to Bernie.'

'I know, how about I say to Fi I'll be in charge of the camera for the weekend incase they lose it when they're pissed?'

'Don't think will work, babe, them kids are gonna wanna keep the camera to take their own snaps,' Oli said rubbing his chin.

'What then?' Shirley asked worriedly.

'I don't know, I don't know. Pray?' Oli sighed. 'At least if all else fails we have got these pics haven't we, kid?'

Shirley got herself and her bits and bobs for the night out together, constantly thinking about how they could ensure the camera and its contents were kept safe from harm.

'Quick, it's nearly seven,' Fiona shouted from outside the room.

The duo put the finishing touches to their already perfect appearance and headed out the door to join the rest of the gang.

'Hey, hang on a sec, I've forgot me camera,' Shaz protested rushing back in to the next room to pick up the camera that Oli and Shirley had hoped she'd forget.

Shirley looked at Oli and she raised her eyebrows guiltily.

'Oh, here it is, babe.' Shirley announced sheepishly.' I must have still had it in my hand when I left yours.'

Shaz didn't bat an eyelid. 'Ta Shirl,' she said reaching out for the camera. Reluctantly, but with no alternative, Shirley handed it over.

'Watch that friggin' camera like a hawk tonight,' Oli warned her as they locked their door and slowly followed the girls who had marched off excitedly.

'Hey, you, it's my hen night, I'm meant to be enjoying meself. I know I should but you should keep an' eye out an' all. I wanna let meself go, might be my last chance,' Shirley protested.

'Aye, I will, but four eyes are better than two, babe.'

'Well, I'm sure we can find you a pair of specs.'

'Aww, come on, babe, we're in this together aren't we?'

'Aye, ok, ok. Let's enjoy the night, though, eh? We're not here for long are we?'

Back on the ground floor, they joined the gang of girls who by the look of them had been down at the bar long before the allocated nine o'clock rendezvous they had given Shirley and Oli.

'Hey, you lot, how long you been here?' Oli asked looking at the giggling group of girls enjoying their smart cocktails.

'Not long. Got here about ten minutes ago. We were thirsty, though, eh girls?' Angie laughed and twirled her pink paper umbrella under his nose.

More drinks were ordered and the gaggle got louder and rowdier. Half an hour later, after yet another round of drinks was guzzled, Angie piped up, 'Come on kid's let's gerroff, it's only dead cheap for the ale in this Viking club down the road and they've got some entertainment and food on an' all. The barman's been tellin' us all about it.'

'Great, let's go then,' Oli said, finishing off the dregs of his blue lagoon cocktail. 'I can feel a Shirley Bassey moment coming on, bit of karaoke, eh girls?'

The gang made their way raucously to the promisingly themed club, hopeful of a night of seriously Scandinavian entertainment.

'Right, now we're here, do you notice something different about this hen night?' Oli asked trying to be serious.

'*We're on our hols as well.*' Shaz shouted out, putting her hand up simultaneously obviously still in school mode, well, it was still Friday, just.

'No, good answer though, Shaz babe,' Oli said taking on the role of teacher.

'I know,' Susan said, knowing what Oli had up his sleeve. 'We've got no hen have we?' She winked at the others.

The gang all sat looking at Oli expectantly.

'Correct, Susan, ten house points to you.' Oli pointed at Susan who looked on smiling proudly.

Shirley groaned. 'Hey, I told you lot before, no tacky veils and L plates.'

'Hey you an' all,' Angie protested. 'Nothing wrong with veils and L plates on a hen night.'

'I know, I know, sorry I didn't mean it like that.'

'Well, let's face it, Susan love, it didn't bring you any luck did it? Your wedding was called off after you had the veil and L plates,' Ali pointed out.

'Don't be worrying there, girl, I wouldn't do that to you would I?' Oli assured Shirley.' But you can't have your hen night dressed quite like that.'

'I wanted you to be dressed as a chicken,' Angie said.

'What?' Shirley was horrified, surely they wouldn't...

'Don't worry, Mum, I put a stop to that.' Fiona grinned.

'Oh you're in on this an' all, are ya?'

'Well, I was trying to protect you, Mum, you should have seen some of the ideas.' Fiona pulled a face.

'So, anyway, we had a few ideas but the obvious choice had to be...' Oli revealed a carrier bag previously concealed under the table.

'Oh God, what?' Shirley asked terrified.

'A sexy school mistress. Wahay!' Oli revealed pulling a black gown, mortarboard and cane.

'Oh God, no!' Shirley exclaimed taking hold of the black gown.

'Look at the back, Mum.' Fiona giggled.

'Sexy hen marrying a sexy head.' Shirley read out. 'Great.'

'Gerrit on, babe. Go in the bogs. You gorra be bra and nicks only underneath,' Angie instructed.

'Oh I don't know about that.'

'Go on… I'll come with ya, Mum,' Fi said encouragingly.

'Ok…' But Shirley's reluctance was plain for all to see.

In the safety of the bathroom Fiona scrabbled in her bag. 'Here ya go, Mum.' Fiona said handing her mother a pair of black shorts and a black vest. 'Put them on underneath – I got 'em for you specially.'

'Awww, ta love,' Shirley said with relief. Bless her, she'd known what Shirley would think of parading about in an open fronted gown with only her undies to cover her dignity.

'Didn't think you'd like it just in ya bra and knickers, so I shoved these in me bag, just put that thing over them no one will know.' Fi said pleased to have helped her less than exhibitionist mother out.

'Thank God for that,' Shirley said pulling on the shorts and vest and neatly folding up the cute little black fitted spaghetti strapped dress and putting it in her handbag.

'You looked lovely in that dress an' all, I know you like it and got it just for this weekend, but you'll just have to go with it now and get into the spirit with the girls,' Fiona said leaning on the hand dryer.

'Thanks for the advice, agony aunt'. You'll be getting a job in them magazines before long.' Shirley teased. 'Mind you I was friggin' freezing in that dress even with me coat on.' She added relieved to be a little bit warmer courtesy of the black thermal vest.

'I know what you're like. And count your lucky stars 'cause you could have ended up boiling ya tits off in a furry chicken suit,' Fiona said sternly. 'Mind you with this weather…'

'Hey, hurry up you two,' Shaz said, coming to see where mother and daughter had got to. 'Hey this place is a bit minging, Shirl, bit dark and dingy.'

'Oh, I think it's meant to be, Shaz love, old-fashioned an' that like the Vikings. Anyway, I'm coming now.' Shirley took a last look in the mirror and ensured her hat was appropriately to one side. 'Ok ready.'

'You forgot this.' Fi tried not to laugh and handed her the cane.

'Oh yeah, ta,' Shirley said breaking out into a laugh.

'The entertainment and food are about to get going,' Oli said poking his head round the door. 'Hey look at you.'

Shirley decided to make the best of it and walked out proudly in her new attire to cheers from her hen night gang.

The posse were all sat around a long table with the special blue lagoon cocktails that they had already become addicted to.

'Come on, kids, the food's about to arrive.' Angie ushered them to the seats she had saved close by her and Susan.

'Oh good I'm starving,' Oli announced.

'Don't be rushing, it looks minging, kids.' Ali announced flatly as they squeezed past her to their chairs.

'Oh, what is it? I saw this programme once about the kind of food they eat here, all sheep's brains and rotten sharks,' Kelly informed the now uneasy group.

'Hey, I see what you mean about the light, Shaz love, but it's the theme of it isn't it? It's a Viking place,' Shirley said looking round the room. Lots of candles in black candle holders adorned the stone walls. Archways separated the various groups of diners and Shirley's gang were seated in the high backed hard wooden bench seats and long wooden table closest to the entertainment area. The venue did look authentic but slightly spooky with it.

'It's all part of the fun, kids.' Oli reassured them.

The food arrived; wafer thin deep fried bread to start, followed by cod cheeks simply poached, served with boiled potatoes and some fresh vegetables.

'What's this, then?' Shaz asked, unsure of anything that didn't involve hamburgers, chips and chicken nuggets or pizza.

'Oh try it, Shaz, it's lovely beautiful fresh fish,' Shirley instructed the teenager, who was poking the cheeks with her fork.

'Aye. It'll give you some brains, babe,' Oli joked.

'It's not bad. I reckon I can just about manage it. Had better in Benidorm, mind,' Ali complained.

'Well looks like it,' Angie said pointing at Ali's empty plate.

'Hey! D'ya know what? I caught Ali washing her friggin' knickers with me best honey and buttermilk facial soap before we came out.' Gail complained to Oli and Shirley as the waitresses cleared their empty plates.

'What? The minger,' Oli announced.

'I know. I walked in and there she was scrubbing the gussets of her massive friggin' pants with me lovely new soap,' Gail went on taking a large sip out of her blue coloured cocktail.

'What did you say?' Shirley asked.

'Oh, I gave her what for; she just said I'm only giving 'em a quick rinse.' Gail said shaking her head.' I've had to throw it an' all now, an' it cost me two ninety-five. I'm mad I am.'

'Why doesn't she take her dirty washing home? We're only here two days.'

Wondering at her behaviour they looked over at Ali who wobbled from one cheek to the other on the chair as if she was relieving an attack of wind.

The group enjoyed their dessert despite the thought of Ali's gussets before settling down to await the night's entertainment. The waitress came round one last time and gave them all a small glass of liquid.

'Hey, what's this, then?' Ali asked smelling the fluid.

'Brennivin.' The waitress announced slamming it down in front of them. 'Svarti dauoi.' She said to others.

'What the hell…? Oh well, when in Rome…' Oli said gulping the burning liquor.

'It's not bad,' Shaz said, finishing the lot before most had even started.

'It's schnapps, isn't it? Mmm, it's ok tastes like caraway seeds,'

Gail said holding her chilled shot glass out for more as the waitress offered top ups.

'Come head, love, we'll have a few more, so you can leave us the bottle,' Susan shouted over. 'It's a special night, it's a hen party.'

Obligingly, the waitress smiled and left the bottle next to Shirley.

'Oh fair do's,' Shaz said, topping her glass up.

'Fair do's? That'll be on the bill,' Shirley muttered.

'Hey you, stop your whining, it's your hen night. Now shut it, the entertainment is about to start,' Oli ordered.

The room darkened and five burly men appeared onstage dressed in full Viking attire: boots, leggings, horned helmets, the lot.

The girls all cheered, but Shaz and Fi looked a bit put off and helped themselves to more of the Brennivin.

One man started banging on a simple drum, the other on wooden pan pipes and the third man started blowing on the whistle. After a few minutes of this and the girls' frantic clapping two other men started singing folk songs.

'Hey, these are ok aren't they?' Ali said clapping furiously.

'Oh, aye, yeah, they're brilliant…' Fi said sarcastically.

'Get into it, babe,' Oli said standing up on his feet and clapping and cheering away.

Another gulp of the Brennivin and Shaz stood up and jigged about to the lively folk music.

With the bottle of Brennivin empty Angie asked the waitress who herself was in full female Viking style costume for another bottle. Laughing nervously she obliged and raised her eyebrows to her colleague who did the same back.

All the girls and Oli were in full swing: clapping, dancing and trying to sing along to the folk duo.

Suddenly the music stopped and the lights got lower and only the candles on the tables lit the darkened room. The Viking on the pan pipes started frantically playing and two of the Vikings came off stage – one of the singers and the one playing the drum.

The one who had been playing the drum grabbed Angie and tried to lift her over his shoulder, then, unsuccessful but still determined, he tried to carry her by holding her in his arms, again without success. Not put off, Angie shouted, 'Come here kid.' And jumped on his back to rapturous applause from the rest of the girls, Oli and the other diners. Triumphant at last, the Viking did a short walk in front of the gang before taking the screaming Angie back stage.

The other Viking tried to pick up Susan, but to no avail. In the end the other three came off stage and helped him. With one Viking holding each arm and one Viking holding each leg they ungraciously lugged Susan back stage.

The room was in hysterics.

'Hey, that has to be the high light of the night,' Oli screamed.

'You could see her drawers,' Jeanette slurred. 'What a tart.'

'Hey, you can talk,' Oli snapped back. 'She was having a laugh.'

Jeanette looked at him, eyes rolling in her head, too drunk to get into a debate.

Ten minutes later Susan returned.' What a scream.'

'You were brilliant babe,' Oli said giving her a kiss on the cheek and throwing a dirty look at Jeanette.

'Yeah you were. Hey, where's Angie?' Shirley asked.

'On her way; she's been chatting to Barry,' Susan replied.

'Barry?' Shirley asked.

'That's me.' The Viking who had been playing the drums was now standing in front of them in jeans and a jumper.

'Meet Barry – he's from Bolton,' Angie blurted excitedly.

'Flamin' 'ell mate, you're a long way from home!' Oli exclaimed.

'Well, it's a long story,' Barry answered.

'Well, come and join us for a drink,' Shirley said realising that

Angie seemed to have developed a soft spot for Barry the Viking.

'Oh, yeah,' Angie said holding the nearly empty bottle of Brennivin.

'Oh God, you haven't been drinking that stuff have you? You do know they call it black death?' Barry informed them.

'Do they, babe, why's that then?' Kelly slurred.

'Think we may find out in the morning...' Shirley answered grimly.

'I'll sit and have a pint with you, though' Barry said and settled down with the gang.

'So what brings you all to Iceland?' Barry asked.

'It's me hen weekend, an' we all sort of work together,' Shirley informed him.

'That's brilliant, it's a great place to come.'

'So, babe, what about you ? What's your story?' Angie was starting to slur a bit, the 'black death' kicking in no doubt.

'Well, I've been here a few years really. Came here for the fish.'

'What, you came all this way on a fishing trip? Did you catch anything?' Kelly asked limply.

'No not a fishing trip; I came here to work.' Barry laughed realising that perhaps it wasn't just the alcohol affecting Kelly's brain. 'Iceland is famed for its fishing industry...or it was.'

'So how come you ended up playing the drums in here?' Shirley was intrigued.

'Well the country's on its arse, so I'm doing two jobs now. To be honest, I'm really enjoying this part loads and it beats being out in all weathers in oilskins.' Barry smiled.

'How did you get into this? I mean it's great fun isn't it?' Oli asked looking around the place.

'I used to come here for a drink and a couple of the lads on the fishing with me they were looking for a drummer for times when we're not at sea, the rest is history.'

'So are ya married Barry?' Angie slurred.

'Divorced. Five years now. It's been all work and a bit of play here.' He smiled.

The rest of the evening passed with Angie getting to know Barry better and one by one the girls and Oli becoming engulfed in the after effects of 'svarti dauoi' or the black death.

SIX

Saturday, April 28
11 am

Oh, me head feels like a washing machine. We shouldn't have had that last bottle. I knew it at the time, just couldn't help meself, plus them girls were not the type to let me get away with being a lightweight. I'm gonna go and sit down in the sitting room for a couple of hours. It's really nice down there. Quiet and peaceful, a coffee maker you just help yourself to and they've got mags and stuff, English ones an' all. Just woke up really, but I have noticed Oli's already gone. The girls are flat out. I'm not surprised cos we were up til 5. The Viking's a case, or should I say Barry. He's off tonight so he's invited himself along with us for the rest of the hen do. He said he'd show us some of the best places for cheap beer. It was a no brainer then for the girls, he just had to come along.

141

Shirley put her diary back in her bag and gingerly made an attempt to gather what she needed for a couple of hours relaxing or maybe sleeping off her hangover in the warm inviting sitting room..

'Hiya, kid,' Oli said brightly, bouncing through the door.

'My God where've you been and how come you're so full of life? I feel like shite.' Shirley put on a pair of sunglasses she'd found in her handbag, hoping it would help her hang over.

'Aww, do ya? Bless you, babe. I feel ok ya know. Don't think I must've drunk as much as you, like. Are the sleeping beauties still asleep?' Oli asked putting Shaz's camera on the coffee table.

'Yeah, flat out. What you been doing with that?' Shirley asked noting the camera.

'Well, last night I asked Barry where I could print off me pics and he told me about a place only down the road, less than ten minutes walk.' Oli showed Shirley the prints of Val and Lenny from Shaz's camera.

'Oh brill! You little star,' Shirley said delighted that their evidence was now official. 'But how did you get the camera in the first place?'

'Shaz was pissed as a fart an' she left the camera on the table last night. I just picked it up when I went to the loo an' she never noticed,' Oli told her.

'Well that was lucky.'

'Aye. So I'll keep these safe, lock 'em away in me case and we can go see Bernie when we get back,' Oli announced proudly.

'What a bit of luck, though, eh? We did well there. Mo is good for something then,' Shirley said, rubbing her throbbing head.

'So, what's the plan today then?' Oli asked brightly.

'You've planned this – thought you'd arranged it all, but *please* tell me we have today to do what we want with.'

'Well, sort of… You've got a couple of hours to yourself then at half-three we're booked in to go to that Blue Lagoon. You know, that geothermal spa. You'll feel a million dollars when they've finished with you,' Oli promised.

'Aww, Oli, how lovely.' Shirley was touched.

'Aye, no expense spared. Me and the girls have covered the bill for you, it's not all tack for us ya know,' he said as she kissed him on the cheek.

'That's so lovely. Just what I need after the black death.'

'You'll be all relaxed and ready for tonight,' Oli assured her.

'Oh God, the way I feel don't think I could touch another drop.'

'Give over, just drink plenty of water today, have your spa, an' you'll be right as rain. Now then, let's go down to the lounge for a bit an' see if we can get a bit of a rest and relax and try and get rid of that hangover.' Oli suggested.

'Ok, I'm gonna leave them kids to it, they'll wake in their own time won't they.'

'Aye, come on, let's see if Ali's got a load of bees buzzing round her lady garden, after her honey and butter milk soapy gussets.' Oli laughed, popping his shades on and heading out the door.

'Hey, thought your head was ok? What you got them on for?' Shirley asked.

'Fashion statement.'

The twosome lazed in the warm and inviting sitting room enjoying the peace and tranquility. There was no sign of any of the rest of the hen party and Shirley didn't mind a bit. The therapeutic sun shone through the window easing her tired body and healing her aching head.

'How you feeling now babe?' Oli asked taking a sip of the water he'd ordered: to make sure they both drank gallons of it.

'Oh, much better ta. How are you? Mind you you were ok, weren't you?'

'It was you knocked 'em back last night ya know. Mind you

with them girls and you being the star of the show you had no choice did ya?'

'I know. Hope it's not too boozy tonight,' Shirley muttered.

'Don't worry babe. It will be.' Oli winked. 'Hey, it's nearly time for us to catch the bus for the Blue Lagoon. We'd best get ourselves off.' Oli jumped up gesticulating at his watch.

Panicking, Oli ran outside to make sure the bus hadn't gone. Relieved and extremely surprised he found all the girls including Fi and Shaz waiting outside the hotel and wondering where the star of the show was – they'd knocked on the bedroom door and found no one home.

'Hey, where's this friggin' bus? We're freezing our wotsits off here,' Shaz complained.

'Well, you should have put a bit more on.' Oli told her sternly. 'It is Iceland ya know and they only have summer for two weeks in July!'

'Well, I haven't got anything else, have I?' She shivered in her skinny jeans and thin pink top, silver dolly shoes and silver bomber jacket.

The rest of the girls were more suitably dressed with coats, scarves and gloves, and Jeanette, Gail and Kelly had hats on too.

The shiny blue bus arrived and pulled to a halt in front of them.

'At last,' Shaz grumbled.

'You'll be all right kid, when we get to that spa,' Ali said, lumbering onto the bus behind Shaz.

'Mmm.' Shaz was still shivering.

On the bus already seated was the middle-aged couple that was on the bus from the airport.

'Oh, hiya kids, you said you were going on this trip didn't ya? Awww, are you enjoying Iceland, then?' Oli asked.

'Superb, what a fascinating place,' the man replied.

'Aww, it is an' all. So what pubs you been to?' Susan asked. 'See if we can advise ya on some better ones.'

'Oh we've just been sight seeing, early to bed so we can get as much in as possible,' the woman informed her.

'Oh, boring…' Susan said plonking herself on a seat. 'So why are you doing coming to waste your time in a spa then?'

'Well this isn't any old spa is it?' the woman said.

'Well, to be honest, once you've been to one spa you've been to them all I think,' Susan said flippantly.

'But in this case the lagoon is surrounded by a moss covered lava field. It's a geothermal spa with naturally arising blue green algae and bubbling silica mud.'

'Aye, they all say that, but I bet they get all that from the bargain shops,' Susan said before settling into her seat and having a nod on the way.

Arriving at the Blue Lagoon they gathered their belongings and made their way to the entrance.

'Stinks a bit doesn't it?' Ali complained.

'That's the minerals,' The woman from the bus piped up as she passed them and got to the front of the queue.

'Oh, maybe they've got cheaper ones in the pound shops here then, ones that don't smell so nice,' Ali grumbled.

'I hope you don't gerra rash, Fi,' Shaz said concerned. 'You know what your skin's like with face masks an' that.'

'Anyway, let's be going in. Follow me,' Oli instructed. Leading the way he marched on to book the group in leaving the girls outside some rather municipal looking changing rooms.

'So can we pick our treatments?' Kelly asked.

'Not sure what it's all about,' Susan said. 'It all looks a bit odd to me. I thought we were coming to some sort of factory to be honest with you when we got into the car park. What with all them pipes an' that. Looks like Runcorn.'

'Here comes Oli, now, he can give us the lowdown,' Angie informed them spotting him coming down the corridor.

'Well, kids, are you ready for this? It is a bit different but that's gonna be all part of the fun.' Oli giggled nervously.

'Oh, my, God. What is it?' Fi asked recognising the look on Oli's face.

'Well it's this beautiful blue green lagoon that is lovely and warm cause of all the molten lava underneath and full of relaxing and revitalizing minerals. I can guarantee that it will make everyone who bathes in it feel years younger and a million dollars.' Oli smiled, bigging up the experience.

'Ok, so what's the catch?' Shirley asked.

'It's outside in the fresh air. Come on kids...' He started marching off again before anyone had a chance to tackle him about it.

'Outside? Outside? It's friggin' freezing outside!' Susan exclaimed. 'I've got two vests on.'

'I thought it sounded dodgy, when that woman went on about algae,' Ali moaned. 'Isn't that what you get when stuff goes off in the fridge?'

'Oh, come on, it's all part of the fun.' Shirley smiled trying to encourage them. 'It's famous, so it must be good. Doesn't Bjork come here? She's from Iceland, isn't she?'

'Aye, ok, Shirl, just for you... Anyway, come on, it'll be a laugh,' Angie said dragging Susan along.

'Won't be a laugh if we're all off next week with pneumonia…' Ali muttered glumly.

With their dreams of being pampered and spoilt in a series of luxury treatment rooms in tatters the group gingerly exited the warm safety of the changing rooms in their costumes and towels and were greeted by the steamy mists of the Blue Lagoon.

Stepping quickly into the healing waters, Shirley felt all her anxiety melt away. Even her head felt warm despite the frigid air temperature.'Ooh that's lovely,' she sighed.

After a lot of pushing and shoving and mutterings about

chilblains, there were groans of delight and pleasure from everyone as the surprisingly warm blue water swallowed up all their concerns and negativity about the experience. They weren't used to finding their way about in the steam and kept bumping into lumpy lava rocks and other bathers.

'Hey, look, those two from the bus are putting that mud on themselves.' Shaz waved at the skinny middle-aged couple. 'Hiya.'

They looked over, gave a small smile and carried on covering themselves with the therapeutic silica mud.

'Let's have a go then, shall we, eh Shaz?' Fi said giggling.

Within minutes the whole group were covering themselves in the mud, laughing and joking.

'Here, what's this remind you of?' Oli winked at the girls, 'They say hippos like playing in mud.'

'Hey, you cheeky git, are you saying we're hippos?' Susan protested. 'I'll have you know I've lost a stone since Christmas – only another five to go and I'll hit my target weight.'

'Would I...?' Oli giggled slapping the mud on Susan's back and giving her a good old rub down.

6 pm

I feel like a million dollars, now, that's for sure. Just great. It was the business, pure heaven. I feel fantastic now with all the stress and strain gone. I think I had a lot of built in tension, to be honest, what with the wedding details and all that. I don't think all of it was hangover. It was so funny though, when we found out it was outside!! Oli knew all along, but he said he didn't know when was the best time to tell us so he just kept quiet, then he thought it was too late, so he just kept quiet till we were there. That was the best thing an' all, I reckon. It was lovely, a totally different experience. I've really enjoyed me hen weekend so far, I really have.

I'm back in me room, now, on me own. Oli's still down by the bar and Fi and Shaz apparently went to join him. I just called in and had one on me way back up to the room. They're gonna stay down for a bit longer. I just wanted to have half an hour's shut eye after that pamper to get ready for tonight. I've found a t shirt on me bed with 'Shirl's Hen Night' printed on it and there are another three on the chair so I take it they are for us all to wear tonight. I'm relieved especially after last night's get up. A t-shirt like that will be a piece of piss. Half an hour of some power zeds and I'll be ready for action. Gonna be a bit chilly tho' in just a t-shirt.

She stripped to her pants and a t-shirt and slipped under the thin cotton sheet. While they had been out Oli had put on the heating and the room was like toast. Even though it was warm she felt comfortable under the soothing cool cotton. Letting out a sigh she closed her eyes and drifted off into a pamper induced sleep.

'Shirl, Shirl… Wake up babe.' Oli whispered softly in her ear.

'Mmm… What...' she murmured quietly rolling on her back.

'Come on babe, it's nearly seven. We've left you for as long as we can, the girls have gone down to the bar already,' Oli said quietly.

'Oh God, I must have gone right off after that Blue Lagoon thing.' Shirley informed him. 'I only meant to have forty winks.'

'Aye, well away you were. Come on now. You won't need to be long 'cause you had your shower after the lagoon sesh, that's why I left ya,' Oli said putting the finishing touches to his hair.

'Ok. I take it these t-shirts are for tonight?' Shirley had noted that Oli was wearing his with a pair of white skinny jeans and his moon boots. He was determined they were going to get an outing, snow or no snow.

148

'Aye, they're great aren't they, and not too tacky…' Oli said. 'My idea,' he finished off, smugly.

'Yeah, they're ok.' Shirley smiled, looking at the white t shirt with red writing on it. 'And it will go with me nails.'

'I don't mean to mither you hon', but you're gonna have to gerrup, now. D'ya want me to wait for you or make me self scarce?' Oli said spraying his aftershave on.

'Ok babe, you go on down. Just me make-up, put me hair up and I'll be dressed in no time. You get off an' get the drinks in and keep an eye on Fi and Shaz till I get there,' Shirley said dragging herself out of bed.

'Ok babe. Hey, I had a text from Marc while you were dozing.'

'Oh. Everything ok?' Shirley asked.

'Oh yeah, said he misses me loads.'

'Oh that's good news then.' Shirley smiled, rolling on her deodorant.

'Oh, yeah, think he's having a hard time though with Apple,' Oli said, pulling a face. 'Said he'd been up all night with her crying. Only way she'd stop was if he put her in bed with him.'

'Oh he's started something now, then. You'll have to make it up to him when you get back.' Shirley suggested.

'Don't you worry I will.' He winked salaciously then headed out of the door.

Before she carried on with getting ready Shirley looked at her mobile phone and was delighted to see that she'd had a message from David while she was asleep.

Smiling she read the text: *miss u so much my gorgeous darling having a great time hope u r 2 boys getting on great love u always xxxxxxxxxxxxxxxxx*

Smiling Shirley got ready to text back: *Havin a mad time, not all tack been 2 that blue lagoon out again in a min. Miss u so much and J glad they getting on love u loads can't wait to c u xxxxxxxxxxxxxxxxxxxxxxxxx*

Finishing off her make-up Shirley felt really happy. She was in love with David and knew he felt the same. Not long and they'd be together every day.

Taking a last look in the mirror and a deep breath, Shirley left the toasty room and made her way to join Barry from Bolton and the rest of her hen night gang.

'Here she is, the star of the show.' Barry announced as Shirley joined them at the bar.

'Hiya, you lot,' Shirley said joining the group.

'Hey, Shirl, Angie was just saying she's ordered a tattoo kit off the internet and 'cause I'm creative she wants me to do a tat for her when it comes.' Oli announced proudly.

'Flamin' hell. Make sure it's not a night after he's been out on the ale and got the DT's,' Shirley warned.

They group laughed and Shirley waited in anticipation to find out what was in store for her. Though she matched the top half of the rest of the group in her white and red hen night t-shirt, Shirley had teamed hers up with tight, red, tailored trousers that hugged her newly toned size twelve figure perfectly. Together with red ankle boots and red jewellery and her shoulder length hair loose she looked casual but very style conscious.

'We did have another bar crawl planned for ya, babe, and a few more dares, but lucky for you Barry's come to the rescue,' Oli said excitedly.

Shirley gulped. 'Ok, what we doing, Barry?'

'Well I have got a few connections here and lucky for you lot me mate Gunni's got a limo hire with no one booked for the next hour, so it's about to arrive to take us lot in two trips down to one of the hotels that's got a casino,' Barry said flashing complimentary casino entry tickets at all the girls.

There were shrieks of delight all round as the girls realised that yet another classic factory girls night out was in the offing.

'So Shirl, Oli, Fi, Shaz and, of course, me will go first,' Barry announced.

'Hey what about us?' Angie complained.

'Next trip, babe, more room for the lot of you.' Barry informed her ushering the first bunch out of the door.

'Hey, who's this one think he is? Better watch it, Oli, I think he's trying to take over from ya kid. You're meant to be in charge.' Susan said quietly, a bit miffed that she was left behind with the likes of Ali, Jeanette and Gail.

'Hey don't be like that, queen; if it wasn't for him we'd be doing the same thing again tonight,' Oli consoled her and sailed off in the part-time Viking's wake.

'Mmm,' was all Susan could muster in response.

The white limo soon pulled up outside the group's hotel.

'Won't be long, girls, say 'bout half an hour. Finish off your drinks then come on out. We'll be waiting in the casino for ya,' Barry shouted to the slightly irritated pack waiting at the door.

'Come on, kids, time to get another couple of rounds in.' Susan stomped back indoors.

'Here we go, in you get.' Barry said opening the door allowing Shirley first entry to the luxurious car.

'Oh, ta Barry, how can we thank you…' Shirley giggled her way in to the cavernous interior of the limo.

'Just have a good time. A drive around first before dropping us off, please driver.' Barry cracked open a bottle of bubbly that was chilling in the silver ice bucket.

'What about the others? They're waiting.' Shirley protested.

'What, those miserable sods? Let 'em wait. I'm with Bazza. Come head an' drive round the place.' Shaz said holding out her glass for the bubbly.

'I must admit it is nice to have a break from that lot for a bit,' smirked Oli.

'Aww…' Shirley guiltily sipped her champagne. She settled back in the luxury of the limo and thought it was a far cry from last night's antics. All of them screaming like wild banshees up and down the street, all linking arms as they drunkenly made their way to the Viking bar. They'd frightened half the male population to death, the other half thought it was hilarious and had shamelessly encouraged them. However, Shirley had the feeling that tonight was going to be a classier affair.

'The only thing is, will we be okay going into the casino with these t-shirts on? I mean, what's the dress code, Barry?' Shirley inquired, trying to sound a bit posher than usual.

'What?' Oli said noting her change of accent. 'Hark at this one with her telephone voice on.'

'What dy'a mean, like,' Shirley screeched in her broadest scouce accent ever and laughing. The bubbles must be going straight to her head.

The gang burst into raucous laughter and Barry opened the second bottle of champagne.

'What about the girls?' Shirley asked.

'What about them?' Barry giggled.

A drive around town and two bottles of champagne later they arrived at the casino.

'Hey, this looks a bit more like it, eh Shirl?' Oli said scanning the place.

'Hey, come on, let's go and have a flutter.' Shirley grabbed his arm and in they went.

An hour later the second half of their posse arrived none too happy. 'Hey we're gagging for a drink, you tight bastards, drinking all the bubbly an' that,' Susan complained.

'Hey, come on, I'll get them,' Shirley said guiltily, they were her mates, after all.

'No way, you're the hen. How about Barry Bollox, he's the best thing since sliced bread...' Susan replied properly miffed.

Overhearing the debate, Angie said, 'Hey you, Barry owes you nothing, he's gorrus all a lift here and in for free.'

'Mmm...' Susan replied.

'Ladies… I've got us a couple of tables and some drinks on order,' Barry said. He hadn't heard the disagreement but noted some animosity in the air.

'Hey, have ya seen Ali? She's like a loon on the slots. She's winning an' all,' Shaz said turning back to the crowd. 'I'm going over to her,' she said and trotted off to join her unlikely new friend.

The night at the casino was shaping up to be a much more civilised affair than the Viking night and Shirley was enjoying every minute of it.

Barry and Angie seemed to be getting closer and spent much of the night chatting and giggling together.

'Hey, there'll be tears there tomorrow,' Oli said to Shirley and looking over at the pair.

'Angie almost looks sweet next to him.'

'Well they do seem to get on. I think it's what she needs, someone like him.' Oli said.

'What, to be firm with her you mean?' Shirley asked.

'Too friggin' right,' Oli laughed.

Sunday, April 28
2 am

We just got in. What a brilliant night. It made the hen weekend for me. I do feel a bit tiddly but I'm not like I was last night. It was nice to see how the other half live!

Barry, bless him, had arranged a limo to take us all into town. The factory girls were a bit pissed off though cos they had to wait for the limo to drop us off and come back. I suppose we could have all squeezed in but the size on Angie, Susan and Ali, well it would have

153

been hellish tight for space. It was nice to relax and spread out. We had all the champagne and they complained like hell that they were gagging for a drink when they arrived at the casino. I was a bit worried it wouldn't be their thing, but we all really enjoyed it. Ali was like a monster on the slots, couldn't move her. We looked ok an' all in the t-shirts, no one seemed to mind and cos I'm the hen they gave me some complimentary chips to have a flutter meself. Lost the lot like, so they got it all back, but it was a bit of fun.

Anyway, I'm ready for me bed. Oli's snoring away beside me, although he says he never snores!! The girls are flat out sleeping next door.

Had a lovely night tonight, really really lovely. Glad me hen night wasn't all tack, a bit of both's brilliant. That limo and casino was the icing on the cake. I know Oli arranged almost everything and I bet he put a word in with Barry for the limo and casino bit. Gonna get me head down, now, we got an early flight tomorrow, well, midday we have to be in the airport, flight home at two. Ah, I feel dead happy and a bit relieved it all went so well.

'Come on sleepy head, last morning, so I've pushed the boat out. We're having a champagne brekkie!' Oli said warmly to the half asleep Shirley.

'Ah, have ya babe? Oh God, more champagne...' Shirley said stretching out in the bed.' I don't know if I can handle any more.'

'Well, here's a nice cuppa to start with.' Oli said handing her a mug of hot sweet tea.

'Ah, ta.' Shirley said taking hold of the mug. 'I need this. I didn't over do it last night though.'

Fi and Shaz knocked on the door and Oli let the pair in.

'Morning girls, you look a bit worse for wear.' Shirley smiled. 'I feel great today.'

'Well, you took it easy didn't ya…' Shaz complained. 'I was teamed up with alcy Ali.'

'Wanted to remember it all and enjoy me last day,' Shirley said, taking a large sip of the tea.

'Any tea going?' Shaz sheepishly asked Oli.

'Oh God, yeah, I'll put the kettle on again. And you, Fi?' Oli asked dancing around the room.

'Coffee please, Oli.' Fi managed.

'So what's the verdict? Have you enjoyed yourself?' Oli said, finally settling down to enjoy his own cuppa.

'I've had the best time ever, ta babe,' Shirley said warmly squeezing his arm.

'It has been fan-bloody-tastic.' Oli giggled.

'I can't tell ya how much I enjoyed it and them girls wasn't sure it'd be their thing but they loved it an' all didn't they?' Shirley said sitting up nursing her mug of tea.

'What? They love gambling. Gail is doing the online Bingo every time Comb Over's back is turned. They love a flutter them lot. Hey did any of them win?' Oli asked.

'Don't know. We didn't see them get home did we?' Shaz pointed out. 'Although Ali was doing well when I was with her.'

Unfortunately the limo was not on offer to return the party animals back home, it was a one way ticket. Shirley, Oli, Fi and Shaz had taken a cab back and had left the factory girls all over Barry like a rash.

'Think they thought Barry was gonna get them home an' all, but he said no way could he get the limo back. It was booked up, we were lucky to get it earlier,' Oli said.

'Well, they'd have been disappointed for the second time in a night then,' Shirley said flatly.

'It's been dead quiet next door. Haven't seen them or heard them yet, mind you they're probably still unconscious,' Oli said grimly.

'I'll go see what they're up to,' Shaz announced, getting up from the edge of Shirley's bed.

Shaz had become very pally with Angie during the weekend as well as chumming up with Ali at the casino.

'They're bosom buddies all of a sudden, what's that about?' Oli asked surprised when Shaz had left to check up on her new best mate.

'Think she sees her as a mother figure and, let's face it, whatever Angie is she's a hell of a lot better than Shaz's own mum,' Shirley commented.

'Don't think Angie would take to kindly to being thought of as a mother figure, more like a *big* sister eh?' Oli said with a smile.

'What time do we have to leave, Mum?' Fi asked slumping back on the bed.

'We have to be at the airport by twelve, flight's at two,' Shirley said looking at her watch. 'Hey it's half nine now.'

'I'm gonna pack up.' Fiona announced getting up and going to wash her cup in the bathroom.

'I'll do them kid,' Oli said thoughtfully. 'I'm all packed up anyway.'

'Aww, ta babe.' Shirley said delighted to have got out of clearing up even if it was just a few cups. She hadn't lifted a finger all weekend and had enjoyed it. 'Just gonna have a quick shower. That was a lovely cuppa, by the way.' She planted a kiss on his head on the way to the bathroom.

Shirley emerged from the shower fresh and bright ready to face the conclusion of her hen weekend, the journey home to the rest of her loved ones.

'No sign of Angie. She's gone awol.' Shaz said returning to tell them the latest gossip.

'What d'ya mean? Where the hell can she be?' Oli asked alarmed.

'No one knows, she just didn't come back last night,' Shaz explained.

'Oh my God…' Shirley was more than a bit concerned. Angie was a long way from home.

'She's probably shacked up with some poor bastard,' Oli sniffed.

'What if something's happened to her?'

'As if.' Oli scoffed.

'I'm going to go round get the low down.' Shirley said slipping her Ugg boots on.

Susan answered the door wearing a t-shirt with 'WAG Wannabe' written across her ample chest.

'Hiya, you ok Shirl?' she said letting her in through the door.

'Nice t-shirt.' Oli giggled following his mate in.

'Aww, ta. Roy give it me,' Susan announced proudly.

'Roy Footie, the Roy who coaches the under-nines five-a-side on the estate Roy?' Shaz asked confused.

'Aye, yeah, him, been asking me out for ages, may give him a go when I get back. Wanted to keep me self young free and single for this weekend, though…' Susan giggled.

'Well like Meatloaf said "two outta three ain't bad."' Oli trilled, singing the last bit.

Shaz and Fiona looked at him as if he was mad.

'You're too young, kids,' he explained. 'So, where's she hiding then?'

'No idea, she didn't come back with us last night. Last we saw she was chatting to this creepy fella by the bar,' Ali said.

'And you left her to it?' Shirley protested.

'Well, you know her, when she's pissed there's no talking to her is there?' Kelly muttered. 'I feel bad now though.'

'She was hammered,' Jeanette added.

'Oh yeah, we saw her stumble a couple of times,' Gail joined in the post mortem of Angie's last known drunken hours. All the girls had congregated into the small room to get the low down.

157

'Well we haven't got a lot of time have we, we need to leave here in about an hour,' Shirley sighed.

'I reckon she's copped off with some fella. She'll be ok. I thought she'd be going for that Barry though,' Oli said.

'Yeah. What about Barry? She was with him when we left…' Shirley added, confused.

'He was about, she must have copped off with someone though,' Susan said.

'Yeah, course she has. Typical of her, we'll just have to leave her to it, we can't miss the flight,' Ali put in unsympathetically.

'I suppose,' Shirley said reluctantly. 'I'm not happy about it though.'

'She's copped off and is sleeping it off in some waiter's grotty flat,' Oli said. 'Now, come head, if we pack up we can meet in the bar for a coffee to wait for the bus to the airport, and hopefully the old trollop will have come back by the time we need to leave.'

'Ok, babe, I've texted her twice, but no reply,' Susan moaned. 'I'll batter her when I see her.'

'Well, twenty minutes, kids, and we'll be down, just got to dry off me cups,' Oli said dancing out.

True to his word, twenty minutes later Oli was carrying a coffee over to Shirley who was sitting out on the deck appreciating the last few moments of peace and harmony.

'Here ya go, hon', enjoy it 'cause this is the last of me waiting on for a bit, when we get back it's back to normal, ok?' he warned, winking.

'Ta babe, I've had a brilliant, brilliant weekend.'

'Me too, it's been great. Oh, here they come,' he said, as Fi and Shaz joined them.

'I've texted Angie, still nothing,' Shaz said disappointedly.

'Hey, don't be worrying babe, she'll be ok, she's a big girl. Bet ya any money she'll come racing in from some fella she's knackered up and tell us all about it,' Oli reassured her.

'Any news?' Shaz asked as the rest of the girls joined the gang.

'Nah her phone is off now an' all, just goes straight to answer machine,' Susan informed them.

'Does she know what time the flight back is?' Fiona asked.

'Yeah, I think she does,' Kelly answered.

'Well then, bet ya she'll join us there, eh?' Oli said confidently. 'Now, come head, the bus will be here in ten minutes, we'd best make our way outside to wait. We can look out for her an' all then.'

'I've packed up her stuff,' Susan sighed, her martyr's voice on. 'I don't know why you lot are so worried, it's Angie we're on about. Angie queen of the parties, the wild one, the one who doesn't give a shit, that Angie. Gerra grip, she's knocking off some poor bastard and you're getting wound up.'

'Heartless cow.' Shaz muttered under her breath.

Still trying to enjoy the remainder of the hen weekend, but slightly troubled at the disappearance of Angie the gang arrived at the airport.

'Suppose we'd best check in. I've got all her stuff here, even her passport. What else could I do? I couldn't leave it there,' Susan said to Shirley.

'No babe you did the right thing she'll be here in a bit.' Shirley was busy looking around the crowded airport in the hope of catching a glimpse of her missing mate.

They completed the customary airport requirements and sat and waited, desperate for any sight of their infuriating friend.

'Well, it's very nearly time to board,' Shirley said despondently.

'Aye,' said Oli, raising his eyebrows. 'We'd best make our way through to the departure gate.'

'Once we do we've got no chance of her finding us. She needs her passport to come through,' Shirley pointed out.

'Ooh I'll friggin' kill her, I will. What shall I do?' Susan said holding Angie's passport.

'Hiya kids, over here.' They heard a familiar voice and turned round to find a grinning Angie.

'Where the hell have you been, you mad cow?' Susan yelled at her.

'Come head, kid, no time for that now,' Oli said, grabbing Susan's arm, 'we're gonna miss our flight you can have a row on the plane.' Oli said ushering the girls towards the departure gate.

'Oh, I'm not coming back with you, I just wanted to come here and get me stuff and tell ya like,' Angie spluttered excitedly.

'Eh?' the girls said simultaneously.

'I went to the hotel, first, but I'd missed ya and the staff said all the rooms had been emptied so I though you must have brought me stuff here with ya.'

'What you on about? You're coming with us, you daft cow, get a move on,' Susan was fuming.

'Hi there. We made it then, thank God,' Barry said breathlessly catching up with Angie. Dressed in his Viking costume ready to go to work later in the afternoon he had taken a while to catch up with Angie – his boots were decorative rather than functional.

'What's going on?' Shirley asked. 'For God's sake! We're gonna miss this flight, hurry up an' tell us.'

'Well, after last night I got left behind in the Casino, luckily with Barry, an' he took me back to his and well we just sort of connected. I'm not saying it's love or anything but there's something. I'm gonna stay on here for a bit, see if it develops further,' Angie said fervently, well stirred up by it all.

'You what?' Susan said. 'You've gone friggin' mad. Get your arse on that plane right now.'

'No I can't kid, I'm gonna give it a go.' Angie was insistent. The two facing up to each other like a couple of maddened bulldogs.

'What about your job, your flat, you life at home?' Shirley asked concerned for Angie's welfare.

'I'm gonna be here a few weeks, see how it goes, then I'll come home. Gonna be there for your wedding party aren't I? I wouldn't miss that for the world, and if it's ok and it works out, I'll bring Barry with me.'

'Final call for flight EJ403 to Liverpool.' Came the announcement over the loud speaker.

'Oh my God, that's us, we've got to go.' Oli said coming all over dramatic.

'Angie, I'm gonna tell you one more time: get your fat friggin' arse on that friggin' plane.' Susan sputtered.

'Final Call for the EJ403 to Liverpool.' The announcement was heard again. 'Would passengers…'

'Give me, me stuff, Susan, love,' Angie said softly, holding Barry's hand.

'I'll look after her, she's a big girl you know,' he said gently. 'Knows her own mind does Angie.'

'You… What the friggin' hell are you anyway? Dressed like Attila the Hun gone wrong. Out the way you freak!' Susan shouted.

'We're gonna have to go Susan hon', we've no choice, she's made up her mind.' Oli was gracious in defeat.

'Whatever… But remember: I told you so.' Susan lobbed Angie's bag at her chest and stormed off passport and ticket at the ready.

The rest made time to give their pal a quick hug and a kiss before running for the gate.

'Bye Angie.' Shaz was in floods.

'Ah don't cry babe, I'll text ya.' Angie said, giving her a big hug.

'All the best Shirl, for the big day an' all, and we'll deffo be there for the big party,' Angie assured her tearful friend as she hugged her good bye.

'You sure you know what you're doing, kid?'

'You know me – heart not head. Gorra give it a go, always wonder otherwise. Love you lots. Don't work too hard in that sweat shop, now girls.'

Angie went to stand by Barry who wrapped his arm round her waist and planted a kiss on her head.

Huffing and puffing from the jog down the walkway to the plane, the factory girls, Oli, Shirley and the kids, settled into their seats. They didn't know whether they'd done the right thing or not, but they couldn't really have frogmarched Angie back to the UK, could they? It was a pretty subdued bunch that fastened their seatbelts for home.

'Who'd have thought it, eh, going back with one less?' Ali said shaking her head.' Mind you at least we can stretch out a bit,' she added unashamedly. Angie should have been sitting between her and Susan.

Shaz, still mortified that her new friendship had only lasted not even seventy two hours, looked at Ali in disgust.

'I can't believe it,' Shirley sighed. 'I really can't. Whirlwind romance, or what?'

'A Viking of all people… Hey, what did they look like the pair of them, him in that get up in the airport?' Oli giggled.

'I know.' Shirley smiled. 'What an eventful weekend. Hey, and with all the dramas I nearly forgot we even solved a case.'

'Oh, hell, yeah, that had fallen to the back of me mind with all this Angie commotion. We did didn't we. Well done, babe.'

'Think I could do with a drink – just to finish off the weekend and have a toast to Angie.'

'On me.' Oli announced it: 'Hey girls put your orders in, this round's on me. It'll settle our nerves from that bit of a drama. 'S worse than Corrie.'

By coincidence David's stag flight was due to land at Liverpool,

John Lennon Airport half an hour before Shirley's hen flight and the welcome sight of her future husband, son and two step sons waiting in the arrival's hall was overwhelming. Even Marc had arrived to meet Oli, Apple all wrapped up snugly sleeping in her bag under his arm.

There were tears all round as the gang met up with their loved ones.

'Hey, what's up with you, babe, you'd swear we'd all been gone for months not a weekend,' David said holding Shirley tight.

'Me hen night started off with tears, the middle bit was great, loads of laughs, and now it's ended up in tears,' Shirley blubbed.

'Come on then, let's go home and you can tell me all about it.' David gave her one more squeeze before picking up both their cases.

'Did you have a good time? Sorry, I forgot to ask,' Shirley asked guiltily, having waved off the factory girls.

'Yeah not as eventful as yours, though, by the sounds of it.'

They made a lovely sight Shirley and David wrapped up in each other, Oli and Marc together with Apple and trailing behind them Fi, Jason, and Shaz who had made a miraculous recovery from mourning her lost friend by flirting with David's Ben and Josh.

Shirley looked round at her current and new family and smiled, thinking she was a very lucky woman to have such a great future ahead. 'Bring it on,' she thought.

<u>11.45pm</u>
Oh thank goodness for that. I'm in me bed all tucked up an' I'm absolutely knackered.

Thought I'd be in bed ages before this time. Don't mind too much, though. I'm taking the day off tomoz. Just to get over it.

I'm late cos they all came back here after the

airport, David and the boys I mean not the girls. They were all still a bit shaken up I think after Angie's announcement. Still can't believe it.

No, David, the boys and Marc (who seems to have more or less moved in here now) I mean all came back and we had a takeaway for our tea, an Indian, and we caught up on both our weekends.

It was nice to have a chance to catch up with Ben and Josh, again, and although we were all knackered we did have a quick run through of any last minute wedding stuff before they went back off home.

Shaz was itching to come back with us so she could have a flirt with the boys, but luckily Fi managed to put her off and reluctantly she agreed to go home.

Oli was made up to see Apple and him and Marc have got her sleeping in the bed with them, which I think is a big mistake and I've told them so, but they won't listen.

Fi is lying here next to me snoring quietly. She looks done in bless her. I'm so glad she came with us, though, it wouldn't have been the same without her. It was an eye opener even for Shaz and that kid's seen a lot with a mother like hers!!

I sent Angie a text, just to say we're back ok and to see if she was ok. She texted back to say she was fine and was heading to the Viking club to watch Barry do his show. I still can't believe it. I'm sure she'll be back by the end of the week, begging old Comb Over for her job back.

Oli texted Bernie an' all, to tell her we've got the evidence on Val and her ex. He's calling in to give her the photos in the morning and to pick up our payment, so that's another one in the bag for us. That was easy money to be honest, we really didn't do that much to earn it, but, oh yeah, how could I forget? We did nearly get arrested for it!! Anyway, I'm gonna have to put that to the back of me mind until me wedding party when I have to see that sarcy copper again. I'll just have to get pissed and stay away from her, let Oli handle it!! Don't want David to get even a whiff of what happened in that car park.

We still haven't got a thing on Hard Des though have we? I really hope we don't have to give in on this one. We've always managed in the past, but this one, well it's a hard nut to crack that's for sure. We'll just have to keep on at it. Jan his missus is getting pissed off, I'm sure, but he's a crafty one and she knows it.

Anyway, me eyes are starting to get heavy. Gonna have to get some sleep, now. I'm off tomoz but I still have to get up early to get the kids to school, then I think I'll go straight to the gym an' get a bit of the weekend's over indulgence off me tum and bum before I come back here and do a bit of cleaning. Jason's room is like a pig sty and it's not fair on poor Oli, so I'll give that a going over but for now it's the land of nod for me.

SEVEN

'Hurry up you two, I'm heading out to the car,' Shirley called to Jason and Fiona, picking up her car keys from the little table in the hallway before heading out of the door.

Waiting not so patiently, she hooted her horn a few moments later and Fiona came running down the path stopping only to put her left shoe on.

'Jase get your arse into gear.' She shouted to her brother who was just slamming the door.

'I'm coming…what's your hurry, it's school not a flamin' shopping trip.'

'Mum wants to go the gym,'

'So?'

'And Fi wants to catch a glimpse of some boy, I suppose…' Shirley smiled as they got in the car still bickering.

Jason looked at her and shook his head. 'Not that knob head Chris James?'

'Oh, Chris James, who's he then? Haven't heard you mention him before,' Shirley asked the cross-faced Fiona in the passenger seat.

'Don't listen to him,' Fiona said, putting her seatbelt on.

Twenty minutes later Shirley pulled up outside the school

'That's Chris James,' Jason said pointing out a tall thin boy with jet black hair, a long fringe and wearing drainpipe black trousers.

'Oh, is he one of them emo's?' Shirley asked.

'Freak show more like,' Jason said getting out of the car. 'Ta Mum, see you later.'

'Piss off Jase.' Fiona leant over to give her mum a kiss. 'Ta mum.' And the she got out and went towards her gang of friends.

Shaz waved frantically at Shirley who smiled and waved back. Shirley looked around in the hope of catching a glimpse of David. He was on yard duty today. Over by the gate the love of her life was talking to Sally the other deputy head. There was no way they could see Shirley and she knew Fiona would never forgive her if she got out and went over to have a chat, especially as she was all dressed up in her gym clothes, so Shirley decided to head off to the gym. She never much felt like going but once she was there, she usually felt all right. Looking round today, Shirley saw the same familiar Monday morning faces. She rarely talked to them, just smiled or said hi. Occasionally she would talk to some of them in the changing room, they couldn't really be bothered with exercise but they all reckoned they felt much better for it afterwards.

Today Shirley had booked herself into a bums and tums class and spent the next hour getting very red, very hot and very sweaty.

'Why do we bother, eh, girl?' A woman of about fifty spoke to Shirley as they both puffed their way out of the class.

'Well, I'm getting married in a few days, that's my excuse.' Shirley laughed.

'Married? Oh, you poor cow, I wouldn't bother. Give you five years you'll have let yourself go; he'll be the same: burping, farting and slobbing about the place in your matching joggin' pants and baggy t-shirts,' the woman said discouragingly and went off into a cubicle to get changed.

Shirley didn't get a chance to ask the woman what her reason for such pessimism was and she ignored her in the changing room. An hour's relax in the pool, spa and steam room area was called for and moments later she was happily relaxing in the jacuzzi. After a quick six minute sun shower, to maintain the healthy glow she was trying to maintain for the wedding, Shirley was back in the car heading for home to clean up Oli's house.

'Hiya babe, good work out?' Oli asked when she arrived back.

'Eww, it was hard but the spa bit was worth it. Lovely. What you been up to then hon'?'

'Well I popped round to Bernie's with the photies… Here's your cut,' he said, handing Shirley a wad of twenty pound notes.

'Oh ta, that was a weird one wasn't it? I feel we earned it, yet in one way we didn't actually,' Shirley said counting the money.

'I know what you mean. We did earn it though babe, we did. Anyway, Apple's having a little sleep, thank God, an' Marc's gone to work, so I may go and have a bit of a lie down. I love her to bits, but that Apple keeps me up all night long. I'm knackered.' Oli yawned as if he couldn't get his mouth open wide enough.

'Yeah, why not catch up after the weekend an' all. Hey, any texts from Angie?'

'I texted her this morning and she's ok, so she says. Bit upset, though, about Susan. She said she's ignoring her texts.'

'Aww, that's a shame they've been mates for years. We'll have to have a word with Susan. I know she's worried about Angie and all annoyed, but I think she's only being like that 'cause she's gonna miss her so much.' Shirley was concerned for them both.

'Aye. I phoned Gail this morning, just to see how they all are after the weekend. Gail said they're all flat as hell and Comb Over did his nut because Angie didn't turn in. Moaning he was, apparently, that he'll have to get more staff in,' Oli informed her.

'Oh, will he now? I bet he'll get another one of his ladies from overseas. Cheap labour or is it a bit of the other he's after? Trying them out one by one then packing them back off.'

'Aye, well, Gail said that a girl from Russia was in this morning. The other one's gone again. God knows who the hell this one is.'

'Never... What's he doing? Pick a country any country...' Shirley asked.

'Right, I'm gonna go up for a bit. What you up to now then, same?' Oli inquired.

'Nah, I feel ok, now, after me gym class and I slept well last night. Thought I'd tidy up a bit, but you've done down here.'

'Well just a quick going over when everyone had gone.' Oli blushed.

'Aww, Oli, you've got a little palace here. I know we're making a mess. You're not used to it are you? Sorry, Oli. I'll have a word with the kids.'

'Hey, you're ok, babe.'

'No Oli, it's not fair. I'll have a word. Gonna tackle Jason's room, now.' Shirley was determined not to let her children's untidy habits undermine her relationship with her best mate. They were more than friends, they were partners, maybe not in love but in pretty much everything else. There wasn't much she couldn't say to Oli (and when there was something, there was always her little pink diary).

EIGHT

<u>12 midday</u>
Well that's me gym done for the day. I feel great now. Felt really bad when I came home. Oli had cleared up all the stuff from last night's meal. The kitchen and living room were spotless. He always keeps such a lovely clean and tidy place. I bet he's having kittens on a daily basis with us lot here. Marc is pretty messy too, I noticed, don't know how Oli's gonna cope with that for long and Apple peeing all over the show an' all. Poor Oli I bet he's close to a nervous breakdown with us lot.

I've spoken to David about it and when we move out I'm, or should I say *we're*, gonna treat Oli to a weekend break in a proper spa. Oli would love that. He's always going on about it, so thought I'd do that for him. Don't think he'd mind going on his own, but think we'll get it for two people. One of the teachers David works with,

170

well, his wife's sister works in one in Cheshire and she said she could get us a special rate for two.

I'm gonna make a start now on Jason's room, it's a disgrace. Me and Fi keep our room ok, why the hell can't he?

Armed with a roll of bin bags, Shirley set about picking up dirty clothes, hanging up clean clothes and moving the debris of many a late night snack from underneath the bed. It was while she was moving the remains of a week old pizza that Shirley came across a letter, a letter that rocked her world.

Shirley read and re read the letter again and again. She knew she shouldn't have but when she saw the envelope addressed to Jason at their old house and recognised the handwriting she couldn't help herself.

Hiya Son,
Long time no read, eh lad.
I'm not a man of many words and I know I haven't been much of a dad to you or your sister over the years but I want to make it up to you and her, son. I'll understand if you don't want to, but I'd be made up if you would get in touch.
Me mobile is 00769512456.
Dad

Shirley was in a state of shock. So many questions went round in her head. When had the letter come? She looked at the envelope and the post mark revealed it had been posted two months ago. Had Jason got in touch with Mike? Why hadn't he told her? What did Mike want? Did Fiona know? Had they spoken? So many questions… How could she find out without Jason guessing she'd been snooping around in his room?

Shirley put the letter back where she'd found it and went through to Oli's room, peeping round the door; he was fast asleep on the bed with Apple snuggled up on his neck. Not wanting to disturb her friend Shirley left him to it and went through to her bedroom, she felt it would help if she got her thoughts down on paper, so she got out her second best friend, the little pink diary in which she confided her most private thoughts. Only that would be up to this job. Why now? Why had Mike chosen this special time to rear his ugly head?

1pm

My God I can't believe what I've just found. How could that slimeball Mike get in touch after all these years? No phone calls, no nothing, yet he expects to just walk back into their lives like this. The bastard – how could he do this to us?

He stopped with the birthday cards and Christmas cards a long time ago, so why bother now? It's just not fair. Not on the kids and not on me.

Why the hell hasn't Jason said anything and has he told Fi? Maybe the pair of them have been talking or texting Mike for months now, getting all pally with him. My God, maybe they'll move away to Scotland, that's where he was living last I heard, and move in with him when I get married. Maybe they think I won't want them around any more, not now I'm with David. Oh my God, I'm getting all worked up now. I can't lose me kids to that scumbag. What am I going to do?

Tears pricked up in Shirley's eyes and she put her diary away and got up to take a look in on Oli, who stirred this time when he heard the door.

'Hiya, babe. Friggin hell what's up with you?' he asked. 'You look like you've seen a ghost.' He sat up in the bed accidently upsetting Apple who rolled off his stomach onto her back then frantically wriggled back into a more comfortable position.

'Oh, Oli what am I gonna do?' She cried crumpling in a heap on the end of the bed.

'Tell me babe what's up we can sort it.' Oli leaned over and hugged her tight.

Shirley eventually managed to tell him the whole story after having a good old sob on his shoulder and they went through to Jason's room and Shirley showed him the letter from the kids' dad.

'Hey, no way would Jase get in touch. He knows how Mike treated you in the end. Jason would never hurt your feelings like that. That's why he hasn't said anything, 'cause he just didn't bother to get in touch with that git. You've got nothing to worry about, just leave it.'

'Do ya reckon? What, not bother even saying anything?'

'Well, you can, but then he'll know that you've been in his room won't he? Mind you, he'll know you've cleaned the room 'cause he'll notice the stench is missing. Oh, I don't know Shirl. Why don't you just ask Fi if he's said anything to her?' Oli suggested.

'I don't know what to do for the best. Oh, I could do without this stress, so close to the wedding an' all.'

'Listen… Let's go out for a walk, now before they come home. We'll take Apple,' Oli said picking up cuddling his new baby who'd followed them into Jason's room.

'Oh… Can she go for a walk? I thought she had to have her injections…'

'Oh, no, she can't *walk*. I'll have to carry her in her bag, but she can get a bit of fresh air and maybe meet some new friends.'

'Ok, let me just put a bit of make up on,' Shirley told him and got up off the bed and went to sort herself out wondering what kind of friends Apple was going to make from her position tucked under Oli's arm.

'No hurry…I just need to dress her first.'

Shirley sighed and smiled as she touched up her make-up. Despite her worries Oli always managed to make her smile, there was just something about him and his hilarious obsessions she couldn't resist..

'The pink t-shirt with *Bitch* in sliver glitter writing or the white one with *Princess* in pink glitter writing, Shirl. What d'ya reckon?' Oli called through.

Shirley laughed out loud. '*Princess* today I think.'

Ten minutes later they were receiving admiring glances from passers by, who thought Apple looked adorable in her new outfit. Oli, very much the proud father, smiled regally, thrilled with all the attention they were getting.

'Aww, see, I'm not the only one who thinks she's gorgeous.' Oli grinned. 'But, hey, we're meant to be thinking about you, babe. Sorry.' He pulled her close and planted a kiss on her forehead.

'I'm a bit calmer now, Oli, it was just when I saw the letter I kinda panicked a bit. I'm sure you're right, no way would Jason get in touch with his dad,' Shirley said trying to convince herself.

'No way! He won't have even told Fi, bet ya,' Oli said. 'Now tell me; how was the gym, any buff fellas there?' he asked adroitly changing the subject.

'Nah, just some old crow advising me on the joys of marriage,' Shirley said flatly.

Enjoying the fresh air, Shirley tried to let the warm spring sun relax her and soak up her worries, but in the back of her mind the niggling thought remained: was she about to lose her son and daughter to the man who had already broken her heart once.

'Hey look! There's Hard Des. Look…going into the park.'

'Oh God yeah it is,' Shirley said, momentarily forgetting her own problems. Quick, let's follow him.'

In a cross between a walk and a jog, with Apple swinging wildly beneath Oli's arm they crossed the road and entered the park.

'He's over there, sitting on the bench,' Oli pointed out.

'Oh, aye, yeah. Maybe he's waiting for someone,' Shirley replied. 'Let's go and sit over there by the tree and wait.'

The couple made themselves comfortable under a huge oak tree within sight of Hard Des sitting on the bench. They had a bit of a job trying to concentrate what with Apple trying to jump out of her carry bag, though.

'Oh, look, he's getting up.' Oli got ready to move if need be.

'To put something in the bin,' Shirley answered flatly.

The pair sat for half an hour just waiting and watching Hard Des sit reading a newspaper on the bench. That and petting 'Princess' Apple who was getting a bit restive despite being given more than a few doggy treats by her lord and master.

'He's getting up again,' Oli announced hitting the dozing Shirley on the arm.

'What to the bin?' Shirley asked, eyes still closed.

'No, kid, he's on the move, target on the move,' Oli said, frantically trying to get her up.

Jumping to attention, but still half-asleep, Shirley tried to focus on Hard Des as he walked off into the distance.

'Come on babe.' Oli grabbed the bag with the whimpering Apple waking her just when she'd nodded off.

With some distance between them Oli and Shirley, and of course Apple, followed Hard Des around the park and back to the bench where he started.

'Well that was worth the effort,' Shirley said flatly.

'Oh, I think it was. Did you see all the people looking at Apple?' Oli asked proudly.

'Yeah,' sighed Shirley, 'but I don't meant to be funny, hon', but that wasn't the idea.'

They settled themselves back under their oak tree and half an hour later both were woken up with a start.

'Oh my God!' Oli screamed. 'Gerroff, gerroff.'

'Hey get lost.' Shirley shouted as two geriatric Rottweiler dogs started licking their legs and sniffing at the whimpering Apple's bag.

'Hey, come here! Max! Vinnie!' A hairy biker type man shouted. 'Don't worry, they're harmless, like two little pussy cats.'

'Well, they don't look it,' Oli said horrified, hiding behind Shirley and holding Apple's bag up to his chest.

'You should have them beasts on a lead...' Shirley scolded.

'They're harmless enough,' the man repeated, reluctantly putting a lead on them.

'Come on Shirl,' Oli said. 'Let's go while they're trapped.'

'But…' Shirley said, looking over at Hard Des who was still sitting on the bench.

'I'm sorry, babe, but I'm shaken up now. And poor Apple's all of a quiver.'

'Ok .' Shirley said not really wanting to give up on this rare chance to keep an eye on whatever Hard Des was up to.

'See ya, then,' the burly biker said holding the still straining Max and Vinnie on their leads.

Creeping past them, Oli still clutching Apple's bag tightly, they made their escape to the safety of the road.

'Oh, typical...' Shirley sighed.

'Well, I'm sorry, babe, but I had to get away. What if more vicious monsters had come after them two. No. Sorry, I know we want to get Hard Des, but Apple's safety is my priority.'

'I know. What with all that excitement I forgot about me own troubles, mind. I've remembered them again now.'

Oli still traumatised by the Rottweiler incident and Shirley deep in thought, the remainder of their walk passed in near silence (apart from the tooting of a little dog whose digestion had been badly affected by the biggest fright of her short life).

'What's for tea, Mum?' Fiona asked as soon as she walked in through the door. 'I'm starving.'

'Oh I haven't thought yet. We've not long got in… We took Apple for a walk.'

Ten seconds later: 'What's for tea, Mum? I need something quick 'cause I'm going out at six,' Jason said, throwing his school bag on the floor and looking in the fridge.

'Oh, aye, where you going?' Shirley asked suspiciously and looked over at Oli, who by the look on his face was thinking along the same lines.

'Only out with Digo, why?' Jason answered shutting the fridge door.

'No reason,' Shirley lied.

'How about I put in a couple of pizzas garlic bread and a few wedges?' Oli piped up trying to sidestep a stand off.

'Oh, ok,' Jason said. 'Any chance you could make a start Oli, don't mean to be rude but I'm starving.'

'Hey! Why don't you do it if you're in such a big hurry? It's only getting them out the freezer. What did your last slave die of? Oh, sorry I'm still alive aren't I,' Shirley said, thinking about the letter and taking it out on her son.

'Who's rattled your cage?'

'Think she's a bit tired. You know…the weekend catching up with her an' all. And we had a traumatic experience in the park. Apple was nearly eaten alive by two savage dogs,' Oli said, getting the pizzas out of the freezer.

'Oh my God. Really?' Fi flung her bag behing the sofa and drifted up the stairs to change out of her uniform.

'No…don't be daft,' Shirley muttered.

Oli looked at her, agog, but decided it was perhaps best not to say anything. His pal was obviously not in the best of moods.

'Mmm, maybe I'll make a salad,' Shirley said, banging her way around the kitchen.

'Aye, well, we're all tired after the weekend. Don't take it out on me. Go to bed early tonight,' Jason said and walked out of the room.

Shirley took a deep breath and started frantically chopping up a cucumber.

'Shirl, love, take it easy. I thought you said you were calm about it now,' Oli said quietly.

'Well… I thought I was but when I saw Jason I couldn't help thinking I wonder if he's been lying to me an' that an' I got all mad.'

'Come on, Shirl, you can't get stressed like this, you'll come out in a pile of zits or summat just before the wedding,'

Shirley smiled, 'A pile of zits?'

'Or something. You have to let it go or you're gonna go mad.'

'I know I know. I'll let it drop. Now…is Marc here for tea?'

'Yeah, I think he's almost moved in hasn't he?' Oli giggled.

'I thought that… Is he gonna give up his place? It's still early days,' Shirley warned.

'Aye, I know. No way will I let him give up his flat. Not yet. Time will tell. I mean, it's all well and good, now, while the house is full with you lot, but what will it be like when it's just me, him and Apple?' Oli said looking a bit more concerned.

'Very wise hon'. Hey have you thought what you're gonna do with the money from Bernie?' Shirley asked, preparing the salad had soothed her frayed nerves.

'Well, I've seen these gorgeous shoes in town – two hundred and fifty quid they are.'

'My God, that's loads!'

'I know, but this money from our sideline, it's my play money, money to do what I want with, not pay the bills an' that, so what the hell, eh?' He laughed. 'What about you?'

'Thought I'd get a pressie for the kids and David with mine. Probably clothes, take them shopping…'

'You should treat yourself; get something nice just for you babe,' Oli said, checking on the pizza and other frozen delights he had popped into the oven.

'How long?' Shirley asked, getting the knives and forks ready.

'Ten minutes and we're good to go.'

Oli laid the table for five, Marc arrived not far behind the teenagers and equally as hungry.

'I'm starving today,' Marc announced taking a potato wedge from the baking tray.

'Hey…go sit down,' Oli scolded him.

All sitting down together, the kids opposite her, Shirley could feel her insecurity about Mike's letter creeping in.

'So…where you off to tonight?' Shirley asked Jason.

'Only down to Digo's. His dad's got him some DVDs knock off. Said I'd go and watch some with him,' Jason said tucking into his pepperoni and wedges.

'Oh, his dad, eh? Does he see much of his dad?' Shirley asked.

Oli looked over at her and discreetly tried to shake his head.

'Ok, ok, what's going on? I know there summat. You've been like a bear with a sore head since I got in and Oli's been making faces like a loon trying to stop you saying something, so come on what's going on?' Jason said putting his pizza down and looking at Oli and Shirley.

'Naah, nothing babe, come on eat up or you'll be late going out,' Oli said nervously. 'More wedges?' He added offering Jason a bowl still half full of potato despite them all claiming to be starving.

'Nothing, I'm just asking,' Shirley said with a tinge of annoyance in her voice. 'Just interested in you that's all.'

'Mmm…' Jason said taking the bowl of wedges and pouring most of them onto his plate.

'Thanks for that,' Fiona said snatching the remainder of the wedges and piling them on her plate before anyone else had a chance.

'Sorry, babe,' Oli muttered to Marc who had no chance of seconds.

Thankfully the ordeal was soon over and Shirley left Jason, Fiona and Marc to clear up and went to sit with Oli in the living room.

'He knows something's wrong babe. You've got to control yourself, get a grip or just come out and tell him.'

'I'm gonna sleep on it and decide tomorrow what I'm gonna do.'

Tuesday, April 30th
8am

Tossed and turned all night. I spoke to David on the phone last night and I nearly told him, but then I didn't know how to so it's only Oli that knows. I don't think I want to mither David with it all. Then I thought that I could maybe ring Mike up, find out what he's playing at. Oh, I still don't know what to do. Maybe I should just be straight with Jason, ask him out right, or maybe I should ask Fi. Oh God... I'm still none the wiser and Oli will be asking me today what I'm gonna do. Best get meself ready. After we've dropped the kids off today we've got Sapphire to do God help us!!

The journey to school was a little quiet with Shirley deep in thought.

'Well what's happening?' Oli asked her as soon as Jason and Fiona were out of the car.

'Still don't know... I had thought about ringing Mike meself.'

'What? Are you mad?' Oli was shocked. 'Why on earth would you want to get involved with him again?'

'Well... I don't know what to do for the best. It's on me mind though, Oli...all the time. I've got a lot of questions and lots of things were left unsaid, you know, after the split.'

'I'm sure there were, babe. There often is I suppose after a divorce like that, but you'll have to forget it for now 'cause we've got Sapphire first.' Oli smiled.

Arriving at Sapphire's estate, they made their way up the graffiti covered stairwell, having left the car in sight of the block, and knocked on the door.

'Hiya kids,' Sapphire said answering the door. 'How's the hen?' She giggled and ushered them into the tiny living room.

'Knackered, but we had a great time.'

'Oh, babe, I would have loved to join you for the weekend but what with me sister having her fiftieth party in the social club I had to go to that, didn't I?'

Oli looked at Shirley as if to say, was she invited? Shirley sensing his question smiled and shook her head.

'So how was it, Sapphire? How's the hangover, queen?' Oli asked getting his equipment out of his bag.

'Well… I've gone through five bog rolls and a can and a half of air freshener since Sunday morning.'

'Oh, so it was a good night then?'

'Aye.' Sapphire settled down to her brush through.

'So what's the goss', then, queen?' Oli asked dragging the brush through her hair.

'Well, we had a great night. Me sister wore a pair of enormous fake boobs on the outside of her clothes the whole night. She started to get a bit fed up though when everyone kept saying I bet you feel a right tit.' Sapphire laughed.

'Who was the clever dick who gave her *them*?' Oli asked.

'Me!' She sniggered. 'Got 'em from the quid shop in town. She did look a right tit an' all.'

'Was there food?' Shirley asked.

'Well we did the food between us. I've still gorra few sausage rolls left over if you want to take 'em with ya for yer dinner.'

'Yer all right, ta. I've got me butties and Shirley's slimming, ya know, for the wedding…' Oli said anxious to avoid death by second-hand sausage roll.

'Oh, yeah. How long to go now, kid?' Sapphire asked.

'May 12th.' Shirley smiled nervously.

'Won't be long now, kid. You're cutting it a bit fine. How much d'ya wanna lose?' Sapphire inquired.

'Well, she doesn't wanna lose any more. Just maintaining aren't ya, babe? So don't be tempting her now with yer sausage rolls.'

'What about you, Oli? They went down like hot cakes on the night. Mind you quite a few were used in the food fight at the end. Our Bobby was nearly knocked out when he got hit by two at the same time, one from each side of the room. Bless him. He was lucky: his hearing aid saved him really.'

'Well it sounds like a right classy do, queen.' Oli chuckled.

'Hey you…' she complained. 'But I know what you mean.' She laughed, seeing the funny side with them.

Oli received a text message on route to their next call.

'It's Susan at the factory, asking us to call in over dinner – just for a cuppa. Comb Over's going out dinner time today,' Oli said brightly. 'Aww, that'll be nice, see how they've recovered from the weekend.'

'Aye, and try and talk some sense into Susan about Angie,' Shirley said.

<u>6pm</u>
Managed to get through the day. We were quite busy so it took me mind off this whole Jason and Mike thing. We called into the factory at lunch time; there was

this Russian girl in today. No sign of the other one, just like Gail said, it looks like he's palmed that other one off an' all.

This one could speak a bit of English, though I don't think she had a clue what we were doing there. She just looked at us, smiled and put the kettle on. This one was meant to be a cleaner. He's going through them like a dose of salts.

He's not really giving them a chance is he? Only a few days and then it's on to the next. Nobody seems to know if he's getting them in as a slave labour kind of thing or if they're there for a bit of the other. Gail reckons he's doing the mail order bride thing. Only time will tell.

Anyhow, I think we managed to talk some sense into Susan, who admitted she's missing Angie like hell. The place wasn't the same without her, that's for sure. I was looking out for her the whole time. Her little space, or should I say big space, looked very empty today. Susan promised she'd ring Angie tonight when she got back in from work to make amends.

Sounds as though it's a case of so far so good with Angie and Barry, though. Angie seems to be supporting him; she's texted Gail to say she was off to the Viking Club tonight to watch him again.

'I think she wants to get in on the act and do a bit of singing there,' Gail said to us.

Susan did defend her mate and say Angie's gorra lovely voice and to be fair she has – when she doesn't shout that is!!

Anyway, at least Susan seems set to try and make it right between them. The girls looked like wet weekends in Blackpool, mind. The thought was there, they'd put on their slap, but the bodies were knackered after hours of partying over the last few days. I think we drank enough to sink the Titanic between us.

Susan told us that Angie's tattoo kit had arrived at her house this morning. So cos Angie is away herself Susan has decided to make use of the tattoo kit and is going to set up shop in her house. Apparently, one night when they were both off their heads they went on eBay and Angie ordered the tattoo kit. £64.95 plus £2.95 postage and packing. She gorra DVD with it and paid an extra £6.95 for a pot of Fire Cracker Red ink!! Oli told her she should send it on to Angie, after all it was quite expensive.

Think that's why Susan's gonna ring Angie tonight, clear it with her. Plus she knows Angie will let her have it cos she feels so bad for leaving the way she did. Whatever Angie is, she's gorra heart of gold that one. A heart of flamin' gold.

I tried me best with Jason when we got in but I can't help meself, it's eating away at me.

I try not to let it but I can't help it. Me mind is working over time with it all.

I think I'm gonna have to ask him about it. I may do it after tea, before I go over to David's, that way if it all goes tits up I'll have somewhere to go and escape.

Taking a deep breath Shirley knocked on Jason's bedroom door and walked in.

'All right?' he said briefly looking up from his laptop.

'Hiya, Jase. Can I have a word?' Shirley asked quietly.

'Course. What's up?' His eyes remained glued to the screen.

'I know I've been a bit…well, you know…' Shirley said nervously.

'What? Picky?' he said, abruptly.

'Well, yeah. I suppose you could put it that way.'

Still looking at the screen he said, 'So what's going on?'

'Well, now… Don't take this the wrong way, and I wasn't snooping…' Shirley tried to assure him.

'You been in my room, I knew you had tidied the place. What you found?' He put the laptop on the bed and looked Shirley straight in the eye.

'A letter from your dad,' Shirley blurted out.

'Oh, that…' Jason said and picked up the laptop and put it back on his knee to carry on checking Facebook.

'What do you mean "oh, that"?' Shirley asked expectantly.

'Well, what about it? He wrote to me. So what, he is me dad.'

'Have you got back in touch?' She steeled herself as she asked the dreaded question.

'Yeah…' he muttered, unable to look at her. 'Sorry, but I had to.'

'Oh.' Shirley took a deep breath.

'I had to Mum. I'm nearly eighteen and… I didn't even remember him.'

'"Didn't", you said "didn't". That means you do remember him now, so you must have met up with him to remind yourself what he was like.' She couldn't help herself, she was so on edge.

'I have, yeah, just the once mind.'

'And Fi, has she?' Shirley asked, almost unable to bear to hear the answer.

'No, she doesn't know a thing about it. Wanted to check him out before I dragged her into it, just in case she got hurt.'

'And?'

'I'm gonna tell her. Listen, Mum, I didn't want you to find out till after the wedding. I didn't want you to worry,' Jason said, squeezing her hand.

'I know it's only natural that you want to get to see him I suppose. I've just dreaded this day for so long.'

'Nothing will change. Why are you so worried and upset?'

'I'm worried about you; you're not replaceable are you?' Shirley sighed.

'I'm going nowhere, Mum and nor is Fi.'

'Does he know about the wedding?'

'Yeah, he was gutted.'

'Yeah, right...' Shirley couldn't believe her ears.

'No, Mum, he was, really. I told him David's a good fella and treats you well. He seemed ok then, though.'

'I'll leave you to it, Jase. I need to get it straight in me head. That ok, love?'

He nodded and with that she left the room.

8pm

Been going over and over it in me head. I'm shaken up, but I suppose deep down I knew this day would come. It's only fair to the kids that they have the chance to get to know their dad. I can't believe that it's happened so close to the wedding. Talk about timing! I think the best thing for me to do is to leave them get on with it and be there for Fi and Jason when he lets them down, which no doubt he will cos he always has done in the past.

Anyway, gonna spend the rest of the evening with David that will give me a chance to take me mind off it. I'm really shaken up by it though. Can't believe it. Now of all times!

NINE

8am

Had a gorgeous evening last night with David. He made me feel so much better about everything. I know if I try and stop the kids it will all go tits up and I don't want any hassles before the wedding. Just keep me head down till after then. I've gone over it all with Oli, an' all.

I've got to get me mind back on the wedding – only twelve days to go. Gonna call round me mum's with Oli this afternoon. She keeps saying she hardly ever hears from me these days. I do feel dead tight, but I've got so much on me plate at the moment. I know that's no excuse but I'm gonna go and see her today, that's the main thing. We may even call there at dinner. Oli and I could pick up a few rolls and a cake, that should do her, only thing is on a Wednesday Auntie Dilys goes over there for dinner and they have a few of the oldies over for a cuppa later on in the afternoon. Mind you, we'll be long gone by then. We will have to put up with Auntie Dilys, though. Never mind, it gives me a chance to give them a bit of fuss before the wedding, I haven't seen them since the tapas bar.

'Hey, did Fi tell ya Shaz and her mum are thinking of trying out for that tele talent show thingie, you know, it's on a Saturday night? I keep missing it 'cause of me manic social life.' Oli laughed as they both sat in the traffic on the way to their first job of the day.

'Never…is there nothing that that mad Mo won't do?'

'Aye, she's a right one isn't she,' Oli said looking in the appointment book. 'I'm looking at this now 'cause if I do it while we're on the go I'll feel sick again.'

'I know, babe, you've got Sapphire this morning an' all. Are you in the mood?' Shirley asked moving on as the traffic lights turned in her favour.

'Yeah, I suppose. Don't know why we're going back there so soon. Mind you, we can get more on her sex phone lines 'cause she didn't tell us much did she? Too busy telling us about her sister's do.' Oli closed the appointment book, sighing before throwing the book over his shoulder onto the back seat.

'Careful!' Shirley scolded. 'She double booked us by mistake but thought she may as well keep the two.'

'Soz. Oh right.'

Shirley and Oli were surprised to find four strange women in Sapphire's living room, all typing away happily on laptops.

'Hiya, kids,' Oli said brightly. 'What's going on here?'

Shirley smiled uncomfortably.

' Oli, Shirley meet the girls.' Sapphire grinned.

'Hiya.' They were both bewildered. About as puzzled as the four girls behind the laptops.

'Don't be worrying, girls, these two are sound, very discreet, they can be trusted,' Sapphire assured the nervous looking girls.

'So what's going on here then, queen?' Oli asked.

'We've got a little gold mine growing here, haven't we, eh girls?' Sapphire said proudly.

The four girls, who ranged from mid forties to late sixties, looked up momentarily from their laptops and agreed.

'Come on…spill the beans…' Shirley urged.

'Well… You know I do the sex phone lines – well these four are doing the same but on the laptops. They can't do it at home 'cause they don't want anyone else to know, so they come here.'

'Oh great,' Shirley said, trying to sound enthusiastic.

'It's a great set up.' Sapphire beamed.

'Well, don't mean to be rude girls, but what's in it for you babe?' Oli asked Sapphire, well aware she wouldn't do anything for nothing.

'I charge them rent and for the use of the electric,' Sapphire revealed. 'Ya see, Christine over there, well, she can't do it from home 'cause her hubby's retired and he's home under her feet all day.'

The sixty-something, grey-haired grandmother waved at Shirley and Oli, barely looking up from her typing.

Shirley and Oli waved back.

'Then there's Jane… Well, she's got six kids and six dads who are right poor bastards for paying. All her kids're in school now – well apart from the teenagers, who either lie in bed all day or lie on the sofa watching TV. That's why she has to come here.' Sapphire went on, introducing her posse one by one, including Jane, a mid-forties mother of six, in skin tight top and tiny mini skirt, which revealed super skinny, stick-like legs.

'Then we've got Pauline over there. She's the dark horse, vicar's wife and mother of four, comes here just for the thrill of it.' Sapphire smiled her encouragement.

Pauline, conservatively dressed in a navy blue a line skirt white blouse and navy cardigan waved at them, looked up very briefly from her lap top, she seemed utterly engrossed in what she was doing.

'And last, but by no means least, is the busiest one of the lot: Beanie. Beanie's in uni'.' Sapphire said.

'Uni?' Oli gasped.

'Aye, I know. She's been round the block a few times but she's a mature student gone back to it after her divorce. Poor cow's more or less penniless after her divorce, she's had to move in with her elderly parents. Pay off though won't it, girl, in the end...'

Beanie waved. It looked as if she had taken on the whole student lifestyle: multi-coloured dreadlocks, tie-dye baggy pants and oversized tie-dye t-shirt was not the most attractive look on a woman in her early fifties.

'What's she studying?' Shirley asked.

'Law.' Sapphire answered and raised her eyebrows.

'Friggin' hell, queen, so you're the next Cynthia Payne then, eh?' Oli giggled.

'Well in me dreams maybe.'

'So what we gonna do today, then? We'll have to do you in the bedroom.'

'Promises promises,' Sapphire cackled as she pushed Oli into the bedroom.

'I can't believe that one. My God she gets friggin' worse. Mind you it kept me mind off the Mike thing,' Shirley said with a half laugh as they trundled down the block stairs.

'Well, that's good then, and guess what babe...? You're about to have your mind taken off it again in a bit, we're off to your mum's,' Oli sniggered.

'Great.' Shirley muttered grimly.

Armed with a large Victoria sponge, four white rolls, four brown rolls and a large packet of thinly sliced ham Shirley and Oli arrived for lunch and a chat with her mum and Auntie Dilys.

'Oh, Shirley, you haven't bought any of that thin ham have you?' Shirley's mother asked looking disappointedly at the packet.

'Yeah, sorry. I thought ordinary ham lay heavy on Auntie Dilys.' Shirley answered, well aware that what ever she'd got it wouldn't have been good enough.

'No it's the pork products she can't do with. Pork plays havoc with her stomach. Up all night she is with it. In agony poor thing she was last time you brought that pork from that shop over the road from you. I'm sure it was off an' all…' Her mother grumbled.

'Nothing to do with the fact that she'd eaten the whole packet and half a loaf, I'm sure…' Shirley mumbled under her breath.

Ignoring, or oblivious to, Shirley's comments her mother inquired, 'What's the sell by date on that thin ham? Hope it's got at least a week, or it'll start off my irritable bowel an' all.'

Shirley ignoring her mother continued to butter the rolls then added the ham.

'How you been keeping then?' Shirley asked tentatively, knowing she had to ask but doing so with reluctance as she knew what the answer would be.

'Well, you know me, not one to complain am I, but I haven't been meself. I only hope me legs will hold out for the wedding.'

'So do I,' Shirley said, plonking the last lid on the thin ham rolls.

'Oh and Auntie Dilys was wondering if she could have her hair done after dinner, hope you've got time…' This last said with a hint of sarcasm.

'Aye, of course we have. I'll do it for her.' Shirley hid the fact that she was a little annoyed not about having to do her aunt's hair, but with the fact her mother thought she might not.

'You're all right Shirley, she wants Oli to do it, reckons he does a better job on her hair than you.' And with that she carried a pot of tea through to the waiting Oli and Auntie Dilys who were having a laugh about something or other.

'Aww, here they come, the waitresses...' Oli announced.

'Yes. Here we are.' Shirley pulled a face at Oli.

'Auntie Dilys wants you to do her hair, Oli love, if you have the time...' Shirley's mum said brightly.

'Yes, you always do such a good job.' Shirley added with just a hint of sarcasm.

'Aww...do I? Ta. Ta Auntie Dilys. Mmm, lovely butties these,' he said, taking a mouthful of the brown roll.

'I was in bed by nine last night,' Auntie Dilys announced to the assembled gathering.

'Were ya, queen? That's an early one.' Oli said, sounding interested.

'Yes, I was, and I didn't bother with supper, just a cup of tea. Nothing to eat.' Auntie Dilys went on.

Shirley's mother looked surprised.

'No nothing to eat, only a Cornetto.'

Shirley and Oli looked at each other, trying not to laugh.

'Now this ham is lovely, Shirley, where did you get it from?' Auntie Dilys asked.

'The shop over the road from me,' Shirley answered, looking over at her mother.

They spent the next hour finishing off their dinner and styling Shirley's mother's and Auntie Dilys's hair and they left the two old dears happy and contented with their new hair cuts ready for the wedding.

'Ooh, I feel ten years younger,' Shirley's mother said, admiring her new do in the hallway mirror as she took the pair to the door.

'Yes, I'm nearly as good as Oli now, aren't I?' Shirley winked at her mother over her shoulder so that she could be seen in the mirror.

'You're better,' her mother said, turning round and giving her daughter a hug. She had enjoyed Shirley's company and now she'd been given some attention all was forgiven.

'Oh, ta!' said Oli, stood holding the bags in the doorway.

'Right, best be off. Come on, you,' Shirley instructed Oli, sweeping out in front of him.

'Ok, ok, you're the boss.'

With that they were on their way home back to the chaos of a house full of Fi and Jason, not forgetting Marc with a c and Apple the miniature dog.

Thursday, May 2nd
1pm

I really don't know what's come over me, but I've just sent the kid's dad a text. I can't believe I've done it. Haven't told a soul, not even Oli!

I just said: *Jason's told me u been in touch not sure what ur playing at just make sure u don't upset them Shirl.*

My God! I nearly pressed the cancel button, but I did send it and now I'm thinking why the hell did I do that?

Can't do anything about it now, I'll just have to wait. Only thing is that now he'll have my mobile number and I didn't really want that. I wasn't thinking straight. Oh God why did I?? Maybe he'll just ignore it, but at least he'll sort of know how I feel.

Shirley slipped her diary back in her oversized handbag as soon as she saw Oli dance his way back to her parked car.

'They only had egg on white, Shirl, so I got you tuna on brown,' he announced breathlessly, getting back in the car.

'Oh, that's ok, I'm not that hungry,' she replied.

'Well, you've got to eat, so here you go.' Oli tossed the carefully wrapped brown tuna sandwich in her direction.

'Ta. Hey, listen, I think I've made a tit of meself.' Shirley blurted.

'What now?' Oli asked.

'I've texted Mike.'

'What the friggin' hell for, you daft cow?'

'I don't know.'.

'Well has he answered?'

Shirley checked her phone and shook her head.

'Oh, well, you've gone and done it now. *And* he'll know your mobie number.' Oli shook his head.

Knowing she had probably made a big mistake, Shirley unenthusiastically took a bite out of her tuna on brown and re-read her sent message.

The afternoon dragged on with a visit to the residential home, where even the usually hilarious old dears couldn't take Shirley's mind off the unfortunate text and she checked her mobile every five minutes.

'Anything?' Oli asked, catching her at it once again.

'Nah.'

'Maybe he won't bother babe, now that'd be ok wouldn't it?' Oli suggested brightly.

'Maybe…hopefully…' Shirley said, checking one last time before popping her phone back in her pocket.

'Hey, come on, chin up babe. It'll be ok. He would have texted by now if he was going to, it's been three hours. Forget it and let's have a drink in town on the way home.'

'Why not? It's a Thursday. Shall we text David and Marc and ask them to join us?' she asked, feeling a little more cheery.

'Aye, why not… Tell them 5 o'clock at The Bell, in town.'

'Ok I'll text them both and I'll text the kids to tell 'em what we're up to and that we'll bring something in with us for tea.' Shirley smiled, getting her phone out for what seemed like the hundredth time that afternoon.

The Bell was full of people enjoying a pre-going home drink. David was already sat at the bar enjoying a pint with Marc when Shirley and Oli arrived.

'What you having?' David asked after giving Shirley a 'welcome' hug and kiss.

'Hey! I'll buy, I asked you two along.'

'Come on…you look like you need it. You two been busy?' David asked.

'You know us, rushed off our tiny little feet,' Oli announced dramatically. 'I'll have a G and T, David, ta.'

'Coming up… White wine, Shirley?'

'Just a small one.'

Shirley felt the stress of worrying about the dreaded text drain from her body as she sat chatting and quaffing with her friends.

'Feeling better babe?' Oli asked very discreetly, when Marc and David were busy discussing the football.

'Much,' Shirley smiled and squeezed his hand.

'Aye, aye, what's going on with you two?' Marc asked jokingly having spotted the gesture.

'Looking after me mate, not jealous are ya?' Oli winked mischievously.

'Hey, look at the time, we'd best be off. It's nearly half six,' Shirley pointed out.

'We're calling in for a takeaway, you coming David?' Oli asked.

'Why not? It'll beat doing a heap of marking.'

'Just gonna pop to the ladies,' Shirley said picking up her handbag and squeezing her way past Oli.

'Hurry up babe, I'm starving now,' he moaned.

'Ok, ok,' she said and quickly raced off to the ladies.

The familiar ring tone rang out while she was in the cubicle: home.

'Hiya Fi, we're on our way.'

'We're starving, Mum, what we having?' Fi moaned from the other end of the phone.

'Chinese, yeah?' Shirley asked hopefully.

Getting an answer in the affirmative, Shirley said good bye and hung up. It was then that she noticed the little envelope on the screen. Maybe Fi had texted as well as ringing. Just to be sure. Shirley's heart skipped a beat. What if it was Mike? Tentatively she opened her inbox and read the message.

Shirl long time no read. Hope u ok. Thought loads bout u ova last few months. I'm in Lpool 2moz 4 wend would love to catch up.

Taking a deep breath Shirley read and re read the message over and over again. It was Mike.

'Hurry up hon'.' Shirley heard the well known voice of Oli frantically knocking at the door of the ladies.

Shirley met him at the door mobile in hand.

'Oh God!' Oli exclaimed, having seen the look on her face, and took the mobile from her hand.

He read the message and said, 'Ignore it. There's no way you're gonna go, is there.' It was a statement rather than a question.

'Course not,' Shirley insisted.

'Good. Now come on, or they'll think you've got the wild shites you been in here so long.' Oli's joke failed to raise even a smile.

Trying to put it to the back of her mind, Shirley put all her efforts into trying to maintain a jolly carefree exterior in front of David and the kids as the evening progressed.

'You're doing a great job, babe,' Oli said warmly as the two of them got the plates and other necessary items together for their meal.

'It's hell though, Oli. Why the hell is he coming here at all? Is he coming to see the kids? They haven't said anything…'

'You don't know he is. Maybe he hasn't told them he's coming.'

'Oh, I don't know. Have we got any wine, Oli? I think I feel the need.'

'Just for you, babe, ice cold Pinot Grigio just as you like it,' Oli said taking the wine out of the freezer.

'Oh, lovely. Did you put it in there as soon as we got in?' Shirley was impressed.

'No, even better, I texted Fi and asked her to do it for us, so it would be icy icy cold just like you like it, babe. And just for good measure, we'll put this one to get the same way while we're getting through that one,' he said, putting another bottle in the freezer. 'Now listen babe, I really think you should keep your gob shut, wine or no wine, tonight. Don't say a word to the kids, let's just enjoy our tea.'

'Ok, ok. I promise.'

'At last. Thought you'd gone back to China for it,' Jason complained.

'Sorry, just getting all the stuff together,' Oli explained

'Get the wine open, eh Oli…' Shirley instructed.

'You're keen,' Fiona noted.

'Well, I was driving I only had a small one in The Bell, unlike some.'

'Hey, I only had three, so I'm gonna have a few more.' Oli filled his glass to the brim.

Forgetting her promise, taking a large sip of wine, Shirley asked, 'So what's the plan for the weekend with you guys?'

Oli looked as if he'd been hit by a bus. Shirley looked innocent, convinced she had not really broken her promise as she hadn't asked the kids directly if they were meeting up with their father.

'Me and Shaz are going to the cinema Saturday, nothing else planned though. We could go shopping?' Fi said looking hopeful.

'Yeah, maybe. Jase?' Shirley asked looking him straight in the eye.

'Dunno,' he answered blankly.

'More prawn balls?' Oli inquired brightly, offering the tray to everyone.

Shirley shook her head and took another large sip of wine.

'Hey, you're not getting pre-wedding nerves are you, love?' David asked, noticing his wife to be's thirst.

'Course not. I can't wait.' Shirley smiled reassuringly and squeezed his knee.

With the help of most of a bottle of white wine Shirley managed to eat her food without problems and after the stern looks from Oli she even managed to keep her mouth closed about any potential family reunions, resulting in a fairly enjoyable evening for all.

'You gonna stop over David?' Oli asked as they got down from the table. 'You're more than welcome.'

'Thanks mate, but I'd best be off, think it'd be easier.'

Shirley went to the door with David to see him out after an hour or so's chat in the living room.

'Why didn't you want to stay, you know you can?'

'I know, love, I don't mean to be funny, but there's no room here is there and to be honest I don't think my back can take a night on that trendy sofa he's got, lovely as it is to look at.'

Shirley looked disappointed and he gently kissed her on the lips. 'It won't be long now sweetheart, we'll soon have the house, and I'll have my new family with me every night. We're going to have the best life ever, I promise you.'

A tear pricked Shirley's eye, she was so in love with David, she only wished she didn't have this Mike thing lurking on the horizon.

'Hey, what's up? Why the tears?' David asked gently wiping them away.

'Oh, just a bit emotional. I can't wait for us to be together, that's all. It's hard being away from you. Plus I've probably had too much wine an' all.' Shirley raised an eyebrow.

'Off to bed now, then, I'll see you tomorrow. You did remember didn't you that I'm off to Manchester on Saturday? To see the boys and my mum and dad...'

'No, I'd forgotten.' Shirley sighed.

'You can come, you know. If you'd like to.'

'I know, but I'd better stay put. Don't like to put on Oli, leaving the kids here with him an' that. Don't want to take the piss, do I? He's been so good with all of us, letting us stay here for so long. I'm sure we drive him mad.'

'All the more reason to get rid of one of you... He wouldn't mind. Come on, Shirley, it would do you good.'

Although very tempted, Shirley was extremely keen not only not to exploit her best friend but also keep an eye on what was going on at the weekend. She wanted to be around just to do some extra-curricular detective work involving her own family this time. 'Thanks, babe, but I'll have to be here for Fi and Jase. If Oli's out, who knows what that mad Shaz and Digo might talk the kids into.' Shirley reckoned she'd come up with the perfect excuse.

'Ok, but how about I take you out for a nice meal tomorrow? Just you and me, taxi there, taxi back, couple bottles of wine – nice and romantic.' It was an enticing offer.

'I'd really like that.'

Kisses and hugs over, Shirley said goodnight to the rest of the household and within minutes she was snoring lightly safe in the land of nod.

Me head was a bit fuzzy this morning after all that wine last night. I've taken some painkillers and I've got some more at the ready. Got a lovely meal booked with David for 8 o'clock tonight. We're going to Freddie's, a little bistro that's become one of our favourite places to eat. It's the place David proposed to me, so it's really really special to us. Gonna dress up really glam and Oli's gonna put me hair up and I'm gonna try and put some false eyelashes on.

Just having our break now. We've got the factory girls in an hour and then we're calling it a day cos I want to be home by four for a bit of a lie down before tonight. Surprisingly, I've hardly thought about Mike coming over this weekend, I'm just going with the flow. I'm so up and down, though, anything could change.

It's all come flooding back to me now as I sit and write this down. There are things I want to ask Mike about the split. We didn't have it out face to face, he didn't have the balls to do that. All I got was a 'Dear John' letter saying how it wasn't me it was him, he was young, couldn't handle the responsibility, blah, blah, blah. Yeah right, but he wasn't too young to go off and have a relationship with someone else was he? And why did he drift away from contact with the kids? Think that hurt me the most. They were the innocent ones in all this, they had to grow up with the thought their dad didn't want to be bothered with them. Too busy with his new woman, his new life. Oh I've been through all the emotions over the years I'm mad with him for stirring things up for us right now. As if I didn't have enough to come to terms with, with me new wedding and me new life. I'd love to give him a piece of my mind! Let all the years of hurt and upset out. It'd be a chance for me to have my say, finally, and to show him I've come through it all and not only survived but done all right, better than all right.

'So you ready to go then, babe?' Oli asked. 'You ok?'

'Yeah, let's go for it. I want to be back home by four, so please don't offer to do a pile of them today.'

Nipping her burgeoning bad mood in the bud Shirley quickly refocused on her plans for the day and the evening to follow.

'Aye, ok, babe. Why four, though?'

'Well I want a little head down and relax before tonight. David's got us a table booked at Freddie's for eight.'

'Vey nice, I must say. Now come head an' let's see who Comb Over's got in today.'

They were greeted by Susan, eager to tell them that she had spoken to Angie who was more than happy for Susan to give her tattoo kit a new home. 'So, Oli babe, I think Shirl can do me hair first, then if you wanna have a go at a tiny tat just on the bottom of me back then I'll be made up.'

'I don't know about that, queen,' Oli said horrified.

'Why not? Come on, you were all for it before.' Susan looked wounded.

'Well I'm not a tattooist, am I? Friggin' 'ell, Susan, what if you collapse or summat?

'I wouldn't trust him,' Shirley added.

'Oi, I thought you were me, mate.'

'But I thought you didn't want to do it,' Shirley protested.

'Well I don't, but I don't want you saying you wouldn't friggin' trust me. Come head, Susan let's see what you had in mind.' Oli was suddenly keen not to let anyone think he mightn't be up to the job in hand.

'I'm the first aider, Oli, love, if you need any assistance,' Ali said, taking a bite out of her sandwich.

'I'll be fine…what's up with you all?' Susan assured them. 'Now, come head, Oli, can you do fairies?'

'Hey, no foreigners here today. What's the latest on his posse?' Shirley asked looking for Comb-over's latest visiting female.

'Gail's the one knows all about it,' Susan said, too busy with her tattoo for gossip.

'Oh, aye, Gail, what's the latest?' Shirley asked eager to hear the lowdown.

'Well, I saw them first few he had here, you know, the Malaysian ones and the Russian one, in town together the other day.'

'What all together?' Oli looked up from the picture Susan had given him to try and copy.

'Yeah. So he must have them all still living with him as sex slaves,' Kelly put in.

'What?' Shirley laughed.

'I know it sounds a bit far fetched, but you do hear about this sort of thing don't ya? Why are they still here, then, why haven't they all gone back home?' Gail added.

'Didn't you ask them anything?'

'No I was in the car just caught a kip of them,' Gail replied.

'Sure it was them?' Oli asked, much to Susan's annoyance.

'Oli, do ya mind? Yes it friggin' was them. Who gives a shite? Just get on with making a tracing of that pic onto that special paper, that's the first step.'

'Hey, I'm not sure I've agreed to this yet have I?'

'Come head… What are you a man or a mouse? Don't bother answering that. Aww, come on, babe, just do it, eh? I've bought a new top especially to show it off.'

'Susan, I'm not being funny, but I'm not sure we've got the time for tattooing today, we're on a bit of a tight schedule,' Shirley said, trying to ease Oli out of a potentially calamitous afternoon.

'What d'ya mean? You're always here Friday afternoon till chucking out time.'

'She's got a date, hasn't she, and needs her beauty sleep,' Oli explained.

'Oh charming. Well sod the hair, I'll just have the tattoo.'

'I'll make a start on the hair, Oli. It's up to you what you do, but I'd be very careful,' Shirley warned him.

'Don't worry, babe, I will. Susan: let's be having ya, babe. Gail, can we go into his office there's a couch in there isn't there? Susan can lie down an' all.'

'Aww, I'm dead excited, let me just go the loo first.' Susan giggled her way off the factory floor and into the corridor to the ladies.

'I'll set up. No one's to come in, though, I'll need total peace and quiet so I don't cock it up.'

'You sure you know what you're doing, babe?' Shirley asked Oli.

'Think so.' And then he winked before disappearing into the office.

Shirley got on with the hairdressing for the rest of the girls and caught up on all the usual gossip.

'So, how's your Ray, Ali?'

'Oh he's had a bad do, Shirl. Been up every night this week with the shites, poor bastard.'

'Aww, hell of a bug that Ali.' Shirley sympathised with the poor man's predicament.

'Oh no, it's not a bug. He's been a volunteer, you know, a human guinea pig for some new tablets on the market for constipation.'

'Aww, well, at least we know they work,' Kelly noted.

'I can't wait to see this tattoo,' Shirley said still a bit worried about the outcome of Oli's first foray into body art.

'Well, you won't have to wait much longer, here they come,' Jeanette said dryly.

'Ta da! What d'ya think?' Susan announced showing them the perfect little pink and purple fairy on her back. 'And it never hurt one bit.'

'Well…it looks great,' Gail said not quite succeeding in hiding her surprise. 'Hey, well done Oli.'

'Yeah, well done, babe.' Shirley gave him a hug, somewhat astounded at the results of his experiment.

'Now, remember no shower or bath till at least Monday, Susan,' Oli instructed her.

'No, I won't. I wanted it today 'cause I'm off out with me sister tonight and I'm gonna wear me new top that has that part of the back cut out of it.'

'Right Shirl, are we ready for the off?'

'Yeah, all done here, Oli. Hey, you take care, Susan, don't over do it now and take a couple of pain killers if it starts to sting.'

'Aye, I will. It's starting to a bit, but it never hurt anywhere near what people told me it would.'

Once they were in the safety of the car, Shirley wanted the gory details.

'Hey you did a good job on Susan, I'm not blaming you babe – but it must have been the cheap ink Angie bought, it looked a bit light, you know. Normal tattoos are brighter if that's the right word. And don't they usually look a bit scabby to start with?'

'Well, I didn't really do it Shirl.' Oli couldn't help but confess.

'Eh? What d'ya mean?'

'I didn't have the guts. What if she had some reaction to the ink or I did it wrong? When I got into Comb-over's office I saw a pack of thin tipped markers. Pink and purple they were, which was lucky, he must have been using them to underline or summat so I thought, right I'll use them. Told Susan I was mixing colours with that red they ordered.'

'Oh my God. And she didn't suspect?'

'She was out like a light once I started doing the tracing, fast asleep and snoring away, it's a wonder you didn't hear her from out here. She told me she wanted the tat for a weekend out and for this top she's bought, so she's got what she wanted.' Oli laughed. 'Won't last, mind, if anyone tips their drink down her back!'

'She'll either kill you next week or thank you. You know what she's like – always changing her mind about stuff. Bet she would have with that tattoo an' all: had it then regretted it. Well done you. It did look real apart from that colour thing and the blood, mind.'

'Right, home now for your nap before a night on the town. I'm gonna do your hair lovely.'

7.30pm

I'm all ready. Taxi'll be here any minute now. Feel full of energy after me nap and I'm dressed to kill. I've chosen a fitted white skirt with a white and silver skimpy top and a pair of gorgeous silver killer heel sandals. Oli's done me hair lovely, put it all up, and he's put a silver and diamante clip in to hold it all together. Even me false eyelashes have turned out well. I've done me eye make-up heavier than normal an' it looks dead glam with the false eyelashes.

Gonna have a lovely romantic night tonight. I just know it. Time just for me and him and it's the count down now to the wedding. This weekend is the last time David will have to see his boys and his side of the family before the wedding, so it's dead important that he goes.

I've been wondering what Susan made of her tattoo. Wonder if she's sussed yet that it's not real. My God, I can't believe Oli got away with it like that.

Anyway, kids all out tonight so Oli will have the house

to himself and Marc, and of course his baby Apple who is getting worse if anything on the potty training front.

Marc came home tonight and said to me quietly that he's getting pissed off with all of Apple's pissing!!! So he's been on the internet in work and has found some doggy nappies. He's put an order in for them and Oli's made up, he thinks it's more like a cute fashion statement but Marc told me it's he's so cheesed off with all the accidents. It was the last straw for him when he put on his fave t-shirt this morning and realised Apple had used it as a doggy toilet while he was in the shower.

Anyway time to pack up me diary and wait down stairs now for the cab. David just texted to say it's just left his place and he's on the way.

The restaurant was full when they arrived but their special table had been reserved in a corner of the cosy bistro. Shirley was thrilled with the table setting, the dim lighting supplemented by a tea light in a red glass holder. A small vase of red and yellow flowers had been placed in the middle of the perfectly set table.

'Champagne?' The waiter asked picking up the bottle David had ordered earlier from the ice bucket alongside the table.

'Aww, lovely. Thanks,' Shirley smiled.

The evening passed in a haze of champagne, loving heart to heart conversation and they left the bistro feeling warm happy and contented.

'I love you Shirley Cartwright, can't wait to love you Shirley Wilmore,' David said as they waited just inside the door for the taxi home.

'I love you too, David. I've had the best night ever. So romantic... I'm so lucky.' Shirley snuggled up to him. The evening had got chilly and with no jacket Shirley was making the most of getting close to David. 'I hope you have a good time in Manchester,' she said.

'I'll be back before you know it. You don't mind me going do you?'

Shirley knew that David would have to see his ex-wife but she'd stopped worrying about that. She knew how much David loved her, and that he had long since moved on from his life with his ex.

'Course not, give my love to everyone, especially Josh and Ben,' she said. 'Taxi's here.'

They cuddled up in the back like two teenagers.

'I would say young love…' The taxi driver said, dryly, winking into his rear view mirror, 'but…'

'We're getting married in a few days,' Shirley informed him, proudly.

'Well, enjoy it while you can you poor sods. It'll soon go down hill,' the taxi driver joked.

Shirley was dropped off first vowing to keep in touch over the weekend by text.

Saturday, May 4th
12 midday

Can't believe I've slept in till now. Must have been even more knackered than I thought. Marc brought me in a cuppa, bless him, when he did Oli's. He's got Marc well trained, has Oli, I'll give him that. They've gone out shopping now and then they're out to lunch. They did offer to take me along, fair dos, cos they know David's gone away, but I don't want to be a goosie do I? Leave them to it, I say.

The house is dead quiet. They've taken Apple with them, thank God, she cries like hell if they leave her behind. Mind you, Oli wouldn't leave her for anything. Oh yeah, the doggie nappies have arrived. Bless him, Oli marched into me bedroom this morning just before they got off to take a look. He was looking fab himself. He was wearing his black skinny jeans, grey and black t-shirt, sunnies: massive black rimmed with diamante on the arms, black boots and carrying Apple in her designer doggy bag. Apple looked just as good in her black and silver t-shirt with 'I'm the boss' written in silver glitter on the front. Oli'd put the doggy nappy on her. I have to say it did look a bit odd but if it saves a pile of accidents then I suppose it's all well and good.

Gonna get up now make me self some brunch. Jason must still be flat out. Think Fi's downstairs watching telly in peace.

Shirley pulled on her white fluffy dressing gown, slipped her perfectly painted red toes into the white slippers that waited by her bed and went in search of sustenance. She put the kettle on and called out: 'Fi, you having a cuppa love?'

Nothing, no sound, not even the television could be heard.

'Fi?' Shirley reiterated, investigating the living room. But there was no sign of anyone, the only telltale sign that Fi had been in there was a coffee mug left on the coaster and a plate with a few discarded toast crusts left on it.

'That's odd,' Shirley said aloud. 'Jase, Jason...' she called out loudly from the bottom of the stairs.

Nothing.

Shirley marched up the stairs to see what had happened to her first born. His bed was empty. That was odd, Shirley thought neither had told her that they were going out first thing, which was really unusual because they always told her if they had something planned. Shirley's mind started to work overtime – her two precious children were nowhere to be seen and her ex-husband, who after years of no contact had now found a conscience and got in touch, was in town. Was it a coincidence or what?

Shirley tried to ring both children on their mobiles, but both went straight to the answer machine.

Pacing the floor Shirley decided she had no alternative but to call Mike's mobile and find out if they had gone off with him. She didn't want to – really she didn't, but now she couldn't find the kids her imagination had gone into overdrive and she wasn't going to be able to relax until she had ruled the possibility out.

Looking through her her mobile's number listings she came across the M's, Oli's Marc first, then it was Mike. Nervously she pressed the call button.

'Hello.' She heard his voice at the other end.

'Mike it's me, Shirley, are the kids with you?'

'I can't hear you too well, love, what did you say?' It sounded like he was shouting, but she could hear him perfectly well.

'Are the kids with you?' Shirley shouted back.

'I can't hear you, Shirl, I'm really sorry. Listen… I'm on me way to the burger bar in town, come and meet me there 'cause I can't hear you.'

'But…oh, ok,' she said reluctantly and Mike hung up.

She certainly didn't want to meet up with her ex-husband, but if he was meeting the kids in the burger bar then she wanted to be there as well. She had initially thought it best to let them decide what to do but she couldn't help it, she had to be there to see for herself what Mike was playing at.

She would give him a piece of her mind, tell him how much he'd hurt her and the kids and her revenge for hurts past would be him seeing how they were all doing fantastically well without him. Jason and Fi would see for themselves what a scumbag their father was and then she was sure they'd vow never to have anything to do with him again. That way she could make sure her nightmare of losing the children to their dad would never be realised.

Forgetting all about her need for food Shirley quickly applied her make-up – there was no way she was going to let Mike think that she had let herself go. She wanted him to know what he'd been missing out on all these years. Coping with hunger pains would be easy if it meant he would see her in all her glory. She let her hair hang loose and thanks to Oli's perfect way of putting her hair up the previous night it looked properly bouncy and wavy today.

She pulled on a pair of white skinny jeans, a red t-shirt and patent red dolly shoes. She took one last look in the mirror and with a deep breath headed out to meet the man who'd broken her heart all those years ago.

Bravely she entered the crowded café. She wondered if she would still recognise Mike, it had been years. She looked out for Jason and Fiona, but they were nowhere to be seen.

Sitting on his own nursing a coffee, at a table for two, Shirley spotted Mike; she'd have known him a mile off, after all. He looked almost the same. His dark hair was greying slightly at the sides but he had the same olive skin that their children had and he looked sun-kissed as if he had just returned from a holiday in the sun.

'Shirley. You look fantastic.' Mike stood up as she approached him.

'Where are the kids?' Shirley asked, ignoring his compliment and looking around the room.

'Jason and Fiona? I thought you'd be bringing them.' He looked disappointed.

'No, I thought they were you,' Shirley said feeling a little uncomfortable.

'No I haven't seen them yet. I was hoping…'

'Oh. I thought they had come out to see you. Wonder where they are, then?' She said, thinking aloud.

'Sit down.' Mike gestured towards a chair.

'No, I don't think I should.'

'Come on, you've come into town, why not just give me ten minutes.'

Not sure she was doing the right thing, Shirley pulled the plastic chair back and sat down.

'Let me get you a coffee,' Mike insisted and immediately got up to get one before Shirley had the opportunity to refuse.

She watched him go. Mike was still as good looking as she remembered, better looking in fact. He'd aged well. He suited the slightly greying hair and had always had great skin. Just a few tiny wrinkles around his eyes, which made him look sexy rather than older, and he'd lost weight to what she remembered, gone was the beginning of a beer belly – he looked slender under his white t-shirt and blue-black jeans. All the anger she had felt and the long speech she had mentally prepared ebbed away as she contemplated the man rather than the ogre of her imaginings.

'Here you go, do you want anything to eat?' Mike asked handing her the coffee.

Shirley shook her head.

'Do you still take sugar?' He asked handing her two sachets of white sugar. 'I wasn't sure, so I brought these.'

'Yeah, same old me,' Shirley said taking the sachets from him.

'You haven't changed a bit, Shirl, you're still as gorgeous as I remember.' He smiled at her.

Shirley looked at him and raised her eyebrows: 'So what's all this about after all this time?'

'Well, I'm getting older and wiser, I've been a dickhead for years an' I wanted to make it up to you all.'

'And you think that you can just walk straight back in to our lives?'

'No, I know I can't. I just want to see the kids, make it up to them. I've missed out on so much.'

'Whose fault is that?'

'I know, I know.'

'And what about the lovely Cheryl, what happened to her?' Shirley asked sarcastically.

'That ended a couple of years ago... I realised no one could compare to you Shirl.' He reached out for Shirley's hand which she quickly pulled away and tucked neatly on her lap under the edge of the table almost spilling her drink in her haste.

'Think I'd better go.' Shirley informed him. 'Find out where the kids have got to.'

'Please don't go, we've got so much to catch up on, let's have a walk. Come on, please Shirl, just give me that.' It was getting even more embarrassing. People on neighbouring tables were beginning to look their way, attracted by the prospect of a domestic drama in the offing. Shirley didn't want to be the subject of their rubbernecking any longer.

She looked at her watch, 'Oh ok then, but first I'll have to have something to eat. I'm starving. But not here.' Although she knew she was risking opening old wounds again, a chance to talk things over might lay some old ghosts to rest. She'd never really known why he'd left.

'Ok, let's go somewhere better than this. How about the Red Lion, is that still ok?' Mike asked.

'Haven't been there for years not since...'

'Well let's give it a go; we used to spend hours there didn't we?'

'Yeah.' Shirley smiled at last, remembering that there were a few happy times.

'Come on then, let's go.' There were twelve years to catch up on. That ought to see them through lunch.

Thought I'd have a catch up here while I'm waiting for the kids to decide on the takeaway we're gonna have tonight. We're all home, so I've left them with Oli and Marc and a pile of menus. To be honest, I still feel a bit full after me dinner with Mike. Seeing as he was paying I had the works, three course meal: soup, steak and ale pie, chips and peas, and the apple crumble with cream for afters. Mike said he didn't know where I put it all!!

Had a really lovely afternoon! I can't believe it. Mike's changed so much. Gone is the selfish bastard he was, the kind caring man I fell in love with first time round seems to be back. We had a good long chat about everything, he said he's dead sorry for the way it's all been these years. He's grown up loads. Think that Cheryl had a lot to do with it an' all. She always was a cow that one.

Told him all about David and the wedding. He went a bit quiet, then, but he wished me all the best.

Apparently Jason had texted him to say he wasn't going to say anything to Fiona until after the wedding and for the time being he didn't want to meet up with Mike. I was surprised. Mike reckons Jason didn't want to do anything that would upset me an' that made me feel dead happy.

Anyway he's back to Scotland tomorrow and is gonna wait now till the kids get in touch with him. I gave him my blessing, but I'm not gonna tell them I've met up with him till after the wedding. I just want to concentrate on that for now. I did get great pleasure telling him all about me new life. How well I've done for me and the kids, with me mobile hairdressing. How I'd met a wonderful man who loved and adored me. I told him straight an' all, told him what a git he'd been, how hurt I was, especially because he didn't bother with the kids. He tried to make excuses about how he was young an' that, but I was young an' all and I told him so.

I thought I'd hate Mike forever, but I think today gave me some sort of healing...if that makes sense. Maybe it's me age or the fact I've got David, but I don't hate Mike anymore. I don't have any feelings for him at all. You can't stay full of anger for ever, you have to let it go. It's the only way to heal. Not gonna say anything to Oli or David either. Just forget it for now.

'Mum...? Come on, we're starving.'

'Coming...' Shirley yelled back, carefully stashing her pink diary out of sight of prying eyes and going down stairs. 'What is it we're having?' she asked, joining the others.

'Pizza!'

That'd make a change then...

'Shirl... I saw Hard Des in town today,' Oli muttered over his shoulder as he helped he get the plates ready.

'Did you? What was he up to?'

'Well, just out and about in town with Jan,' Oli answered. 'She did smile at me and give him the evil eye.'

'I think she's getting pissed off. Do you?'

'Yeah, probably. Look, I know you've got a lot on but we really have to nail this one. It's gone on for ages now.'

'Ok, how about a visit to the gym in the morning. We've seen him there before. It could be worth a go.'

'Ok, and if we don't see him, then I'll text Jan an' see if we can meet her on the way back. That might be enough to keep her off our case, if we have a bit of a meeting with her about it all, yeah?'

'Sounds like a plan...' Shirley smiled and gave him a quick hug.

'Hey, I was thinking, today, Shirl, a week to now you'll be Mrs Wilmore!'

'Oh my God you're right, friggin' hell, I will.' This came out more nervously than Shirley had intended.

'Are you excited?' Oli asked. 'Or scared?'

'I can't wait; be sad to leave here, though. You've been so good to us, babe. I really appreciate it you know.'

'I wouldn't have it any other way, hon'. Love you loads...' He pulled her close and planted a kiss on her forehead.

'So, where did you kids get to today?' Shirley asked as they all settled down to an array of pizza, garlic bread, hot and spicy chicken wings and enough chips to feed the whole street.

'I went out with Shaz. You were snoring away when I left. I did try and wake you. We went to the cinema; I did tell you we were going,' Fiona spluttered through mouthfuls of food.

'Oh, yeah.' Shirley remembered, now, too late for regrets.

'I went to play footie with the lads,' Jason said. 'They asked me out tonight, but I can't be arsed now, too knacked.' He took another huge slice of pepperoni, must have had empty legs what with all that football.

'Well... The three of us had a lovely shop, didn't we?' Oli said smiling warmly at Marc and tickling Apple who was frantically trying to tug her nappy off.

'Did you get anything?' Shirley asked.

'Got a new hi fi, for the bedroom...' Oli said excitedly. 'We can have a bit of music going when we get going, eh Marc?' Oli giggled while Jason groaned and made barfing noises. Marc just shook his head in dismay.

'Hey, talking of hi-fi's, did you hear about Digo?' Fiona giggled.

'No, what kid?' Oli asked keen for a laugh at the poor lad's expense.

'Well, Shaz told me that Digo met this lad, who asked if he

215

wanted to buy a car stereo from him for fifty quid. Digo said, ok, 'cause he wanted a new one.' Fiona was trying hard to keep a straight face and tell them the story.

'Go on, babe.' Oli said giggling in anticipation.

'Give over, pack it in.' Jason said, knowing what was coming and feeling bad for his mate. 'What does that mad cow know anyway?'

'Shut up an' let me tell them.'

'Yeah, Jase, we wanna hear what that Digo's been up to now.' Shirley always enjoyed hearing tales of Digo or Shaz's latest mishaps.

'Well, anyway, he agreed to buy this car stereo from this fella for fifty quid and when he got back to his car his own stereo had been nicked. When he had a proper look at the stereo he'd only gone and bought his original one back.'

'Aww, bless him, poor Digo,' Shirley said sympathetically, while the others laughed.

'Don't mean to be tight, Jase, but it could only happen to Digo couldn't it?' Oli giggled.

'Well, no, not really 'cause the same thing happened to his dad a week earlier. You'd have thought Digo would have been on the look out for that scam, wouldn't ya?' Fi chuckled.

'The lights are on, but there's no one home,' Oli said, raising his eyebrows. 'Sorry, Jase.'

Jason just shook his head, took a last large slice of pizza and grunted, 'Think I'll go out for a bit, seeing as you lot want to take the piss.'

'Aww, Jase...' Shirley objected.

'Leave him. I've got a load more stories from Shaz about Digo.' Fiona smirked.

'Oh, ok then. See you, Jase,' Oli said swiftly, teasing him.

'See you later...' Jason said grumpily and left them to hear all the exaggerated stories Shaz had told Fiona about his best mate.

<u>11pm</u>
Just come up to check me phone and I've got two messages. One from me gorgeous David saying how much he misses me. The other one from MIKE! Saying how much he enjoyed today and could we see each other again tomorrow before he goes back to Scotland!!

Oh my God, what am I going to do? I thought that was it till after the wedding. I can't understand why he wants to see me again. I thought we'd put a few ghosts to rest and that was it till after the wedding. Maybe he wants to sort something out with the kids, some sort of access, or maybe he's had second thoughts about them and has decided that he doesn't want to bother and he's leaving it to me to tell them...That's more like the Mike they knew!! Oh well, I don't suppose it will do any harm will it. I'll have to ring at least, to find out if it is something to do with the kids. I'll tell him I'll meet him after dinner, it'll give me a chance to sort out this Hard Des thing first.

I wanna text David, to tell him how much I miss him and love him, an' all.

TEN

'Here you go, Mum,' Fiona said, placing a cup of tea on the bedside cabinet.

'Aww, ta love. Listen, I've been thinking, it's less than a week now till the wedding. The house will be ready on Thursday, so we need to think about packing up our stuff.'

'God, the time has flown, here, Mum. I can't believe it's the wedding can you?' Fiona said excitedly.

'I know… David's gonna move into the house on Thursday, all our stuff from storage is getting delivered there then an' all. Jason told me he wants to move in on Thursday, too, but I thought you might like to stay here with me till the wedding.'

'Oh god, yeah, I'm not moving in there with just them two. We'll have a couple of days here together before everything.' Fiona reassured her mum.

'You ready, queen?' Oli pranced into the bedroom all togged up in his gym gear.

'Gimme five and I will be. We were just talking about moving out of here and the wedding an' that.' Shirley smiled.

'Oh girls! What am I gonna do without you? I'm gonna miss you three so much. It'll be so quiet here.' Oli sighed.

'You've got Marc,' Shirley said.

'And Apple,' Fi added.

'Yeah, I know, but I've got used to having you three around now haven't I. I'll miss you lot loads.'

'It's still ok for me and Fi to stay on here till Saturday, isn't it? Jason is still keen to go Thursday,' Shirley explained.

'Course it is. I thought Thursday we could have a little drink here, just us. Nice meal… I'll cook. I'll be home all day 'cause we only doing Monday and Tuesday this week, aren't we.'

'Yeah, finish lunchtime Tuesday, actually, give me the rest of the week for any final details that need attending to.'

'Aww, that'll be lovely,' Fiona added.

'Yes: a farewell dinner. You two, me, Marc, Jason and David, of course. A gorgeous meal, champagne an' all, and then Jason and David can go back to the house. We'll blow it and get a taxi for them. Can't see them cooking, can you? Not on the first night in the new house, anyway.'

'Oh that sounds lovely, Oli. I'm gonna enjoy that. That'll be the last time I see David before the wedding.'

'What about the rehearsal?' Oli asked.

'We decided against it, there's no time, really. David's brother isn't getting here till late Friday with his mum and dad, so we're gonna wing it. It's only a really small do isn't it, an' we've both done it before, what can go wrong?' Shirley said raising her eyes and looking to heaven.

'Come head, then, let's go the gym now an' get it out the way. You can stop all this lark after the weekend, eat like a horse and let yourself go,' Oli joked.

'Ok, ok… Let's go then, gym and the afternoon to ourselves.

What you up to Fi?' Shirley asked, not wanting her daughter to be at a loose end.

'Got a pile of homework to do, so I'll be bust with that all day long unfortunately. Go on, off you go, have a good work out...'

2pm

Had a really good workout, today. We both really went for it. Last pull now before the wedding. Did fifteen minutes on the ski machine, fifteen on the cross trainer, then I did 2,000 metres on the rower, which took me about ten minutes. I did twenty minutes on the treadmill then before I hooked up with Oli. Oli and I went on the bikes after I'd done me bit. We joined up and got them next to each other so we could have a chat. I try and do my own bit for the first hour cos Oli, to be honest, just prances about the machines going from one to the other doing five minutes max on each. He get's easily bored. He's ok if I'm next to him, cos he likes the chat, but it kind of defeats the object if I go there and chat to him the whole time. I don't mind if I've had a good hour's work out first, and I do still go for it when I'm on the bike, mind. I go at level ten. Oli bless him does his at level two. We do that for about fifteen minutes while having a goss, Oli slagging people off in the gym for doing exactly the same as he is – bugger all!! Then I go round some of the machines, just to tone up me arms, abs and that.

We did the works today, cos we'd got the time, and who did we see in the jacuzzi afterwards but Hard Des. Well, there was just the three of us in there so it was an ideal chance to ask a few discreet questions. Well, when I say discreet questions I am talking about Oli and he went in with all guns blazing... 'So what brings you to the gym. Trying to impress the ladies?' Oli giggled. Hard Des didn't look impressed, he just looked at Oli and said, 'Just to relax.'

Oli did try and get a bit more info but nothing. It did give us a chance to get a closer look at Des, though, and he's got this scorpion tattoo all down his left arm from his shoulder to his elbow. Not sure how that's going to help. Hard Des wasn't interested in making convo and Oli was given short shift when he tried to prise anymore info out of him. In fact, he must have thought Oli was some kind of strange weirdo or trying to come on to him. Hard Des had enough and got out and went to get changed. We sent Jan a text just to say we'd seen him and she said she didn't know he was in the gym he'd said he'd had to go to do a few extra hours in work.

Anyway, I'm back in now. David's due back later tonight, so I won't get to see him tonight. I've decided to go and say bye to Mike and to see what he wants, in case he is trying to get out of seeing the kids and leaving his dirty work to me!! I'm meeting him down by the docks at three so I'd better go and get ready. Not gonna say a word to anyone here, though. Fi's still busy with her homework, Jason's still out and Oli and Marc have taken Apple to the park. They still can't let her walk, mind, she has to go in the bag cos she still hasn't had all her injections.

Best go and get meself ready.

Waiting patiently outside the Museum of Liverpool Life, Shirley was the first to arrive but not wanting to appear too keen she carried on walking a bit further along the dock. She bumped into Mike coming towards her.

'Hey you're going the wrong way. Not standing me up are you, changed your mind?'

'No, no, I thought I was a bit early that's all.'

'May as well go up this way then, do you wanna go for a coffee?'

'Not yet, let's just walk,' Shirley said. 'What's up then? Why did you want to see me? Thought we'd said it all yesterday.'

They walked along in silence for a few moments, then suddenly Mike stopped, reached out and took Shirley's hand and said, 'Listen Shirl… I've thought about nothing else since I saw you yesterday. I know it's hell of a timing, what with your wedding an' all, but I just couldn't go back with out telling you.'

Shirley looked at him. 'What the hell are you trying to say?'

'I know…I know…it's friggin' awful timing but I had to tell you, love. I still love you Shirl… Seeing you yesterday I realised I love you more than ever. I want to give it another go: you, me, the kids. We can make it work, I know we can.' He stood in front of her and looked at her, his eyes pleading.

'Forget it. No chance. I'm getting married in six days' time. I'm in love with David.' Shirley marched off. She wasn't just shocked, she was horrified; this just wasn't happening.

'Please Shirley just think about it love, I know we can work it all out, we had some happy times didn't we? I'm not that same person. I've grown up realised what a fool I've been and what I've missed out on.' He went on and on, desperately trying to catch up with Shirley, who was nearly jogging by this point. Trying to get away as fast as she could. Then she stopped equally suddenly and turned back to face her ex.

'I'm off. Listen…get in touch next month sometime with the kids, not before. And leave me out of it. You can see them but you won't be seeing me again. Goodbye Mike.' She left him standing alone, her tone unmistakeable.

Walking away from Mike, Shirley was surprised by the tears springing to her eyes. Why would that affect her, she thought, after all he had put her through? Surely she didn't still have feelings for him. She felt confused and sad, and angry to boot. The cheek of it...

Next morning Shirley woke up to what seemed like the hundredth text from Mike. He was continuing to declare his love for Shirley and the kids and saying he wanted to start afresh. In amongst the texts from Mike was a text from David saying that he was back home, tired but desperate to see her as he'd missed her so much.

Shirley reached for her diary hoping that by writing her experience down on paper she could make some sense of the last twenty four hours.

<u>Monday, May 6th</u>
<u>7am</u>
Been lying here awake for hours going over everything in me head. I have to be strong. I love David. We're gonna have a wonderful life together. He's nothing like Mike. I have so many memories with Mike good and bad. I've been dead emotional for a bit, now. What with the wedding coming up, I'm not thinking straight. Me head's all over the place. Once the kids have got off I'm gonna have a chat with Oli, tell him the lot. I need to talk to someone and I know he'll help me as best he can. He's the only one I can trust not to blab and to be honest with me. Maybe I shouldn't have gone to see Mike, but I wanted to put a line under our relationship, see him, let him see I was doing well and then for us both to move on. The last thing I wanted to do was lead him on. I suppose I knew one day he might want to see the

kids, he did think the world of them when they were tiny – at least until he left! I think I was blaming Cheryl for keeping him from them, thinking that it was all her idea to lose touch. I really wasn't expecting what happened today. I mean – I know we got on yesterday we had a chat about old times the good and bad, but I had nothing more in mind We managed to behave like grown ups so I didn't think anything of it.

'I need to talk to you babe, when the kids have gone off,' Shirley said to Oli, quietly buttering some toast.

'Ok hon'. You ok?' He asked concerned picking up on her serious tone.

'I don't know,' she replied honestly.

Oli looked at her anxiously, but Shirley carried on buttering the toast deep in thought.

Settled safe from teenage ear shot in the car to their first appointment of the day, Shirley spilt the beans on what she had been up to over the last twenty four hours.

'I can't believe you'd do such a thing. What the friggin' hell possessed ya, Shirl? Is it a full moon?'

'I know, I know… I just did it for the kids and to lay a few ghosts to rest.'

'Well, just leave it, now. Less said the better.'

'I've had twenty texts from Mike this morning, alone,' Shirley confessed. 'All saying how much he loves me.'

Oli shook his head.

The remainder of the journey took place in silence, Shirley deep in thought and Oli lost for words as to how stupid he felt his best friend had been.

'We're in the factory today instead of Friday, Comb-over's off today.'

'Right,' said Oli, obviously still annoyed with Shirley.

'Look, please don't be mad,' Shirley pleaded.

'Mad? Too friggin' right I'm mad. At this rate you're gonna chuck away probably the best thing that's ever happened to you. David is a fantastic fella. From what you've told me, and what bit of him I know personally, Mike is a waste of space. Wake up and smell the coffee Shirley...'

By the time they arrived at Henshaws you could cut the atmosphere with a knife and it was obvious to the whole production line that the usually happy-go-lucky pals had fallen out.

'So what's up with you two?' Susan asked.

'Nothing.' They both said simultaneously.

'Well, listen here, Oli I don't know quite how to tell ya, but Susan's regretting that tattoo you give her.' Ali said, as eager to stir things up as ever.

'Hey, you!' Susan scolded. 'Not really, Oli, but...ya know...' she stammered.

'Oh yeah, let's have a look. Still there is it?' Oli asked surprised.

'Still there? What d'ya mean?'

'Let's have a look,' Oli demanded.

Susan lifted up her top to revel the by now rather smudged fairy.

'Not too keen on the shower, then are we, queen,' Oli noted.

'Eh? Only every day,' Susan lied.

'Don't think so babe. Not if that's still there,' Oli said, wiping the remains of the marker pen 'tattoo' off with one of the facial wipes he always had handy in his hairdresser's bag of tricks.

'What the—?' Susan asked.

'I know what yer like and I didn't want to cock it up, so I did it in felt tip,' Oli confessed.

'Ergh, when did you last wash, Susan?' Jeanette asked horrified.

Susan looked all embarrassed. 'It's not good for your skin if you have too many showers – or the planet...'

The rest of the girls looked at each other, they were more than

225

a bit disgusted that Susan hadn't washed for the last four days, longer possibly, she wasn't admitting to anything. Of course, to be fair to Susan, Oli had told her not to take a shower too soon after her 'tattoo' for fear she'd wash it off before her big night – four days, though, was pushing it by any standards.

'Anyway, enough about me. What's up with you two?' Susan was keen to change the subject.

'Oh, Shirl has only had her ex on to her, wanting her back an' that,' Oli declared.

'Oli! Ta a bunch,' Shirley yelled, horrified he had divulged her secret. He might as well have got a megaphone and stood on the steps of City Hall. Now everyone would know before the week was out. She could only hope the news wouldn't find its way to David before their big day.

'Well, nothing happened, he just wants to see the kids.' Oli quickly realised he was well out of order, but it had just popped out without him meaning to dump Shirley in it.

All the factory girls looked on eager for more information.

'An old flame is like a pair of old slippers, comfy, safe you know them well but then you feel you need a new pair; at first they don't feel as comfy as your old pair so you go back to your old slippers, but then you realise that your old slippers pinch your toes, the soles are all thin and worn out and you know why you put them in the bin in the first place.'

Everyone looked at Ali, amazed at the pearls of homespun wisdom coming from such an unlikely source.

<u>11pm</u>
Just got in from David's. I felt dead guilty 'bout this Mike thing. I haven't done anything, but I still do!! I didn't say anything to David, cos I didn't want to upset anything before the wedding. It's on me mind, though.

I'll tell him when the wedding's over, make sure he knows I'm being truthful. I've had a load of texts from Mike again tonight. I haven't answered them, just ignored him. He even sent me a pic of us on our wedding day. He must have taken a pic of it with his phone. I'm gobsmacked that he's still got one. I threw all of the ones I had out, all except two – Fi wanted one to keep and took one for Jason an' all in case he wants one when he's older. Fi said it was to show her kids who their nan and granddad were. Talk about making you feel old!! Anyway I thought it was a nice thought, her wanting a picture of her mum and dad in happier times. They're not out on show or anything Fi's got them locked away in a draw somewhere. I don't know what he's playing at but he's doing my head in, so close to the wedding an' all.

I'll just have to be strong and keep ignoring him. He's told me he's got no intention of going back till he's seen me again. Thank goodness I've told Oli everything. At least I've got someone to talk to about it all otherwise I think I'd go barmy.

David had a great time in Manchester and he's come back with a pile of wedding pressies, gifts that friends who haven't even been asked to the wedding had given us. People that I've never even met... You know, like his parent's next door neighbours and the woman who does his mum's hair, they've all given pressies, bless them. His mum and dad have given us vouchers to buy whatever we want for the house. We've already got some stuff from them, cos they gave them to David earlier knowing we wanted them for when David moves in.

We opened the presents together, tonight, we had

glasses and towels: white ones so they'll go with everything. One little old woman who lives over the road from his mum and dad – she used to give David piano lessons when he was a kid – gave a pack of three t-towels, bless her. At this rate we're gonna have all new stuff and will have to skip the rest or give to Oxfam or something.

I really feel it's happening now; it's the countdown, not long at all to go. I just can't wait for the day to come. I only wish Mike would go back up north, it's playing on my mind that he's hovering.

Only got half a day in work before the wedding, just tomorrow morning then tomorrow night – well tea time – we're all going for a final fitting and to bring the dresses and Oli and Jason's suit home. Wednesday is the day to check on the flowers, and me and Oli are going to that Lyn's to pick up the cake and take it straight to the reception place. It's a bit early but I want to make sure it's there and we've no time Thursday or Friday, really, what with the move. We can check up that everything is ok with the reception as well, the menu, wine and that.

Thursday is the big move. David has got a half-day he's finishing work at twelve then we've got the lovely meal and Friday is a pamper day. That's the week gone and it'll be Saturday before I know it and I'll be Mrs Wilmore. Lovely!!!

Right, beauty sleep time or David might take one look at me marching up the aisle and do one!!

Tuesday morning seemed to race by and a few of Shirley's regulars added to her wedding gifts with presents of their own. She was thrilled that they had been so kind and Oli was equally delighted and kept himself busy carrying everything to the car for her.

'Hey! Shows how much they all love ya, babe, all these pressies,' Oli said piling the last of the clients' gifts in the car.

'I know, I can't believe it, fairdo's.' Shirley blushed.

'Maybe they're all after a free hairdo next time,' Oli joked. 'Even Sapphire gave you summat...I can't wait to see what that is.'

'Shall I open it now?' Shirley asked, eager to find out what someone like Sapphire would think was an appropriate gift for such a celebration.

'Don't you want to open them all with David? Oh, go on then,' He said not pausing for breath.

Sapphire had texted and although she didn't have an appointment asked the pair to call in to pick up the present.

Oli had waited in the car while Shirley had quickly popped to the flat. He couldn't be bothered to walk up all the stairs only to be given a few moments rest before having to come down them again to go on to the next job so had chosen to wait in the car. 'Did she still have them sex slaves working there?'

'Oh, aye, yeah; the four of them were still at it. They looked well busy,' Shirley said with a mischievous smile.

'Go 'way. My God I'll give her that, she's resourceful isn't she eh?' He giggled.

'Anyway, let's have a look. I'm not being funny but this wrapping paper's seen better days hasn't it?' Shirley said looking down at the square parcel wrapped in slightly battered and a little dated 'congratulations on your wedding day' paper.

Oli raised his eye brows. 'I did think that, yeah. Come head, let's have a look.'

Gingerly, Shirley opened the white and silver grey packaging and inside she found a box, which she opened in trepidation. Inside she found coloured glass salad bowl.

'Aww, look, she's put the gift card inside it to make sure it doesn't come off and you know for sure who gave it to you,' Oli noted.

Shirley picked up the tiny card and read it out: 'To Rita and Jack. Congratulations on your wedding. Tamed him at last! Jim and Caroline.' Who the friggin' hell are Rita and Jack?'

'Oh Rita's her sister. She was due to get married must be about eight years ago, to this bloke Jack. She jilted him at the altar. Don't you remember her telling us once?'

'Well what's this about?' Shirley asked picking up the salad bowl.

'Sapphire must have bagged the pressies and recycled them. But she obviously didn't even bother re-wrapping this one. She probably doesn't even know what she's given you, babe!'

'Oh well, I suppose it's the thought that counts,' Shirley said grimly.

'Some thought. Typical of that one. Wait till I see her. I feel like texting her now,' Oli announced.

Shirley started laughing, almost hysterically, and picked up the bowl again. Oli watched her distate turning to humour and burst into of laughter himself.

4pm

Well, I've dropped off all the pressies we've already had at David's on the way home from work. I've got a key so it's quite handy to just move them all to the new place from there in one job lot. Then all we'll need to move on Thursday from Oli's is our clothes – oh, and Jason. I've told Fi she has to pack up most of her stuff to take to the new house, just leave enough things at Oli's to last till the wedding.

Showed the kids the salad bowl. Fi wants me to give it to a jumble sale!! Knowing my luck I'd get rid of it somewhere and Sapphire would go along buy it and give

230

it me back to match the one I've already got... Oh no, she couldn't, could she, cos she doesn't even know who she got me!! The cheeky cow... Well, I suppose it <u>is</u> the thought that counts. Hey, I could give it her back as a pressie one day, couldn't I, seeing as she doesn't even know what it is!!

Anyway, we're off in a bit to the fitting. I'm dead excited, hope I haven't put any weight on...

'So, not long to go now. Are you all set?' Maj at the dress shop said as she carefully got Shirley's dress out of the packaging.

'Well, I think so. As ready as I'll ever be.' Shirley smiled, her tummy fizzing with excitement as she eagerly waited for the finally finished dress to be unveiled.

'Here it is, again.' Maj smiled encouragingly as she spoke.

Oli and Fi sat and relaxed on the cream sofa sipping the crisp white wine Maj had given them. Apple slept soundly in her designer bag. Jason had decided he wasn't needed; his suit fitted perfectly and he was far more interested in having the house to himself than oohing and aahing over his mother's dress.

'I hope it still fits...' Shirley muttered.

'What with all that gym and slimming, course it will,' Oli enthused, wine in hand.

A few moments later, Shirley emerged from the dressing room her dress ever so slightly baggy around the waist area.

'I think I've lost a bit too much,' Shirley said disappointed. The stress of the last few days must have taken its toil and the once figure hugging dress looked almost a size too big.

'Ooh, have you been overdoing it love?' Maj asked, quickly getting out her pins and pulling the dress tight again and adjusting the darts. 'Happens to lots of women, what with the stress of the organisation and everything.'

'That looks better,' Shirley said, as the dress once again hugged her perfectly toned figure.

'Aww, yeah. It looked ok before but, after all your hard work in the gym an' that, it's only fair for you to have it all fitted like that and show it all off,' Oli encouraged.

'Will you be able to do make the changes in time though?' Shirley asked Maj.

'Of course we will.'

'Thank God for that. Otherwise I'd have had to eat six meals a day till Saturday.'

'Your sister still away then, Maj?' Oli asked, ever the gossip.

'Oh no she's back but I've had such a great time here while she's been away, and she enjoyed the break that much thatI do three days here now and she does two. It's great. I love meeting people and making a fuss of them.'

'Do I need to call in again, just to double check?' Shirley asked.

'No need love, it will be perfect, trust me,' Maj assured her.

Shirley took her beautiful dress off and settled back on the sofa to enjoy her glass of wine. Oli and Fi wanted to try their outfits on again and both fitted as perfectly as they had the last time.

'Hey, Shirl, what about a ribbon for Apple, in the same colour as my suit?' Oli suggested, looking through a range of coloured fabrics.

Oli had asked if Apple could come along to the wedding as an extra little bridesmaid. He'd already ordered a pure white designer doggy bag from the internet as her wedding transport.

'Aww, is she going to the wedding, too?' Maj asked.

'Yeah, littlest bridesmaid,' Oli announced, ever the proud dad.

'Aww, bless… If you want I could run up a little top for her, same as Fiona's – well same material anyway, and a lovely bow for her collar,' Maj said excitedly.

'Oh Maj, you're a star. Can ya, babe?'

'No probs; do it in no time.'

'Come on, queen, have a glass of wine with us to celebrate,' Oli said handing Maj a glass of wine.

'Oh, don't mind if I do.' She raised her glass to them all before taking a sip.

'Great…' Shirley looked at Fi with eyebrows raised. 'David will be dead chuffed.'

Wednesday, May 7th
10am

Taking it a bit easier today. Oli's just brought me up a cuppa. I'm gonna enjoy this then get up and start on the jobs for the day. Still getting a load of texts from Mike; he still hasn't gone back home…said he's refusing to leave til I meet up with him again. I think I'm gonna have to, just to get him off my case. Thought I might do it today and take Oli with me, maybe see him on the way back from all these jobs we've got planned. David's sorting out the photographer, so that's one less thing for me to worry about, but I've got the flowers, the cake… Oh my God the cake!!! And the reception. I hope to God the cake's ok.

'I've made you a bacon buttie, try and fatten you up a bit,' Oli joked.

'I can't put any weight on, can I? Maj has pinned the dress to the size I am now,' Shirley protested.

'Oh, yeah.' He sighed. 'Well, a bacon buttie isn't gonna do much is it? Anyway you need to make sure you don't lose any more, babe. Now, come on, get it down your neck so we can get going. I've made a list.' He sat down and showed it to her.

'Oh, what would I do without you, hon'?' Shirley smiled, looking at the organised plan of the day ahead.

'Well, hurry up then so we can get off...'

With the flowers arranged to be picked up on the morning of the wedding, it was on to Lyn's to pick up the cake.

'Oh my God, I'm dead nervous about this, you know. Why didn't I go somewhere else, somewhere a bit more reliable?' Shirley moaned when they pulled up outside the neat 1950s semi.

'Well, the house looks ok, nice and tidy from the outside. Come on, don't let them factory girls put you off, it'll be ok.'

Shirley nervously made her way down the path, followed eagerly by Oli. She knocked on the door and waited patiently for an answer.

'Shirley...hiya, come on in,' Lanky Lynda greeted her. 'It's ready for you.'

Anxiously they walked in to see what the final result looked like.

'Oh...my...God...' Oli said breathlessly.

'Oh, Lyn... It's beautiful,' Shirley managed.

The cake stood proudly boxed on Lanky Lynda's dining room table. Delicious chocolate covered cake with the cutest bride and groom made out of icing Shirley had ever seen.

'You've got a real talent there, Lynda,' Oli said. 'It looks brilliant.'

'And I can guarantee you it will taste even better,' Lynda said proudly.

Shirley carefully carried the box to the boot of her car, while Oli frantically danced up the path trying to guide her route.

'Well, it's better than I could have hoped for,' Shirley said thrilled with the finished product.

'Aye, and not a chocolate button in sight.'

The journey to the venue for the reception was a painstaking process with every step on the brake pedal a near heart attack for Shirley, who in the end stopped the car, got the cake out of the boot and made Oli sit in the back seat with it on his lap.

'Sorry, babe, but me nerves can't stand it, you're gonna have to look after it.'

'Aye, ok, kid, but still take it easy, yeah?'

Relieved to arrive at their final destination without mishap, Oli carried the prized possession into the beautiful country pub, this time with Shirley frantically guiding the way.

'You did great with this place,' Oli said looking at the location.

'Isn't it just the best place ever?' Shirley sighed.

Situated inn the middle of nowhere, the ideal venue for Shirley's romantic vision of her wedding reception was a far cry from their usual working locations. The white thatched building, embellished with the most gorgeous plump pink early roses around the door, stood in front of a beautiful walled garden. The floral display had rewarded the attentive gardener with the most wonderful show of spring colour.

Cake in the safety of its new home for a few days, Shirley and Oli looked around the charming inn. The sun was shining so they decided to wander outside and enjoy a much deserved drink in the walled garden.

'It's gonna be gorgeous, here, babe. We're all gonna have a lovely day.' Oli squeezed her hand.

'I'm so happy Oli; I just hope nothing will spoil it,' Shirley said, sounding a teensy bit worried.

'Hey! Like what kid?'

'Well… Mike's still texting me, I was gonna ask if you'd come with me to see him on our way home. He said he won't go back till he sees me one more time.'

'No Shirl, you're not to see him. He'll keep on at you if you go, he'll think he can worm his way back into your affections. You'll have to say no and stick to your guns. Just leave it Shirl,' Oli insisted.

'D'ya reckon? Ok, if you think that's best. I just wanted to make him go home before the wedding, I'm worried he might turn up.' Shirley sighed.

'Yes, I do. Now, let's see if we can have a look at one of the rooms, here, seeing as that's gonna be your bed for the wedding night!' Oli grinned and winked.

David had arranged for him and Shirley to stay over in the pub. Everyone else was going home, and Jason and Fi were in two minds as to whether to sleep at the new house or go back to Oli's.

'Think we're having the four poster bed. The room overlooks the garden.'

'Come head, then, let's see if we can have a look.'

'I know we're not going on honeymoon, but at least we get one romantic night away.' Shirley smiled contentedly.

Oli winked at her.

'Do you know something I don't?'

'Who me? Nooo, I know nothing…'

7pm

All our errands went well today, I was dead chuffed. The cake is fan-bloody-tastic. I'm over the moon with it and the venue for the wedding, well I don't think we could have found a better place for a million pounds. It is the most perfect romantic place I could imagine. I love it.

We went up to have a look at the room David and I will be staying in. Oh my God, it is <u>gorgeous</u>. Four poster bed in the middle of the room and it even has a roll top bath, yeah right in the bedroom. Oli thought it was a bit odd, that, but I thought it was lovely, so different to the usual.

We decided to stay and have a bit of lunch there, Oli wanted to try out the food. David and I have eaten there before, of course. Oli loved it. The chef is fantastic. He trained in London with one of them celebrity chefs and him and his wife moved up here and out into the country for their kids. Anyway, we were both tucking into our homemade lasagne when who turned up for her dinner but the vicar. She sat with us for a bit and went over a couple of things, so we killed two birds with one stone.

Didn't bother with trying to see Mike on the way home, Oli talked me out of it, but I don't think not seeing him will work cos the texts are still coming. He's trying everything: said he wants me to give him another chance, that he'll make it up to me. It's so hard. I sent him one back saying, 'Please don't text me again till after the wedding and only stuff to do with the kids.' And he sent one back saying, 'Don't go through with the wedding.' I couldn't believe it!!

Anyway nothing planned for the rest of the night just watching a bit of telly. We've got the big move tomorrow. Just me, Oli and Marc to start with, then David will be there at twelve.

I've got the vouchers for that pamper weekend for Oli and Marc from that woman in David's school. I'm gonna give it to them tomorrow night at the meal. I've got Oli his favourite aftershave from the kids: it's like a gift set, aftershave, shower gel and deodorant all-in the same smell, he'll love that. Fi's got Apple a new outfit and cos we didn't want to leave Marc out we got him a bottle of Jack Daniels, so they should all be happy.

I'm really looking forward to the meal. Oli will go to town, I know. I've asked David to bring in a couple of bottles of champagne. Oli loves it so it will go down a treat and it will really show him that we appreciate all his effort.

Shirley looked around the bedroom that had been her sanctuary for the last few weeks. She really would miss living with Oli. She had a little wave of anxiety flutter over her as she thought of her new life. She loved David, but couldn't help think back for just a brief second to Mike and their life together. They had been happy once and been in love. She quickly got up and tried to chase away the dark thoughts that crept into her head by doing something else. She picked up her hair brush and pulled it through her already neat hair.

'Mum! Your programme's on...' Fiona called up the stairs.

Shirley welcomed the excuse to escape her unease and went to join the rest of her family, in the hope it would calm her slightly frayed nerves.

Thursday, May 8th
7.30am
Early start for us: the big move today!!
David texted first thing, wishing all the best for the first half. He'll see us at twelve.

With Fiona and Jason at school, Shirley, Oli, Marc and, of course, Apple waited patiently outside the new four bedroomed detached house for the removal vans to arrive. One from David's place and one from the warehouse in which Shirley had stored all her own furniture.

'Oh, a van's here,' Oli announced.

'All hands on deck…' Shirley giggled with excitement.

By the time David had arrived most of the hard work had been done.

'Just in time.' He winked at Oli who looked flustered.

'Oh – about time,' Shirley moaned.

'Is the kettle on?' David asked.

'Aye, go and make us a brew soft lad,' Oli instructed.

'Ok, I will, looks like you need one, and then you can give me a job to do.'

With only the beds left to make, Shirley sat back on their new cream leather settee and took sip of the hot refreshing tea.

'Ah, lovely,' she said.

'Well, you've worked hard, well done you.' David smiled.

'Once I've finished this tea, me and Marc are gonna get off and leave you two to do the rest. Need to pop to the shops to get ready for tonight's extravaganza,' Oli announced.

'Yeah, you two gerroff. Ta very much for all your help. I couldn't have done it without you babes, both of you.' Shirley gave them both a big hug and a kiss.

'So... What're we having to eat tonight?' David asked.

'Surprise!' Oli announced.' Now, come head Marc-ie, baby, let's go.'

A few minutes later Shirley and David were left alone in their new home.

'Just for us.' David said getting a half bottle of champagne and two glasses out of his bag.

'Aww, David.'

'Just a small one, but we have to toast our new place, and I wanted just you and me here for this.'

They shared the champagne and then a kiss and christened their new settee...

7pm

I've decided on a long white skirt and a green and white fitted blouse and little white dolly shoes. Oli said we had to dress up for tonight. It's a warm evening an' all, so we've got to meet out on the back patio at 7.15 for drinks. I've warned David and Jason to get here by then. Jase decided to stay on with David at the house. He's got his room looking great already. We've put all the wedding presents we've already had in the spare bedroom. I can't believe I've got a spare bedroom!! Me mum asked me to put twin beds in there so that she and Auntie Dilys can come and sleep over at Christmas. We have got it as a twin room, but that's cos David's boys will use it when they come over to see us; not so sure about having me mum and Auntie Dilys over to stay!!

Anyway, Fi's already downstairs an' she looks fab. She's got a lovely pink, purple, blue and white patterned strappy dress on and a pair of silver strappy sandals. I've done her hair up in like a scruffy bun with bits coming down. She looks amazing.

Anyway, nearly time, so I'd best get down there. I've got Oli's voucher and I've put it in a lovely 'thank you' card. Hope he likes it. Got the rest of the pressies too but I'm gonna leave them up here and give them all out after the meal.

Shirley joined the others outside, David and Jason had kept their promise and arrived on time.

'Hey I didn't hear you arrive.' Shirley smiled and kissed them both.

'Well you said to be early,' David said grabbing his very nearly wife around her now very narrow waist.

'Hey, Ma, we're earlier than you and you've only come from upstairs,' Jason joked.

'Here you go, babe.' Marc handed Shirley a champagne cocktail.

'Ooh, lovely, Marc. Ta. Oli said you're a dab hand at champagne cocktails.'

Oli had the best of everything and paid great attention to detail: the cocktails were served in elegant flutes and the patio was lit by insect repellent flares.

'So are we allowed to know what's on the menu yet?' David asked, winking at Shirley.

'Here ya go…' Oli said happily handing David a hand-crafted menu.

'Oh you boys have gone to town.'

'What is it?' Fi asked excitedly.

'Cream of watercress soup to start, with a basket of warm bread…' David said, reading the menu from the perfectly written cream and gold card.

'Ooh, lovely,' Shirley and Fiona said together.

Jason looked at them, then Oli, and smiled nervously – he wasn't sure watercress was his kind of thing. It sounded suspiciously green.

'Then breast of duck with a redcurrant sauce, herby mashed potatoes, and a medley of spring vegetables,' David went on.

More oohs and aahs from the girls.

'Followed by home-made chocolate mousse with clotted cream…'

'You could have made an effort lads,' Jason put in.

'I've not finished yet: filtered coffee and mints to follow and it says here that the meal will be accompanied by a selection of fine wines.'

'Well, Oli and Marc, you have gone to loads of trouble,' Shirley said giving them both a big hug and another kiss.

'We haven't tasted it yet, it might sound good but taste like load of crap,' Jason said smiling, he didn't want them to get too carried away.

'I don't think so…' Shirley said giving her son a maternal poke in the ribs.

'Sounds dead lovely.' Fiona took the menu from David and inspected it.

'Well, let's have a toast,' Oli said picking up his champagne. 'To the best friend anyone could ever wish for and her amazing kids. Not forgetting her fit fella. Love you all to bits, here's to you.' Oli got slightly emotional toward the end of his mini-speech.

Tears welled in Shirley's eyes and after the toast she gave Oli yet another hug and kiss.

'Come on now, this is meant to be a happy time, you pair have been crying on and off for weeks,' Marc chided them.

'Yeah, come on you two.' Fiona grabbed a bottle of fizz and a punnet of strawberries. 'Let's have a few more of these cocktails, Marc, and they'll be all giggly.'

Marc topped them all up.

'I think, to be honest, you can all go and sit down. We can bring out the starter now,' Oli announced brightly.

They all went in through the opened patio door and took their seats at the neatly laid table.

'Aww, look Mum, they've even done our names.' Fi picked up her place name and waved it for all to admire.

The warm evening encouraged them to leave the patio door open and it made for a relaxing summery atmosphere.

Showing their appreciation by sending back clean plates after all three courses – even the usually faddy Jason, Shirley excused herself and went upstairs to collect her 'thank you' presents.

'Now it's my turn,' she smiled as she came back to the table. 'We all want to thank you so much for taking us in and letting us treat this place like home. You're a true friend Oli and we love you very much, me especially.' Shirley sniffed tearily as she handed the voucher to Oli.

'Oh my God, babe, you didn't have to...' Oli blubbed.

'And this is for Apple,' Fiona announced.

'And this is for you, Marc.'

All delighted with their gifts they went to relax outside again.

'I'll put the patio heater on kids,' Oli said struggling to ignite it.

'It's gone a bit chilly now the sun's down.'

'Shaz wanted to come over tonight,' Fiona said.

'Oh hell, no way, not tonight,' Shirley protested. 'Tonight's special.'

'That's what I told her, so she's staying in to practise with her mum.'

'Practise what, the talent show thing?' Oli asked.

'Yeah, they're doing a Madonna and Britney thing, you know, when those two did that song together.' Fiona went on. 'They had thought of doing a Cheeky Girls thing first, but Mo said she couldn't let Shaz wear them gold shorts.'

'Oh, found her maternal instincts at last has she?' Oli asked.

'No, not that, she said it was cos she looked miles better in them than Shaz and they might not get through.'

'More like the other way round,' Shirley pointed out, peeved on Shaz's behalf.

'She thinks she's God's gift, that Mo one,' Oli moaned.

'More like the freaky girls; Madonna and Britney? They're in cloud cookoo land,' Jason protested.

'Mo said Shaz has to take the Madonna part, cos she reckons she's more like Britney. She thinks it'll make a more believable audition cos she says she looks the same age as Shaz, or like she keeps saying they look just like sisters,' Fiona added.

'Yeah…the ugly sisters,' Jason piped up.

'Hey Jase do you remember that time when she tried to—'

'Shut your face!' her brother retorted before everybody could be reminded yet again of the worst five minutes in his life so far…

Friday, May 9th
10am
Oli let me have a bit of a lie in this morning after last night. He treated us all so well, the food was gorgeous

and the wine. Absolutely gorgeous. Oli and Marc did it together, I told Marc he should look into doing catering for events, he certainly has a talent for it, should have got him to do the wedding! Just so long as him and Oli don't join forces: I'd miss him so much and so would Cuts 'n' Curls.

I've got a pedicure, manicure and I did have a spray tan booked this afternoon, but I cancelled it after chatting with David. I was worried I'd look orange next to him in the photies. Anyway, we've had a bit of warm weather and with the help from that body lotion with a hint of self tan I look ok. Sun-kissed David called it. Don't want us to look odd in the photies though do I? I've changed it to a back massage, to relax before tomorrow.

Oli's got a pedicure booked and a back massage. Gonna go for French polish on me hands and me feet cos I think that looks lovely in the summer. Oli said he was gonna have French polish on his feet an' all. Who's gonna see it? I don't know!!

I'm just gonna take it easy this morning, have a bit of brekkie, relax with the paper an' try and take me mind off everything.

Tucking into her plate of scrambled eggs on granary bread and mug of tea, Shirley mulled over the paper. Her mobile buzzed alerting her to a message. Shirley reluctantly looked at her phone, she was almost sure who it'd be. Mike again. Why wouldn't he just go home?

Please Shirl I'm beggin u let me talk to u again.

Knowing she had a couple of hours till her appointment in the salon Shirley hit the reply button and keyed: *Ok.*

Stomach churning, she finished off her breakfast and headed for the shower.

'Morning, babe.' Oli greeted her at the top of the landing. 'Off for a shower?'

'Yeah, listen, thought I'd go and get some petrol after, so we can go straight to the salon,' she lied.

'Oh, I don't mind getting off a bit earlier, we can do the petrol on the way.'

'To be honest I need a bit of air, gonna do it now, if you don't mind, hon',' she said, feeling guilty about lying to her best friend.

'Oh ok kid; you ok, yeah?'

'Yeah, fine,' she said, feeling even more guilty.

Feeling better after her shower, Shirley quickly made her way to meet Mike before she changed her mind again.

He stood waiting for her on a bench in the park. He looked lonely and sad sitting there with his hands on his knees. 'Hiya, thanks for coming Shirl.' He stood up nervously.

He had a desperate look in his eye that made Shirley's insides tug with sorrow. She hated the thought of hurting anyone, even him, despite all the heartache he'd put her through years ago. She knew how he must be feeling and it upset her.

'All right?' Shirley said sitting down on the bench.

'I'm so glad you came.'

'Look: I'm here to say goodbye, Mike,' Shirley ventured. 'I have to. This can't go on, all the messages an' that. I'm getting married tomorrow.'

'You can't, Shirl. Please, please just think about it, we got lost but we've found the way back, now.'

'You got lost! I stayed on the same road, Mike, I didn't go anywhere.'

'I know, I know... It was all my fault, I know that, but you me and the kids we can make it this time.'

'I'm getting married tomorrow Mike and that's all I want to say, except for goodbye,' Shirley told him and got up to walk away.

'Shirley, stop. I just want you to think about it. What if you're throwing away a chance to make all of us really happy, you, me and the kids. We were meant to be together, everyone said we were. Think about it, Shirley, please.'

Shirley looked at him and kissing him lightly on the cheek said, 'Goodbye, Mike. No more texts.'

Walking back to her car tears pricked in Shirley's eyes. He was right; everyone had said they were meant to be together. All Shirley had ever wanted was to be a proper family. She didn't want to get divorced, she'd wanted a happy settled family life. Maybe this was her second chance to keep her family together, the kids deserved to have their father in their lives. Was she denying her children the right to have a settled home life with their real mum and dad? Thoughts raced through her head. Should she give up David, who she had truly fallen in love with, for the sake of making it up to her children? They had never been without in all the years Shirley had brought them up alone, but they did have something missing from their lives. Did Shirley owe it to them, who she loved more than anything else in the world to give their father a second chance?

Shirley's mobile rang, she looked, it was Oli. She wiped the now streaming tears away from her eyes and cheeks, mascara smudged all over her face she sat in her car and tried to pull herself together.

'Hiya, babe, just wondering where you'd got to, we're gonna be late if you don't get back soon,' He said brightly.

'Sorry, Oli, I'm on my way,' she said trying her best to hide her sadness and the fact she had spent the last ten minutes crying like a baby.

'You ok?'

'Yeah, fine, just had a sneezing fit.'

'Well…get your arse back here soon as. Me feet are crying out for that pedicure.'

In the sanctuary of Pamper Plus Shirley felt the trauma of the day ease away with every stroke of her therapist's hands. The soothing oriental music helped the stress and strain on its way.

'A few knots in your neck madam,' the young therapist noted.

'Oh… Pre-wedding nerves…'

'Well, we'll sort that out for you…'

'I feel better already,' Shirley said, letting out a long deep breath.

'Are you and your friend joining up for your pedicures?'

'Oh yes I think so, that will be nice.'

After being allowed to rest and relax for a few minutes after the massage, Shirley slowly pulled herself up, put on the white fluffy robe and went to join Oli for the rest of their treatments.

'Hiya, babe, gorgeous wasn't it?' Oli sipped water slowly as he had been advised.

'Oh yeah… I feel a hundred times better.'

'Me too, didn't realise how knotty I was,' Oli said rolling his shoulders.

Shirley smiled and sat beside him, waiting patiently for her manicure.

'Oh I've decided to have a manicure as well now, babe. Natasha, my therapist, said lots of men have them. I'm not going for any coloured or French polish, though, just clear and the same on me toes.'

'Oh…my…God!' Shirley exclaimed under her breath.

'What? What's up?' Oli asked looking around.

'Hard Des…over there, having his hands done.'

'Oh, hell, yeah, so it is.'

'See, I told you other men have manicures,' Natasha, Oli's therapist, said catching the tail end of their conversation.

'Yeah, we just noticed,' Oli said.

'Told you. Des is here every week,' Natasha went on.

'Is he?' Oli asked, hoping for a bit more information.

'Yeah, he's been a regular of mine for a few months now,' Natasha admitted. 'He likes to look after himself.' She handed

Shirley a glass of water.

'Oh…does he have anything else done?' Shirley asked, much to Oli's surprise –it was usually Oli who tried to dig the dirt.

'He has a spray tan on a Friday every week, and he has a back, sack and crack once a month,' she whispered.

'Oh my God...' Oli winced.

'So he looks after himself and he had manicures…' Shirley raised her eyebrows.

'Is he married?' Oli pushed for more...

'Don't know, he's never said. Never mentioned a wife or girlfriend. Why, are you interested?' Natasha asked quietly. 'I can put a word in for you.'

'Eh? No, you're all right, I've got a partner,' Oli said, horrified at the thought. 'Anyway, he's old enough to be me dad.'

Natasha looked at Oli, then Shirley and pulled a face teasingly.

The duo enjoyed the rest of their treatments and as well as the manicure and pedicure they both opted for a facial to ensure a clear canvas to work on the following day.

'Oh, I feel great now, Shirl, how about you?' Oli said linking arms with her as they walked towards the car.

'I feel better than I did earlier.' She nearly confided in him, but thought about how much she'd just spent getting over the upset and though better of it.

'Why, what was up with you? You seemed ok at brekkie.'

'Oh just a bit jumpy that's all.'

'You've got an exciting time ahead of ya, babe. You're so lucky… David's a lovely fella. Not my type, but perfect for you, of course!'

'Do you think so?' Shirley stopped walking and looked at Oli straight in the eye.

'What, of course he is and so are you for him. You're gonna make a lovely family, all four…no, all six of you,' Oli promised.

'Don't you think the kids would prefer to live with their real dad?'

'Well not their *real* dad Shirl, course not, he's been a right waste of space hasn't he babe?' Oli said alarmed.

'Yeah, he was… But what if he's changed. What if I'm denying Fi and Jason the chance to get to know their dad?' Shirley protested.

'Well you're not are you? You're not stopping them getting to know their real dad are ya babe?'

'I hadn't thought of it like that,' Shirley muttered.

'Listen, Shirl, call it cold feet, pre-wedding nerves or whatever, but whatever it is *don't* listen to it. Don't let Mike ruin things for you, babe. He's done it once, don't let him do it again.'

Shirley wrapped her arms around her friend; he always seemed to know when to say the right things.

'Oh, Oli, I just wish Mike hadn't shown up, he's just made me think about things. Things I thought I'd forgotten about yonks ago, you know…' Shirley confided.

'Shirl, hon', David is the best thing that's happened to you…after me, of course,' Oli winked cheekily, always willing to lighten the atmosphere.

'Hey… Changing the subject completely, what about Hard Des, what do you make of that?'

'Aye, I know, we just can't seem to get to the bottom of it can we?' Oli groaned.

'Well, let's see… He likes to take care of himself, yet he seems a man's man when he's down the pub. I'm sure the fella's we've seen him with would really take the piss if they knew that he has regular manicures and fake tans.'

'We have to nail this one soon, babe. I didn't really want to tell you, in case it stressed you out, but we've had another two enquiries in.'

'Oh God have we?'

'Yeah. I haven't said yes yet, mind. I've told them we're really busy at the moment. Plus we really need to get Hard Des before we can take on anything else.'

'Oh, hell just keep them on hold till after the wedding and the party next week, maybe then we can really get going with Hard Des and take on some new clients,' Shirley suggested.

'Yeah I will babe, don't you be worrying, So, what're we doing tonight?'

'Well… Jason is with David.'

'See, he wants to be in his new house with his step dad,' Oli butted in.

Smiling, Shirley said, 'You're right, you know. So I thought you, me and Fi could have a little go at our hair? Like a dry run for tomorrow.'

'Ok, babe, I know what I'm doing for you, don't I, but I've had another idea for Fi's hair. Hey, and we'll get Marc to serve us a couple of glasses of wine wearing nothing but a little white apron while we're at it!' Oli giggled. 'It'll be just like on the tele…'

Shirley laughed. 'I can't wait.'

8pm

I've had a lovely bath and Oli's done me hair perfect. He put in some Velcro rollers and it's all full and bouncy. I've got it half up and half down with me tiara sitting in the middle. Looks bloody gorgeous, even if I say so meself.

He's working on Fi's now and, bless him, he's got Marc pouring the wine. Marc refused to be naked bar a little white apron, like Oli asked him to, but fair do's he's been waiting on us hand and foot. I'm only having two glasses, though, I want a clear head for the morning. The wedding's at two so I can have a bit of time in the morning to get sorted. Me mum and Auntie Dilys are coming over at 12.30 and are going from here. David family are going from our new place with Jason. I've had a text from David saying how much he loves me and how he's looking forward to tomorrow.

Haven't heard a thing from Mike, so hopefully that will be it, now. I can't bear to have to go through all that again. I hope he's on his way back to Scotland – for his sake as well as mine. He needs to go home and start afresh.

Anyway, Fi's just called me to look at another style Oli want's to try out on her, plus Marc is doing the top ups on the wine. So bye, bye diary I'm back off downstairs.

Cosy and comfy, in her soft cream dressing gown, Shirley sat on the sofa sipping her rose wine and watching Oli put the finishing touches to Fiona's hair.

'Oh Fi, that's gorgeous on you.'

Oli fluttered around squirting a bit of spray to hold it in place. Marc sat drinking beer out of a bottle while watching the football on the telly and Apple snoozed contentedly on his knee.

'I love it,' Fiona beamed, preening in the mirror.

'I'll do it like that in the morning then, kid, yeah.'

Fiona looked beautiful. Her hair was pulled up in a mass of bouncy curls, and topped with a tiara similar to Shirley's only smaller. She had done her own make-up very subtly and couldn't resist trying on her dress to gauge the complete look.

Shirley had sneakily tried her dress on again when she got back from the pamper session. She and Oli had picked up the dresses and suits on the way back. Shirley was keen to ensure the fit was right after the last minute alterations.

'You'd best get that dress off now, Fi, just in case. You don't want to spill wine on it,' Shirley warned.

Fiona went up to change, leaving Shirley, Oli and Marc in the living room. Safe in the knowledge that Marc was utterly engrossed in the football Oli asked, 'Any more messages?'

'No nothing. He must have got the message,' Shirley said well aware she hadn't been totally truthful with Oli. He was still unaware that she had met up with Mike that morning.

'He must be long gone now, babe, it's been a couple of days. Bet he's back to his old life in Scotland. You're well rid of him. Now finish off your drink 'cause you have to get an early night. I'm in charge tonight, remember.

10.30pm

I've been sent to bed like a little girl by Oli. Me and Fi both have. Thinks' he's our mum! Talking of which, me mum did phone tonight – just to see how everything was. She sounded full of it, said she'd had a hell of a time with Auntie Dilys being ill all week. She had a bit of a moan, saying she hadn't heard from me since the weekend. Asked if I'd moved country! I did tell I'd got other things on me mind...like planning me friggin' wedding and moving house!!

Anyway, she was ok by the end of the conversation. She was going on about what they're gonna have for dinner tomorrow. I told her we couldn't be making dinner before going to the ceremony. I told her to have a brunch type of brekkie like we were all gonna do, but she said she couldn't wait till 5 o'clock for the food, so she's bringing a packed lunch for her and Auntie Dilys. I tell ya I can't win; I'll just have to let her do as she pleases. She'd phoned David and Jason, too, just to put her oar in there an' all, obviously.

Well, I'm in bed now, with a nice cuppa. No more

texts from Mike, so I'm feeling relaxed – I think. Hope I can get some sleep. Fi's already flat out. Must be the wine!

ELEVEN

Can't believe I slept till now! Thought I'd be up half the night with nerves, but I've been out like a light till now. Must have been all that pampering and then the bath and hair here.

Fi's up and in the shower; she had to be organised so that Oli can make a start on her hair, get it out the way handy, cos he's only gone and promised to go over and do me mum and Auntie Dilys's hair this morning an' all. He's there now. He said he was gonna try and get there for half-eight. No sign of him here so he must have gone. He shouldn't take too long though, to be honest, we cut their hair already, so it's just a quick wash and blow dry they need. By the time he gets back Fi will be ready for him. Then once he's done Fi he can make a start on me. Bless him, doing all this hair; he needs to get ready an' all!

Shirley snuggled back under the duvet for another couple of minutes before finally getting up. She looked at her beautiful dress hanging up expectantly and smiled. She searched for her phone in her handbag hoping David may have sent her a message.

There were three messages in her inbox, the first from David.

Good morning my darling can't wait to c u. Won't be long and I can call u my wife.

She smiled happily.

Next Oli.

Just got here and the pair of them are already in their outfits and the butties are made to bring ova to ours!!

Shirley laughed, knowing exactly what Oli was going through just then.

The third from Mike.

It's still not too late Shirley please.

Shirley's stomach turned over and she deleted the message.

'Morning.'

She heard Fi's voice behind her.

'Oh, hiya, love you had your shower then?' Shirley asked nervously.

'Er, yeah, I think so,' Fiona answered gesturing to her towel clad body and shaking her head.

'Think I'll go next, Oli won't be long and he'll be back to get started on us so I need to get washed.' Shirley mumbled, still shaken up by the text from Mike.

Was he still here? Had he gone back? He'd told her he wouldn't go back till he'd seen her. Well she had been to see him, so did that still apply? Shirley wondered as she let the hot water and the aroma of coconut and honey envelop her body. She tried to push thoughts of Mike out of her mind as she washed but they kept racing back. She thought of David and how much she loved him. Was she making the right choice? Was she being selfish? Would it ever have worked out second time with Mike?

She got out of the shower and dried herself on one of Oli's big white fluffy towels – he insisted on supplying them with everything but the clothes they stood up in while they were staying. Slipping on her dressing gown she made her way downstairs to find Marc busy making brunch in the kitchen.

'I've been left strict instructions to make sure you eat a good brekkie.' Marc said putting down a full English breakfast in front of her.

'Ah…ta, Marc.' Shirley gave a half-hearted smile.

'So, you ready for the big day?' he asked, sitting down to join her.

'I don't know.' Shirley answered him honestly.

'Well David's ready Shirl…' Marc informed her. 'He's just texted me and said today is gonna be the best day of his life.'

'Has he?' Shirley asked surprised.' I didn't know you texted each other.'

'We swapped numbers a few weeks ago, so we could have a moan to each other about you two.' He winked. 'He's mad about you Shirl, and the kids love him,' Marc said noting her anxiety.

'Do they?'

'Jason told me that he knows it's not cool to like your soon to be step-dad, especially when he's your deputy head, but he thinks he's the best thing that's ever happened to you, hon'.'

'Did he?'

'Yeah, and Fi said she loves having a dad…' Marc added.

'But he's not her *real* dad is he? Wouldn't she prefer to have him?' Shirley asked sensing that perhaps Oli had told Marc a bit more than maybe he should have.

'Shirley,' Marc confided, 'I never knew *my* real dad properly, just saw him from time to time, nothing regular. Then me mum married Jed and he was me dad after that in every sense of the word. Jed looked after me, was there for me when I came out, never judged me, loved me for how and who I was and always showed how proud he was of me and that he wanted me as a son, not just because I came with me mum.'

'But what if I'm denying me kids that?' Shirley asked, tears in her eyes.

'If Mike wants to be their dad and be there for them, fine, don't stop it. He still can. But don't sacrifice your own happiness. Do you want to be with a man you don't love? Would Fi and Jase want that for you?'

Marc's words all of a sudden made sense. Shirley realised she wasn't in love with Mike anymore. Maybe he did deserve a second chance at being a dad, but he didn't deserve a second chance at being her husband. Shirley was in love with David, no one else, and nothing would stand in the way of that.

'Oli's a lucky fella,' Shirley said getting up to give Marc a hug.

'Hey! What's going on here, the minute me back's turned?' Oli asked catching her at it.

'Oli, you've found a good man, here babe. Hang onto him, he's brilliant,' Shirley grinned.

12.45pm

Well, I'm all ready, just waiting for the cars to start arriving. Me mum and Auntie Dilys are downstairs finishing off the butties they brought with them!! They brought a pack of mini pork pies and a pack of mini Scotch eggs an' all. Marc's been helping them polish it all off.

I feel nice and calm and relaxed now. I've just had a glass of champagne... Oli bought it for us to have a little tipple before we go. Auntie Dilys is after more but I've said only one glass each. I don't want them pissed before we get there.

Everyone looks a treat. We got Marc a suit like the

rest of the lads, so they're all the same in a morning suit. Oli looks fab in his blue suit and as for Apple, well... Maj did a fantastic job of the bow! My Fi looks like a princess and as for me, well, if I do say so meself, David is a lucky man.

Gonna really enjoy the day now, all me worries behind me; just gonna think about me, David and the kids.

'Mum… The car's here,' Fiona screeched excitedly up the stairs.

Shirley took a deep breath and carefully tackled the stairs.

'Careful, now, babe,' Oli cautioned her.

'I'm ok, I think,' Shirley smiled, lifting her dress as best she could.

'You look a million dollars, kid,' Oli said, when she finally arrived at the bottom of the stairs.

'You don't look so bad yourself.' She winked. 'So, we all set then?'

'Yeah. Your mum, Auntie Dilys, Marc and Apple have gone, it's just the three of us now in this car,' Oli explained.

'Ok, then, let's go.' Shirley took a deep breath, smiled and stepped out into the street and the three of them carefully attempted to get in the car without disturbing any of their carefully put together outfits.

'Oh this is lovely.' Oli said getting into the 1967 silver open top Alvis.

'Isn't it just?' Shirley was thrilled. She hadn't wanted a limo, too tacky for her wedding, and everyone had a Rolls Royce, she wanted something classy and a bit different.

'Hiya. Oh…thank God we haven't missed ya.' A familiar voice was heard breathlessly coming towards them.

'Susan!' Oli exclaimed. 'Aww, Shirley, look, and all the factory girls.'

'Sorry we're late, kids, we had to stop off twice on the way. Ali's got the wild shites again,' Susan explained.

'Aww, but you made it. Hope you're not too uncomfortable, Ali,' Shirley said looking at Oli and Fiona trying desperately not to laugh.

'Aye couldn't miss this, so I've taken a load of Diacalm,' Ali explained.

'Oh…lovely…well least you're ok now, eh, queen,' Oli pointed out.

'Well—.' Ali started, trying to give out more details.

'Ah looks who's here,' Oli interrupted, keen to avoid hearing all about Ali's toilet habits in Technicolor.

'Hiya, kids, don't you look a treat…Sapphire poked her head over the car taking it all in.

'Aww, you look lovely, Fi,' Shaz said, arriving equally late and with Mo in tow.

'It's lovely to see you all, but you're cutting it a bit fine aren't you?' Oli pointed out.

'But you're here, now. Thank you all so much for coming to see us off,' Shirley said genuinely.

'Hey, and next week it's party, party, party, eh?' Susan happily announced referring to the big do the following week.

'Oh, aye, yeah. I'm looking forward to that, hope there'll be some fit teachers at that do?' Mo looked at Shirley hopefully.

'Oh, yeah, there will. Lots of them are married though or with partners.'

'I'm not arsed about that; it's only for the night,' said Mo, matter of factly. The woman had no shame!

'Ta for the pressie,' Shirley said to Sapphire.

'Oh, did ya like it?' Sapphire smiled with no evident sense of embarrassment.

'Yeah, I wouldn't mind one of them. Where's it from?' Oli teased.

Feeling uncomfortable Shirley butted in, 'Hey, don't you think we should get going don't want to keep me fella waiting more than the traditional five minutes.'

'You give him a big smacker from me love, he's friggin' gorgeous that one. Can't believe I missed out there. If only he'd seen me in time, Shirl, it would have been me sitting in that car,' Mo said defiantly.

Oli looked at Shirley and winked. 'Aye well he'll just have to try and not dwell on what could have been won't he? I'm sure Shirley will help keep his mind off it, and good for you you've still got the pick of the rest.'

The engine revved slightly, the chauffeur indicating that time was pressing on.

'Well, thanks all of you for coming...' Shirley smiled.

As they pulled away from Oli's tidy semi- the three waved at their fans.

'I feel like a princess,' Fiona giggled.

'So do I.' Oli sniffled emotionally.

The journey to the church was delightful with warm still sunny weather and a careful driver so there were no worries about their hair becoming disarranged. When they arrived at the beautiful little church, Marc was waiting outside having a sly cigarette.

'Hey, where's Apple?' Oli asked him, concerned.

'Oh... Auntie Dilys has taken her under her wing, she's taken on full time babysitting.'

'Aww.' Oli was touched.

'Erm, can we get on with this.' Shirley's nerves were beginning to set in.

'Best get back in then. Oh, and Shirl, if it helps, David is shitting himself an' all,' Marc joshed.

Smiling determinedly, Shirley took a deep breath and made her way to meet Jason who was giving her away.

'Now, let's get organised...' Oli ordered the wedding party.

'Is he there up front?' Shirley nervously asked Marc. He just looked at her and pulled a face as if to say 'silly question'.

'Thanks.' Shirley smiled.

'Go and get Apple, babe,' Oli instructed Marc.

Oli ensured they were all sorted out: Jason next to Shirley, to walk her down the aisle, followed by Oli carrying Apple and Fiona next to him.

As Shirley and her proud son slowly walked down the aisle to the soft sound of Mendelssohn, she could see the love of her life looking at her. He'd turned around to watch her gracefully walk all the way towards him. She didn't take her eyes off him, either.

'You look absolutely gorgeous,' David whispered when she arrived next to him.

The wedding was a cosy family affair, the small group of guests sat comfortably in the homely church. Coordinating floral displays filled the building.

Confidently David said his vows while Shirley listened, a tear trickling down her face.

'Shirley, I love you with all that I have. I promise to love, cherish and adore you till the day I die,' he added after his formal declaration was over.

These extra words of love had the whole party in tears.

Smiling but a little wobbly Shirley spoke her vows.

'Thank you my darling for making me feel so loved and for making me the happiest woman alive.'

It was time for Oli to read his poem and he nervously made his way to the pulpit. He managed to get through it without choking and the congregation managed to hear it through Apples cries for her daddy.

Two hymns and a prayer later, Shirley emerged as Mrs Wilmore at last.

'I'm so happy...' she whispered to David in the middle of the photographs.

'Me too, Shirley, we were made for each other,' he said, kissing her softly, as their loved ones threw confetti all over them.

An hour later everyone had arrived at the country inn. David and Shirley in the open top Avis.

'Oh this is beautiful Shirley,' her mother said impressed with the surroundings.

Glad that she had managed to impress her mum, Shirley took a glass of champagne from the tray held out by the waitress and escorted her mum through to see the beautifully set dining room.

'Oh it's gorgeous, Shirley, and all these flowers are the same as in the church and the bouquets,' Auntie Dilys said, taking a sip of champagne. 'Any chance your mum and me can take some home?'

Shirley just smiled.

'Think I'm gonna have to put a nappy on her, now.' Oli said holding Apple stretched out in front of him so as not to spoil his suit. 'She's peeing all over the place. Still at least she didn't go during the service…'

'Aww, she's excited, bless her,' Auntie Dilys said stroking her new best friend.

'I didn't want to put a nappy on her for the ceremony, it would've spoiled her outfit but I think she needs it now, she's like a friggin' hosepipe!' He said still holding the wriggling pup in his outstretched arms.

'Well do it quick, we want some photies before the food,' Shirley instructed.

'I'll give yer a hand,' Auntie Dilys said taking Apple from Oli's arms.

'Aww, ta, queen.' Oli smiled, rubbing his hands together. 'Then we can relax and have another blub at what David has to say about his girl in the speeches.'

Everyone sat in the cosy dining room following a sumptuous meal; the speeches didn't fail to disappoint and the clan were all in a flood of tears. Jason set off an avalanche in his mum and his gran when he gave his.

'I'm not used to this kind of thing,' he said awkwardly, playing with his hair, 'but here goes. Mum: Fi and I got together to put this together and what we want to say first and foremost is thank you Mum, thank you for everything you've done for us. You've always been there for us, you've been our mum and our dad and we love you for it.'

There wasn't a dry eye in the house. Jason picking up confidence as they all made him feel at ease, told his audience funny tales of his mother over the years and added a couple of innocent dating disasters for effect.

'But in all seriousness, David, you've been the best thing to happen to Mum, well, since me and Fi, of course.' He smiled. 'And I wish you all the happiness for the future. The bride and groom everyone.'

With the speeches finished the wedding party carried on celebrating outside in the walled garden.

'Hey, everyone seems to be getting on...' Shirley smiled, looking over at the two mothers chatting away.

'Yeah, it's been lovely, just need to get shut of this lot and we can really start celebrating.' David grinned and took a sip of his drink.

'Well...you won't if you drink too much of that,' Oli warned eavesdropping on their conversation. 'Our bus is due in a bit, kids, so you can do what ever it is you're allowed to do now that you're Mr and Mrs...'

Twenty minutes later, Mr and Mrs David Wilmore waved off their newly joined families and happily started their new lives together as a married couple.

9pm

Oh my God, what a day, what a fantastic day. It was just perfect in every way and now I'm lying on me four poster bed, everyone's buggered off home and I'm waiting for me husband – yeah that's right me husband!! To come out of the bathroom so we can get on with our first night of married life. Anyway gonna call it a night now, I've got a bottle of champagne chilling by the bedside, it is me wedding night after all an' I do have other things in mind. And that's enough of that, there are some things I can't tell even me little pink diary...

Sunday, May 11th
12 midday

Still lying in bed after our gorgeous Bucks Fizz brekkie. God I've drunk loads of champagne recently. I'm getting quite used to it now. David's in the shower, me next, then we're gonna go down and have a bit of lunch here before we head off back to our new home.

Hearing the sound of the shower switching off, Shirley quickly packed her diary away in her handbag.

'That's better,' David said, emerging wearing nothing but a towel.

'Very nice,' Shirley smiled cheekily.

'Hey, you've worn me out! Get in the shower or that lovely big tub. I've worked up an appetite and need to recharge my batteries.' He slapped her gently on the behind as she slipped passed him.

Feeling refreshed and relaxed they both settled down to their lunch in the warm sunshine and enjoyed sharing a bottled of ice cold, crisp white wine.

'What time is Oli coming to pick us up?' David asked.

'I've had a text from him, he wants us to text him when we're ready,' Shirley said taking another sip of wine.

'We have to remember to take the rest of the cake home, don't we?' David reminded her.

'Oh yeah, I was thinking afterwards maybe we should have kept that cake for Saturday's party...'

'Oh yeah, we've got to go through all that again, haven't we?' David raised his eyebrows.

Shirley giggled. 'Shall I text Oli? I can't wait to get to our new home.'

'Me neither,' he admitted. 'This is great, but home's best, eh?'

6pm

Well I'm home in me beautiful, beautiful new home. I'm so made up I can't describe it. David and Jase have kept the place well tidy since they moved in and the kids didn't wreck the place last night, thank God. I've got a feeling Oli and Marc might have called in on the way to pick us up, just to give it the once over, like!

I've got an ensuite for the first time in me life. I can't get over it. I keep going in there just for a look. We've got four lovely big bedrooms, a massive kitchen that you can eat in, as well as an upstairs bathroom and a downstairs cloakroom!! It's just a bog and a basin, really, but cloakroom sounds so much better. Downstairs we've got a lovely through living/dining room and my favourite of all, the conservatory. It's massive, goes the whole length of the back of the house. We've got it set up so David can use half of it as a place to work. The other half has a lovely comfy sofa and we've got our music in there so I can lie on the sofa listening to relaxing music, reading a book and he can be busy at his desk working!! Just the way I like it.

We've still got some boxes to clear and the wedding pressies have taken over part of the spare, or should I say Josh and Ben's, bedroom. I haven't planned a heavy week this week so I can slowly plough through them and write the thank-you notes.

Even though I'm back in work tomorrow, I don't think anything will be able to keep this massive grin off me face. Everything has worked out just the way I wanted, even though I did have that hiccup with Mike. I'm so glad I spoke to Marc about it. He's a wise one that one. I know he's lucky to have someone as fantastic as Oli, but I have to say Oli's damn lucky too.

It's only the four of us here now. Just me, David, Fi and Jason. Just my little family and it feels good. I've even got a roast on the go. David had been to do a food shop after work on Friday so we've got everything in. He's so organised. We can sit down together, enjoy our meal and get used to being a four and not a three. This is our first meal in our new house as a family, so I want it to be nice. Luckily a roast is one of my specialities so I know I'm gonna do a good job on it.

Anyway, best go and check the meat and spend some quality time with me husband!!

Unable to stop smiling Shirley went to finish off preparing the dinner and an hour later the four were sitting down enjoying the fruits of her labour.

'Shirley, go and put your feet up hon', me and the kids will clear up,' David ordered.

'Ok, let's start as we mean to go on...' Shirley smiled at the shocked looking Jason and Fiona.

'She's got you well trained,' Jason complained.

'That's what she thinks...' David winked at Shirley. 'Only joking, love, she deserves looking after, after all she's looked after you two hasn't she? That's what you were saying yesterday...'

Shirley happy and content settled down on her brand new sofa and smiled with pleasure. Life was definitely looking up!

TWELVE

<u>Monday, May 12th</u>
<u>10am</u>

Well me honeymoon's over...well, sort of. I'm still on honeymoon in me head and I can't see that changing for at least thirty years!! I am back to work though and so is David. He took the kids to school today, I'm not sure how any of them felt about it, to be honest, but the three of them set off together anyway. I even made David his butties. Ham and a bit of salad. He said I didn't have to, cos he's so used to doing his own, but I wanted to. Not sure how long it will last, I mean I can see that novelty wearing off, but I'll have a go at it for now, see how long I can last – when do they break up for the summer hols?? Only kidding. I'll try and do it longer than that.

I'd best make tracks to pick up Oli. We've got a late start today, but we're pretty packed up till four. Want to make sure I'm home for when me new husband arrives in from work, so I decided we'd pack up early. Gonna make sure I'm home when he gets back all this

268

week. Finishing with a half-day Friday though, cos I want to pop into town to make sure everything is ok in the hotel for the party on Saturday.

The day passed in a haze of cuts, sets and blow dries. Everyone gave their congratulations and was eager to see the pictures Oli and Marc had taken and already printed off and put in an album. Most of the time was taken up with Oli giving a running commentary on the day.

By half-past three Shirley was itching to finish off her final client for the day so that she could rush home to prepare tea for her family.

'So, what's on the menu tonight then?' Oli smiled.

'Pizza, salad, garlic bread and potato wedges.'

'Hey that Gordon Ramsey must be quaking in his boots, knowing you're giving cooking a good go.'

'Well it's quick and easy. I have been working all day an' all.'

Oli nudged her in the ribs and grinned: 'Come head, babe, let's gerroff then.'

After dropping Oli off (he'd insisted she call in just to say hi to Apple, who he swore was missing Shirley) she arrived back to a wonderful aroma of home-cooked food. Opening the oven door the welcome sight of dinner awaited her and she smiled happily realising David must have put something in the oven and set the timer as she lay happily in bed with a morning cuppa.

'Mmm, what's that lovely smell?' Fi said, the first to arrive in through the door, quickly followed by Jason and finally David.

'Nice one...' Jason added.

'Oh, Shirley, you have been busy.' David winked at her.

Smiling, Shirley gave her husband a welcome home kiss. 'Thank you,' she whispered.

'You've been busy too, hon'. I don't expect you to do everything.'

8pm

Just texted Oli and told him about me tea. He thinks I'm a jammy cow to land on me feet with such a fit and wonderful fella. I told him that I don't expect it every night, me and Daivd, though, we can both do it. I don't want to take advantage of him, bless him.

Oli was asking about Hard Des again. I don't know where to go with this one. I've been thinking we may have to tell Jan that we've come to a standstill. Don't know what else we can do and we can't move on with new stuff can we? Think we'll have to put a deadline on it and if we don't come up with the goods then think we may have to call it a day.

Me mum phoned asking if I'll give her and me Auntie Dilys a lift on Wednesday night; they wanna go and see some show that the Over-sixties have recommended to them. I don't mind.

Had a good day, today, in work. Oli was proud as punch showing everyone all the photies, bless him, he'd got them in a lovely wedding album.

Everyone seemed surprised to see me back in work, they thought Oli would be doing it all on his own an' that I'd be away on honeymoon. I would have loved a honeymoon I really would. But we both agreed that we've spent so much on the new house and the wedding, which cost a bomb between the actual wedding and the party on Saturday, a honeymoon was really out of the question. Least we had a night to ourselves the night of the wedding. That was lovely, really romantic.

Anyway, think I'll go and pamper David a bit now, make him a nice cuppa and go and have a cuddle with him on the sofa.

'Shirl… I could do with nipping into town at lunch time, is that ok, babe?' Oli asked as he tried to comb Sapphire's hair.

'Aye, ok,' Shirley said, struggling equally as much with Beanie's hair.

'Oh, what you after love?' Sapphire was as nosy as ever.

'Mind yours…' Oli said, tugging away at the matted locks.

Sapphire had asked if Oli and Shirley would be willing to do her ladies' hair as they were impressed with their skills.

Shirley peeked over Beanie's shoulder as she continued to tap away on the laptop whilst having her hair done. She was describing to some poor unsuspecting man what she was wearing and how she was desperate for him, stopping only to feed her face from the packet of smokey bacon crisps on the side.

'So, you enjoying this work, Beanie, love?' Shirley asked, eyes on stalks as she read the messages.

'Well…it pays the bills, eh, kid?'

'What do ya do with yerself then, apart from studying?' Shirley said cutting away at the matted hair, which she had initially thought was dreadlocks.

'Well, I've got me mum and dad to look after haven't I? Mind you they look after me!' She laughed. 'I go out an' all, ya know, to the student union, when it's a pound a pint that is.'

'Oh, an' what do they make of you, you being a mature student an' all?' Oli asked.

'Oh, they see Beanie as a bit of an agony aunt, don't they, queen?' Sapphire piped in. 'Now let her gerron with her work, the more she works the more she earns and the more pound a pints she can have!'

'So, are we doing you all?' Oli asked, looking round at Jane, Pauline, and Christine who were all busy describing in minute detail what they wanted to do to their amorous admirers.

'If you don't mind, kids. Hey, I should take a bit of commission off ya, getting ya some new clients.' Sapphire said seriously.

'On ya bike,' Oli scolded.

'I wouldn't mind a bit of a blow dry if you've got the time. I've got a meeting with the Mother's Union tonight. We've got a talk on how we can help our local community,' Pauline the vicar's wife asked politely.

'I think ya doing a pretty good job of that already,' Oli giggled.

Tittering, Pauline put down her lap top and went to sit at the table ready for Oli to work his magic.

'Not for me ta – unless it's free.' Jane the forty-something mum of six looked over the top of her laptop.

'Sorry, babe, we've gorra business to run,' Oli answered.

'I could give you a few packs of panty pads, or some tins of beans and sausage in exchange...'

'Nah,' Shirley and Oli answered at the same time.

Shirley and Oli looked at each other and then at Sapphire, who answered the question that was on both their minds. 'Her brother works nights in the cash and carry, get's her whatever specials he can and she uses them instead of cash. I've got enough bleach and bog rolls to last me till Christmas instead of two months rent here for her.'

Shirley and Oli exchanged their special look again.

'I'll pay for your hair if you want, Jane, and I'll take the beans and sausage. What flow are the panty pads, love? I mean, would they do for me instead of me usual pads, you know for the odd leak I get, only when I laugh and cough like...' Christine the retired grandmother said brazenly, eyes peeping over the top of the glasses that were perched on the end of her nose.

'Oh will ya, queen? Ta. The pads are night time ones, so they'd do ya. They've got wings an all.'

'Ok, love. Do Jane as well, will you. I'll give Ted the beans and sausage for his tea. They play havoc with him. He'll be up and down all evening, tonight, bloody great it'll be, I can watch Frost in peace.' Christine smiled contentedly. 'You could do me a blow dry if you've time, kids. It could do with it,' she added both hands patting her hair.

'Hey, it's getting like Henshaw's mark two,' Shirley commented as they got back in the car.

'I thought that. Can we nip into town now?' Oli asked putting his seat belt on.

'Yeah, but what's the hurry?' Shirley asked.

'Oh, I've ordered Marc a bracelet and it's gonna be ready today, lunchtime, engraved an' all.'

'Oh very nice, he's a lucky one, it's not Christmas and I haven't missed his birthday have I?'

'Oh no, no, just that we've been together four months today, so I'm making us a nice meal and we're gonna celebrate.'

'Four months…that long? It doesn't feel like it.'

I know, well it hasn't been serious for four months, but it was four months ago today that I first clapped eyes on him.' Oli smiled at the memory.

Shirley parked up in the short stay car park and followed the overly excited Oli to the jewellers.

'Hey, after we've been there, I need to go and get mascara.'

'Aye, ok.'

They spent a good ten minutes admiring the silver linked bracelet with a small silver love heart engraved with the words 'with love Oli xx.' Then it was Oli's turn to follow Shirley into the department store's beauty department.

Picking up her usual mascara, Shirley made her way to the till to pay for it.

'Hey, isn't that Hard Des?' Shirley asked, noting a man remarkably like Hard Des browsing in the lingerie department.

'Oh my God, yeah, it is, babe. Come on, let's follow him.'

The pair followed Hard Des around the lingerie department

and noted him picking up and purchasing a black lacy nighty and what looked like black fishnet stockings.

'Well, that's pretty suspect.' Oli said. 'They're not exactly going to be for him are they?'

'Too right it is. But it's still not proof. Text Jan and ask her if Hard Des has ever bought her any sexy underwear,' Shirley instructed.

'Ok, kid; it is a bit tactless isn't it though?' Oli said, feeling a bit uneasy.

'Well, babe, we're desperate now, at least she'll know we're working on it. Get on with it, babe. See if you can get a photo as well.'

Oli frantically texted Jan, unsure whether he was doing the right thing.

Oli's mobile alerted them to a new message.

'Jan,' Oli said grimly. 'No. Never.'

Wednesday, May 14th
5pm

Well, I'm about halfway through me week first week as a (re)married woman. I know it's been a work week, but it definitely hasn't been all work and no play!! I'm so happy being married, still on me honeymoon, really, even in work.

Oli and I called into the hotel when we were in town, just to make sure everything is ok for the party on Saturday night and they're on the ball. It's great, we don't have to do a thing. They've got it all covered. All we have to do is turn up!! A few are staying in the hotel; we got a special discount on the rooms. David's family, of course, are staying, even me mum and Auntie Dilys have decided to stay over. The factory girls have got a minibus booked – that's a blessing, cos I know what they're like over brekkie. I don't really want to put David through all that!! We've got the honeymoon suite and the kids are all a long way off on another corridor!! I know we haven't had an away honeymoon but we will have had two nights in lovely hotels, which is a bit of a luxury.

Promised to take me mum tonight, to this Over-sixties show, and I've been hoodwinked into watching the friggin' thing!! She said she didn't think it would be on long and it'd save me having to go out again to pick them up. She thought Fi and I would like it so got us both tickets, like she was doing us a great big favour! Apparently, Auntie Dilys said that she thought Oli would like it, too, so Betty Smith – this old crow who lives near them, her granddaughters in it – is gonna keep a ticket on the door for Oli!

I'm starting me pick ups at half six, so I'd better get on with it.

'Hurry up, will ya!' Shirley called up the stairs to Fiona.

'You off, then?' David asked giving Shirley a kiss on the lips.

'Yeah, for my riveting evening with Hinge and Bracket.'

'You'll have fun, you've got Oli and Fi with you…' David smiled.

'Mmm,' Shirley muttered, unconvinced.

'Well, you two have fun, we've got a nice evening in planned, a few beers and a DVD, a bit of male bonding…' Jason joked.

'Well, think of us,' Fiona said grimly.

Nearing the community hall where the performance was to be held, Oli excitedly asked, 'So what we watching then?'

'Oh it's fantastic apparently.' Auntie Dilys announced.

'Oh, brilliant, by all accounts. Betty Smith's granddaughter said they've been sold out, you're lucky to get a seat, Oli. Tonight it opens...'

'What's it called, Nanna?' Fiona asked.

'*Hairspray*,' came the response.

'*Hairspray*? Oh my God, I love that one, it's one of me favourites,' Oli announced excitedly.

'Oh, I love that one an' all; I've got the DVD.' Fiona was equally excited.

Taking their seats they waited for the performance to start, all agog except Shirley, who wished she was sitting at home with David snuggled up on the sofa watching crap TV and drinking cold wine.

The village hall was packed for the amateur dramatics performance and the room darkened and the opening number began. Given it was an amateur show everyone seemed to enjoy it and Shirley settled into her seat to enjoy the rest of the show.

It was the turn for the main character Edna Turnblad to come on stage: it was obviously a man dressed as a woman, just like in the movies, and they watched him sing and dance in full make-up. He had an astonishing voice. He was amazing and his dancing was fantastic.

'I dunno what, Shirl, but that Edna looks like Hard Des...' Oli giggled.

Shirley looked and said laughing, 'I know I thought that. He does, a bit.'

'He's good, isn't he?' Oli whispered.

'Yeah, he is.' Shirley said studying the happenings on stage as Edna Turnlad danced around in a black frilly nightdress.

Shirley looked at Oli who was singing and clapping away with the music. 'It *is* friggin' Hard Des!' she said, digging him in the side.

Oli looked again, and then he looked back at Shirley.

'Look at the nightie an' all,' Shirley insisted.

'Oh…my…God,' Oli whispered.

There were complaints from behind and lots of ' Shhhhhhhh' type noises.

Oli turned round and looked at the row behind apologetically.

Shirley's mother looked at the pair and shook her head.

'Mum, Mum…' Shirley said, trying to get her mother's attention and failing, she had to wait till the interval to ask her question.

'Hey, do you know who the lead is, Mum?'

'Oh, isn't she brilliant!' Auntie Dilys butted in. 'And it's all a secret.'

'A secret, what d'ya mean queen?' Oli asked.

'Well he's so shy, that man playing Edna, that according to Betty Smith he hasn't told anyone that he's in the show, they can't even put his name on the programme, well his real name anyway. He doesn't want anyone to know he's into this kind of thing or they'll take the mickey, shame…'

'Oh, so he hasn't got his family here, then?' Shirley asked looking round.

'What's it to you, though?'

'Oh, nothing, just that he's good that's all.' Shirley tried desperately to cover up her real reason for asking.

'So, what do you reckon, babe?' Oli asked when he had a moment alone with Shirley pretending to choose an interval ice-cream.

'Well it makes sense: the manicures and all the treatments in the salon, the keeping fit an' working out. He has to do a hell of a lot of dancing, an' all the practising he must have had to do must have been where he was disappearing to when Jan couldn't find him.'

'And that nightie, we saw him buy it an' now he's wearing it.'

'And the fact he wasn't interested in anyone else. Dy'a remember when we were in the pub and one of the girls tried it on with him.

He was horrified.'

'Well that's not evidence as such,' Oli winked. 'But I know what you mean.'

'So he isn't having an affair, after, old Hard Des,' Shirley said flatly.

'Doesn't seem like it; an' all this time we've been calling him Hard Des, we should have been calling him Dancing Queen.' Oli giggled fit to bust at his own joke.

'Well… Take a few pics with your phone, babe, in the second half, then we can show them to Jan and she can put her mind at rest.'

'Aye, ok, I'll take them to show her tomorrow. Aww, this one has a happy ending in the end then doesn't it. I like it when that happens.' Oli smiled, he was real softie at heart.

'Yeah…it's not all people doing the dirty is it?'

'Hey, and once we've done that we can move onto the next one,' Oli said, excitedly.

'Oh friggin' hell, Oli, at least let me have the weekend off for me wedding party.'

'Ok, hey how about this one, save us giving Jan all the pics, why don't we buy her a ticket for the show. Not tell her, like, that he's in it, just give her a ticket in an envelope and she can see for herself.'

'Oh that's a brilliant idea. Just write on it "all you need to know will be here".' Shirley was impressed with her mate's idea. 'It will all make sense when she sees for herself, and it's a bit more personal.'

'And when she sees how friggin' good he is, she can encourage him, support him an' all that,' Oli added, generously.

<u>Thursday, May 15th</u>
<u>9am</u>
Last day at work before the party. We've got the factory girls today instead of tomorrow. I've got a bit of a pamper tomoz, well, just me nails doing again and getting everything together for the big party on Saturday.

Best get me skates on, I'm running late to pick up Oli.

'Oh my God, thank God you're here, me hair's desperate,' Kelly complained running her fingers through her already perfect hair.

'Oh yeah, you look like a bag of shite,' Oli teased.

'So what's the latest here then, how come Comb-over's not in today?' Shirley asked, setting out her equipment.

'Well, you won't believe it; he's probably on his way to the nick,' Susan announced.

'What?' Shirley and Oli exclaimed together.

'Well, he phoned me at home late last night an' asked me to sort everything out here, that he'd be off today and maybe tomorrow,' Gail explained.

'I had a text this morning from me sister saying she'd heard in the pub that Comb-over's house was raided by Customs and Excise,' Susan blurted out.

'What? He's not a drug dealer is he?' Oli asked alarmed.

'No, nothing like that. Worse...' Kelly insisted.

'What the hell's he done now, then?' Shirley asked, eagerly.

'Well, you know all them girls he had here, he only had thirty five of them cooped up in his house, like sex slaves they were...' Susan said.

'Never...?' Oli said, agog.

279

'Well that's what's going around our estate, some say thirty-five. Lou from the chippy, I saw her this morning, said she'd heard it was fifty of them.'

'Friggin' hell, right little Hugh Heffner isn't he?' Oli said genuinely shocked.

'So what did he say to you, Gail?' Shirley asked. 'Did he tell you what the real story was?'

'Nah, he just said he knew he could trust me to run this place and that he wouldn't be in till tomorrow or maybe even Monday. To be honest, he did sound a bit cagey. I couldn't understand him properly, he was sort of whispering.'

'Well you never know about people, do ya?' Ali piped up.

'That's true enough, queen, who'd know that you were a style icon to all those celebs out there...' Oli said winking at the others.

'So, anyone heard from Angie?' Shirley asked. 'Is she coming to me party?'

'Well, she said she is. She texted me the other day to say she was looking forward to catching up with everyone. Don't hold ya breath, though, Shirl I can't see her making the effort to get all the way here from Iceland,' Susan said grimly.

'Aww, I hope she does, I'd love to see her.'

'And she's still with Barry?' Oli asked.

'Don't know... I didn't ask her that,' Susan muttered.

'Maybe she's making a go of it out there. Good luck to her I say.' Shirley set about brushing Kelly's immaculate hair.

Susan pulled a face of disgust.

'Yeah, you're right, Shirl. We should be happy for her,' Kelly agreed.

'Mmmm,' Susan said, dipping her biscuit into her mug of tea. 'Let's wait and see, eh?'

<u>6pm</u>

We called in to see Jan on our way home from work. Oli gave her the envelope with the ticket in it. She did look a bit confused. She thinks that he's taking someone to see the show and she's gonna catch him out herself an' she thinks we're too busy to go cos of the wedding party. Anyway, she's paid us and she's gonna go tonight. She said she's up for a show down with him!! She'll get a show all right. Hard Des has told her he is busy now every evening starting an intensive computer course in the local college and he said he has a few extra shifts at work an' all. She isn't half going to be surprised when she sees what he's really up to!

I do feel a bit tight that we haven't told her the truth yet, but I think seeing for herself and seeing how great he is will make it all the more dramatic. I'm dead chuffed this one has worked out well. We have to deal with all the cheaters, and it's nice when it all works out well in the end for once.

We haven't heard any more on the Comb-over front. Oli reckons it's all true, but come on...up to fifty women kept in the house, and as sex slaves? Surely he hasn't even got it in him... Jeanette was dead quiet when the girls were going on about it. Well, Jeanette had a bit of a fling with old Comb-over the other year, so she probably feels a bit embarrassed. None of the factory girls know, like, just me and Oli.

I think Susan must be missing Angie loads the way she's so mean about her. I think it's a front and really she misses her like hell, it's just a very big front.

Hope Angie comes for the party cos it would be great to see her. Good luck to her if she has decided

281

to make a go of it and grab herself a new life in Iceland with Barry. She's got guts I'll give her that.

It's my turn to make the tea, tonight. Well not so much turn but I'm gonna make a start on it. Pasta in a tomato sauce, bit of garlic bread now that can't be too hard!! I hope...

<u>Friday, May 16th</u>
<u>10am</u>
I thought pasta was meant to be foolproof. The friggin' lot stuck to the bottom of the pan. I blame Oli, he was on the phone talking to me for ages. I forgot all about the pasta till the smoke alarm went ringing all over the house. We ended up with beans on toast. David said it was just what he wanted, so thank God for that.

Got me nails booked for eleven, then I'm home for the rest of the day. I'll just call in me mum's an' make sure she's ok for tomorrow then just sit back and wait for the party to begin.

Shirley sat back and relaxed in the salon's comfy arm chair following her manicure.

'Mmm, it's lovely isn't it? I could get used to this, babe. Every week, how about it?' Oli said equally relaxed.

'Make the most of it, babe, it's back to work next Friday for the full day. We've had the last couple off.'

'Well, seeing as you said that, I'll have another few minutes.' Oli closed his eyes and snuggled back into the comfort of the soft leather chair.

The newly relaxed couple hampered their chances of remaining relaxed when they called in at Shirley's mother's house.

282

'I could do without this now, really, but I suppose we have to,' Shirley sighed, pulling up outside.

'Ah, come head. Let's see what the old dear's been up to.'

'Oh hello stranger,' Shirley's mother said, greeting her daughter.

'Hiya, Mum.' Shirley looked knowingly at Oli.

'Hardly seen her meself, she's been busy this week; first week as Mrs Wilmore an' all,' Oli said trying to stick up for his pal.

'I suppose…' Shirley's mother said grimly. 'But you have got a phone in that posh new house of yours I take it.'

'I took you to the show this week,' Shirley reminded her.

'Ah yes, so you did. I forgot about that. You pair did talk through most of it, though, didn't you?'

'Anyway… Do you want me to give you a quick wash and a blow for tomorrow?' Oli asked, trying to change her mood.

'Oh will you, Oli, love, ta very much.' She started making an attempt to brush her hair through.

'Well, we can't have David's mum outdoing ya, can we, queen?' Oli said, succeeding in his efforts.

'And Shirl can put some nail varnish on ya, while I'm blow drying your hair.'

Back in the car half an hour later, Oli's mobile starting ringing: 'Gail.'

'Hiya, babe. Everything ok?' he asked, pulling a face at Shirley at the same time. 'Oh my God, no…never…no…oh my God…no, no, no!'

'What's going on? Tell me!' Shirley was desperate to know what Gail was saying. It was maddening only hearing Oli's half of the conversation.

'Shh! Oh my God, no, no, no!' Oli went on.

Shirley tried to grab his phone from him. But he pulled it back.

'Ok, kid, yeah. I'll tell Shirl. I can't believe it, babe. Ok kid, thanks for letting us know. See ya tomorrow, kid.' Oli shook his head as he finally got off the phone.

'Oh my God…' he started.

'Yeah, yeah, I got all that. Now what the friggin' hell's going on?'

'Well… when the girls turned up at the factory today, the police were there.' Oli said.

'Oh my God! Why?' Shirley asked.

'Shh…and I'll tell ya... They said the factory was being searched and would remain closed for the foreseeable future.'

'No…why?'

'Shh, will ya? Well, you know this sex slave thing they were going on about? Well it's not that. Apparently Gail got chatting to one of the coppers and Comb-over's being held for bringing in illegal immigrants. He's in the nick.'

'Never? Oh my God!' Shirley exclaimed. 'What about their jobs?'

'Apparently he had started a side line, getting illegal women over, an' getting them to work for people as cheap labour. He would test them out in his place, in the factory and at home, and then advertise them. He'd gorra website an' everything. Apparently, it was a big operation. There were three businessmen involved. It was like a ring of them.'

Shirley couldn't believe her ears. This was more shocking than Hard Des up in lights in ladies' tights.

'Gail reckons he was getting a bit more than labour out of some of them, but they can't prove that. He'll probably go down, you know, that's what the copper said.' Oli savoured the last titbit of information.

'Ooh the poor girls, are they upset?' Shirley asked concerned for their friends' jobs.

'Well they were all going en masse to the Citizen's Advice today to sort out their rights,' Oli explained.

'So, he was getting all these illegal workers in with two other businessmen and they were advertising them on a website, and it was all cheap labour. Oh my God! What's happened to all the women?

'Oh, they'll all have to be deported.'

'I can't believe it. How did they think they could get away with it?'

'Anyway, come head, let's gerroff home,' Oli instructed. 'We've got lots to do.'

Saturday, May 17th
5pm

Finally got rid of David's mum, dad, brother and his family. They've made their way to the hotel. Pile of them landed here on dinner. David got a text from his brother to say they were on their way. We weren't expecting them till later, thought we were just gonna see them at the hotel. Anyway, we managed to go to the shop and get a few things for dinner. Ended up doing a BBQ, it's been such a lovely day.

Josh and Ben have been here since last night it's like home from home for them two: nice, they have completely taken over the bedroom, so it looks like they will be here every other weekend, if not every, which is great, plus it means no room for me mum and Auntie Dilys!!

Me mum would be most put out if she knew that they were all over for a barbie but what else could I do? I had to feed them. I do want to make a good impression.

The kids cleared up while we all sat and had a glass or two of rosé; his mum and sister-in-law went away from here more than a bit merry. They said they were gonna have a bit of a lie down in the hotel before the party.

Anyway, Oli's gonna call into our room before the party just to do me hair again. We're all wearing our wedding day stuff so everyone else can see. Even Apple is dressing up in her wedding day bow!! He's been trying to talk to me for a couple of days about our next job but I just wanna have a rest from it all now, at least over the weekend. I've told him not to go on about it for now. In a nice way, of course.

Best get me skates on, I wanna be in the hotel by six to start getting ready. The guests are due to arrive at eight!! Hope the factory girls will be in the mood for partying after the Comb-over saga.

The reception room was more than Shirley could have hoped for. It was decorated in the colours of her and Fiona and Oli's outfits and balloons and flowers and ribbons filled the room. They had a second fantastic five-tier wedding cake proudly sitting in the middle of the mouth watering buffet.

'Hey, there's a cake...' Shirley pointed out to David as they inspected the set up.

'Well, I thought you wanted one and they said to leave it to them,' David said kissing her gently.

'Aww, I'm made up this all looks really beautiful.' Shirley was overwhelmed.

'Hey, they've gone to town here, eh? What will the factory girls think of this lot?' Oli asked, impressed.

There were fresh flowers dotted on every table in keeping with the colour scheme of the room. Bottles of red wine and wine coolers awaiting bottles of white wine joined the floral display.

'Oh, I love it, it looks beautiful,' Shirley beamed.

Noticing people start to arrive, Shirley said, 'Hey, come on David, we'd best go and greet our guests.'

'Oh, aye, off ya go, Posh and Becks, your guests need greeting.'
Oli teased. 'And seeing as me and Apple are part of your entourage,
we'd best come with ya, an' all.'

'Hiya, babe…' Shirley turned to see the familiar face of Angie,
looking all happy and refreshed, the best she had ever seen her.

'Angie!' Shirley screamed. 'Oh my God, you look fantastic.'

'I feel it.' Angie beamed.

'And Barry…' Shirley added, noting thankfully that Barry had
joined them dressed as Barry and not a Viking.

'Hiya, love, and congratulations,' Barry said giving Shirley a
hug. 'You look a million dollars.'

'Oh, I'm so glad you came,' Shirley told Angie.

'We wouldn't have missed it for the world,' Angie said, hugging
Oli, too.

'So…are ya back for good? Hey, have you heard the news about
Comb-over?' Oli asked.

Oh my God, yeah. I called in to Susan's earlier today. They were
all there, they'd had a special meeting with the Citizens Advice.'

'Oh, an' how did they get on? Oli asked with concern.

'Here they come, they can tell ya.'

'Hiya, kids. Oh my God, you made it,' Susan turned to Angie.

'Well, I told ya I would,' Angie smiled and started giving all the
factory girls a hug.

'Doesn't she look well?' Oli said.

When Angie approached her old pal Susan for a hug, Susan
grabbed hold of her really tightly, reluctant to let her go.

Oli looked at Shirley and they both smiled, knowing how much
they had both missed each other.

'Hey, come on, Angie said you lot went to the Citizen's Advice.
Well?' Oli asked.

'Well, it may take a little while…' Susan started to explain.

'And we can claim benefits till it's all sorted, by the way,' Ali
piped in.

'Yeah, we can,' Gail confirmed.

'So, what they said was, is there's nothing stopping us from taking over the factory ourselves, you know, if Comb-over goes down,' Susan informed them.

'And it's highly likely he will. Did you see it on the news?' Kelly asked.

'Oh God no, we haven't had time to watch telly, today.'

'Well, you've had more important things to do, Shirley.' Barry laughed.

'So you're thinking of taking it over?' Oli said.

'Well, yeah, I mean it's a great little business and it's busy, it'd be a great opportunity for us. If we all put in have equal shares...' Gail explained.

'How about you two, any thoughts?' Susan looked hopefully to Angie and Barry.

'Well, it's all a bit sudden, we'd need more time but we're keen to think about it...' Angie laughed.

'Oh my God, that's great.' Susan gave Angie a big hug.

'Aww, all back together again.' Kelly grinned.

'Well, I'm so chuffed for you lot. I hope it all goes well,' Shirley said genuinely.

'Come head, then, girls let's find a spot and ya can fill me in on all the latest goss,' Angie suggested to the rest of the girls.

Back together again, the factory girls and honorary member Barry settled them selves on a table close to the buffet ready for a night of chatting, eating, boozing and boogieing.

'Aww, I'm so chuffed Angie made it,' Shirley said to Oli.

'My God, can you imagine the factory with that lot in charge!' Oli exclaimed.

'It'll be a riot.' Shirley laughed.

Next to be greeted were Mo, Shaz and Digo.

'Hiya, babe.' Mo was dressed in a tight, black, satin-effect mini skirt, red low cut top and black patent, five inch wedge sandals.

She had enough jewellery on to sink the Titanic.

'You lot look great,' Shaz said. She was wearing slightly more than her mother, but only just.

'Well, you're a jammy cow Shirley Cartwright and no mistake...' Mo said, slightly miffed.

'Shirley Wilmore...' Oli corrected.

'That's why she's a jammy cow; you were lucky kid, in the right place at the right time...' Mo went on.

'And to think it could have been me.' She looked around the room shaking her head, before sailing off towards the opened bottles of wine on the table next to the factory girls.

Shaz and Digo followed her, Shaz trying not to fall over as she negotiated the slippery dance floor between her and the table her mother was heading for.

Next to arrive were Shirley's mother and Auntie Dilys, who had to endure the trauma of the taxi driver arriving late then under the instruction to put his foot down from Auntie Dilys he had according to them 'nearly killed them' on route.

'Order a couple of brandies for your nanna and Auntie Dilys,' David instructed Jason. 'Sounds like they need them.'

'As we've had such a shock you'd better make them doubles,' Auntie Dilys insisted, following Jason to the bar.

Sapphire arrived next, larger than life. 'Oh you haven't got your pressies out on show?'

'Are you mad, with this lot? They'd wanna keep them,' Oli said, horrified at the thought.

'Aye, I suppose,' she replied looking over at the factory girls. 'Shame though.' Sapphire headed off towards Mo, who was easily halfway through a bottle of red wine.

'Cheek, she'd be the biggest culprit...' Oli objected.

The rest of the guests continued to arrive and Shirley began to feel a bit like a robot repeating the same few sentences over and over again.

'Here's the Head,' David announced noticing his boss John arrive.

'Aww, and where's your lovely wife?' Shirley asked, fingers crossed.

'Here I am, sorry, just had to pop to the ladies...' The lovely Angela smiled smugly at Shirley.

Hugging Shirley and David and thanking them for their invite they left and found a table and joined Sally the other deputy head teacher and her husband Andy but not before Angela whispered discreetly in Shirley's ear.

'Let's hope now you're married that you've got it out of your system.'

Shirley giggled and said, loudly, 'Oh, you shouldn't be telling me all your bedroom secrets, Angela.' That'd teach her.

The room filled up nicely and everyone seemed to be having a lovely time. The dancefloor was never empty and the buffet and complimentary wine had soon vanished.

'Hey Shirl babe, I wanna have a word with ya about our next job,' Oli said as they boogied the night away on the dance floor.

'Not now, eh?' Shirley said just wanting to have fun.

'Well I've made a start on it, and I need next week off...'

'What? Oh, ok. I suppose. I haven't booked much in this week, thought we probably couldn't be arsed after tonight,' Shirley muttered.

'Hey, can I have a word?' David asked butting in to their dance.

'Yeah, what's up?' Shirley asked.

'Well that Mo, look at her, she's after the boys,' David said pointing at Mo who was moving in on not just Josh but Ben as well.

'Don't worry, I'll sort it,' Shirley smiled.

Shirley took Mo to one side and had little chat with her. Moments later Mo was dancing away all over the Headmaster. His wife was giving them daggers before grabbing her coat and storming out. Mo carried on all over him and he seemed to be enjoying all the attention from the over-friendly woman.

'What's up with her? Not her usual type is he?' Oli asked shocked.

'I told her that he's Sid Howell's cousin, you know that talent show king. Told her to get in with him and she'd have a chance of getting somewhere with her singing.' Shirley chuckled.

'You didn't?' David was horrified.

'Well, killed two birds with one stone, got her off the lads, and got rid of his missus at the same time.'

'Why, what's up with his missus?' David asked, confused.

Shirley and Oli looked at each other before saying as one: 'Sourpuss.'

Auntie Dilys enjoyed a dance or two with Marc, and the factory girls tried to get in with some of the teachers and the party was in full swing when David interrupted the song to have a few words on the mike.

'Hello, sorry to disturb you all, I can see you're having a great time.'

'Hurry up, we've got dancing to do,' Mo heckled.

'Ok… ok… Now I just want to say a few words: thank you all for coming and for all the beautiful gifts.'

'It's ok, plenty more where they came from!' Sapphire laughed drunkenly.

'Aye, we know,' Oli murmured.

'Anyway, I won't keep you from your dancing for long, I just want to ask my beautiful wife if she'll do me the honour of joining me tomorrow to celebrate our wedding by joining me on a honeymoon in the Maldives.' He was waving two tickets from his pocket.

'Oh my God, how wonderful. Too right I will.'

Shakily, Shirley got off the stage and joined Oli who was standing cuddling a sleepy Apple.

'Oh my God, I don't believe it, how wonderful is that? I get to have a proper honeymoon after all.' Shirley was blubbing again.

'It's amazing news hon'. I can't believe it meself and it's such a brilliant stroke of luck...' Oli announced.

'What d'ya mean?'

'Well, you know this new job I've been trying to tell you about?'

'Aww, listen, babe, can we leave it for now? Look I won't be able to do anything now, will I, till I get back and that,' Shirley said inspecting the tickets.

'Well, babe, that's where you're wrong. I had a quick word with David before he did his big surprise and it's the same place...' Oli blurted out.

'Oli, what you going on about, babe?'

'Well this next job...it's a fella who's going on a business trip tomorrow with his secretary and they're only setting off tomorrow to the friggin' Maldives.' Oli pulled frantically on Shirley's arm. 'Talk about a coincidence!'

'Oh no, Oli, babe, no way... I'm on me friggin' honeymoon. I don't want to be doing that kind of thing do I?' Shirley objected.

'Well, you don't have to, not really, that's what I was trying to tell you. I told you I'd made a start on this one, and I want next week off, didn't I?' Oli said with a mischievous smile.

'Yeah...' Shirley said, still unsure where Oli was going with this.

'Well me and Marc are booked on the same flight as them tomorrow to the...' he paused... 'Maldives.'

Shirley suddenly made sense of it all.

'It's the same flight as you two, same hotel, the lot. We can spend the week together; I'll do the detective bit and you can too if you're a bit bored. Shirl, I'm gonna spend your honeymoon with ya, babe!'

More Than Just a Hairdresser Nia Pritchard

"Enjoyed it loads. A good juicy read!"
Margi Clarke

"One to watch"
The Bookseller

<u>Tuesday, January 1, 10am</u>
<u>Dear Diary,</u>

"Oh my God, I feel totally wrecked. I've still got the whirlies. What a Party. It was mint! Fireworks in more ways than one!
Loads of peeps came. Oli – he works for me in Cuts and Curls. Bent as a nine bob note but me best friend and I love him to bits. Me kids: Jason, he's 16 and Fiona, she's 14. I think it's Jason's friends who are still lying on me living room floor actually..."

When Shirley catches Oli's boyfriend Gus red-handed, arms around devious two-timing Matt, and gets the evidence to prove it, a couple of her clients are keen for a repeat performance. Within weeks she's on the case of Dave 'n' Mave, looking for clues among the curlers and clinches behind the counter...With her mobile hairdressing business taking off in a new direction, Shirley's little pink diary is the keeper of surprising secrets...

Sit back and relax, while Shirley and Oli take you on a hilarious journey round Liverpool's finest, from the girls on the production line to the perky pensioners looking for more than just a blue rinse.

9781906784126 • £7.99

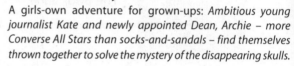

ABOUT HONNO

Honno Welsh Women's Press was set up in 1986 by a group of women who felt strongly that women in Wales needed wider opportunities to see their writing in print and to become involved in the publishing process. Our aim is to develop the writing talents of women in Wales, give them new and exciting opportunities to see their work published and often to give them their first 'break' as a writer.

Honno is registered as a community co-operative. Any profit that Honno makes is invested in the publishing programme. Women from Wales and around the world have expressed their support for Honno by buying shares. Supporters' liability is limited to the amount invested and each supporter has a vote at the Annual General Meeting.

To buy shares or to receive further information about forthcoming publications, please write to Honno at the address below, or visit our website: **www.honno.co.uk.**

HONNO
Unit 14, Creative Units
Aberystwyth Arts Centre
Penglais Campus
Aberystwyth
Ceredigion
SY23 3GL

All Honno titles can be ordered online at
www.honno.co.uk
or by sending a cheque to Honno.
Free p&p to all UK addresses.